EXHIBIT AURORA

Kylie Casino

PROLOGUE

14th Century, Voltav Castle

Aurora huffed as she finally managed to sneak away from her birthday celebration. There were only so many dances with complete disappointments of suitors that she could take. After multiple failed escape attempts—each thwarted by her mother—she had taken the opportunity of a surprise harp performance to slip out. She was grateful; her parents had gone above and beyond with planning and, for the most part, everything had been lovely. But she couldn't escape the unspoken truth that loomed over the night.

This was not just a celebration of her twenty-first birthday. It was her debut as a future wife.

While she knew she was fortunate that her parents hadn't forced her to consider marriage before twenty-one, she remained furious with them for inviting every potential husband from the Seven Kingdoms. Her nurse had always told her that no man would be truly worthy of her. This evening had shown her that the statement wasn't true.

Men just weren't worth her time.

Although Aurora was proud of her independence, general life skills, and education, she always understood that she would have to do the "right" thing one day. Her parents had allowed her to grow into a self-sufficient adult before even mentioning a betrothal. But the moment she turned twenty-one, everything changed. Her independence was to be left behind for what mattered: marriage, queership and producing heirs.

Guards were quick to move out of Aurora's way as she strode down the corridor, her skirts making a light swishing sound against the polished floor. While they probably should have sent her back to her party, they knew better than to interfere when their princess was frustrated. They likely assumed she would wander for a bit, clear her head, and return to the ballroom once she had calmed down.

That was originally her plan.

But as she continued to walk, her frustration only grew. The parade of absolute mediocrity offended her. There had been a foreign prince who wouldn't stop talking about his own accomplishments, abysmal that they were. A duke who treated the dance floor like a battlefield, tossing her around as if she were an attacking threat. A count who, for whatever reason, smelled so strongly of onions that her eyes watered. Was this a glimpse into her future? Giving up her unbelievably fulfilling life to play submissive wife to an insufferable man?

While her mother, Matilda, had been an incredible queen up to this point, her father, Florestan, was the one Aurora most admired. He ruled the kingdom, as they said, with "an iron fist clutching a daisy." He was firm, yet compassionate, expressing a fondness for all subjects which was rarely seen among royalty. An impending marriage crushed Aurora's plans to continue her father's legacy.

The sound of her footsteps echoing grew louder, pulling her away from the thoughts of becoming a stinking turd's wife. She only then noticed how dark and empty the hallway she'd been walking had turned. She glanced around, realizing she didn't even recognize her location.

"Lovely. I got lost in my own castle."

Aurora...

Did someone just call her name? She frowned, knowing her mother would probably appear soon to march her back to the ballroom.

Aurora...

That wasn't her mother. She glanced around, trying to find the source of the voice, and a small door seemed to materialize. Had that always been there?

Aurora...

The voice was loud and clear, but somehow still a whisper. It was smooth, silky, and inviting, seeming to wrap around Aurora's mind as she approached the door. She reached for the doorknob, surprised at the warmth seeping from the metal. It didn't burn; it almost felt like a warm handhold.

Her vision blurred and her mind felt fuzzy. Deep down, she knew she should turn back.

But she didn't want to.

The door creaked open, revealing a small room bathed in a strange green glow, dust swirling in the murky light. At its center stood a silhouette of a cloaked figure, next to a tall wooden structure she didn't recognize—a great wheel, turning ever so slightly, its pointed spindle glinting in the light. The cloaked figure looked up from the object, a hint of a smile crossing their lips.

Hello child.

CHAPTER 1

2025, The Museum of Historical Mysteries

"She's seriously asleep?"

Greg barely suppressed a groan. He was used to that question, but it still grated on him. It implied that people either refused to read the exhibit markers or to pay any attention to him during the tour. He shouldn't have been surprised, considering the current group was a sixth grade class on a field trip.

"Yes," he replied, "she's asleep. She's been asleep since she was discovered in the 60s. Like I said earlier, it's been scientifically and medically proven, multiple times."

The girl who had asked sneered. "All I'm saying is that she looks too good to have really been asleep that long."

The other kids chuckled, and a different girl elbowed the first. "She's a literal mystery. Why else would she be in a museum?"

Greg envied Princess Aurora during times like these. She slept in a temperature-regulated bed under a glass dome, received specialized physical therapy weekly, and had the world's most intelligent minds caring for her. It just had to be the epitome of peace.

A young boy raised his hand. "Can I kiss her?"

A mix of giggles and groans rumbled throughout the group.

"You dumbass! The guy already said kissing wasn't allowed anymore." Greg smirked; at least *someone* had been listening.

Another boy pulled the wannabe kisser close. "Idiot, you want to end up like the Mongoose?" The boy shook his head. "Then keep it in your pants."

Greg paused for a moment before continuing. "Like your friend said, since COVID, we no longer offer the kissing aspect of the exhibit. It would have been difficult to see if the princess contracted the virus and we couldn't risk her getting sick."

Well, that and an outspoken "journalist" had used the opportunity of the pandemic to bring up consent. A retired museum worker had told Greg plenty of stories about the initial popularity of the notorious Sleeping Beauty in 1967. Thousands of people, all genders and ages, had flocked to the museum, hoping to wake the princess with a kiss. Thankfully, the museum team had always been careful with Aurora. It took two years for them to sort through initial applications, screen participants, and monitor the few kisses that occurred. By 1969, the population gave up and resorted to just watching and waiting.

Granted, the initial appeal died down right along with the Free Love movement. But the few who asked to see if they were Aurora's "True Love" had been questionable, to say the least. Greg shuddered, remembering a creep whom they had thankfully ejected before he got his lips on the princess. If a kiss from him hadn't woken her, his breath surely would have.

"Well, if I can't kiss her, how the heck is she gonna wake up?"

"You think you're seriously her True Love? She's too old for you anyway."

Greg actually chuckled. Normally, he would have tried to settle the kids, but this group seemed to be particularly amusing.

"Maybe I *am* her true love."

There was a yelp as the wannabe Prince Charming got smacked. "Even if you were, can you imagine the legal trouble?"

The group's teacher looked up from her pamphlet and offered a halfhearted *shush*. Greg waited for a break in the argument to begin his spiel again. "Even if we had still allowed the kissing, you actually would be too young. You had to be at least twenty-one to participate." That and you had to fill out a lengthy contract covering all the bases. That alone had thankfully deterred some potential suitors.

"The pandemic greatly affected The Museum of Historical Mysteries, but it also allowed Princess Aurora's team to try and research her sleep state at a deeper level. Multiple attempts have been made to wake her up, but as you can see, nothing has been successful." He motioned to the princess. "The most recent theory was she is deceased but was preserved perfectly."

The first girl raised her hand. "But isn't she breathing?"

Greg nodded. "Yes, they considered it might just be air somehow passing through her body, but that was a reach. She has a pulse—barely detectable, but there. She's most comparable to a coma patient."
The kids seemed enthralled, so he continued.

"Only recently, the department received a grant allowing a purchase of electroencephalogram equipment. They could detect brain activity and REM sleep cycles, so she is absolutely alive."

Another raised hand. "Is it true that she doesn't eat?"

Greg nodded once more. "Yes, that's the reason a medical team is on staff here. As far as we know, she hasn't consumed any food or water since she first fell asleep."

"Does she pee?" Laughter erupted as the student who had asked turned pink. Greg waved his hand to get their attention again. "That's honestly a great question. The answer is no. Doctors were initially wary of running blood tests or anything similar, as they weren't sure if Aurora's body would replenish anything. They took a chance and ran a full lab panel, including an attempt at a urinalysis."

"And?"

"Nothing. No stomach contents, no urine, no bodily waste. But she's still perfectly healthy."

He looked at the beautiful young woman again. Despite not having access to essential human needs, she had remained mostly unchanged. Her golden hair remained shiny and full. Her skin maintained a healthy glow. She had not gained or lost a pound since she first arrived at the museum. She was the definition of a mystery, but what kind? Medical? Scientific? Or perhaps, even, magical?

"Dude?"

Greg jerked back to reality. "Apologies. Even after working here for a while, Aurora's story always makes me think."

The group just stared at him inquisitively. He sighed.

"Okay, who's ready for the Bigfoot exhibit?"
Exhibit Aurora was quickly forgotten.

CHAPTER 2

2025, The Museum of Historical Mysteries

Dez growled as he was nearly run over by a stampede of sixth graders. A young, exasperated looking woman, who had to be their teacher, ran desperately after the group. It had to be another field trip. Which meant Greg would be moseying by shortly.

"Christ on a crutch."

Speak of the devil. Dez turned to find Greg walking out from the staff lounge, looking exhausted. He gave a small wave.

"Rough day?"

"Something like that. More like too many kids with too many questions." He pulled a vape pen out of his pocket and took a drag. Dez wrinkled his nose, and Greg chuffed. "Let me have *something* that relieves stress. At least it's not a cigarette."

Dez rolled his eyes. If vaping was the worst of his vices, he couldn't exactly blame him. Even though they very well could be as bad as cigarettes.

"Don't you just wish you had gone into early childhood education like you originally planned?" Dez joked.

"I swear," Greg shook his head. "Were we this crazy? If we were, they were wayyy too trustworthy to let us run around in there."

"Normally you complain the kids are too bored."

"No, I fully appreciate inquisitive minds. It's just difficult when they keep hitting you with question after question after question…"

"I still envy you."

Dez smoothed his custodial uniform. No offense to Greg, but he was far more qualified to be a tour guide. Heck, he was qualified enough to be working on one of the museum's research teams. He had worked his ass off to be awarded a full scholarship to his current graduate program, where he was consistently at the top of all his classes. He'd passionately studied every exhibit at The Museum of Historical Mysteries in his free time. Despite all the hard work, he'd lost out on the only internship position to the niece of a curator.

He knew his future job prospects were still good; he already had a research paper published in an academic journal and his school was currently utilizing a registration program he had created. But being turned down by the museum had still been a hard blow, even if it had been because of a nerd nepo baby. He had loved the museum since he and Greg visited for the first time with their own sixth grade class as children. Having only seen a limited amount of the exhibits on that field trip, Dez had begged his parents to return so much they ended up becoming VIP patrons. It was because he cared so deeply for the place that he applied for his current custodial position. The pay wasn't amazing, and between it and school, he barely slept. But he could spend time—real time—among incredible historical artifacts. Even if he was only mopping the floors.

Greg took another puff of his vape.

"Look at it this way, you basically get the museum all to yourself. Isn't that your dream?"

Dez waved away the artificial cotton candy fumes. "No, I know. I just want to get my hands on the actual research behind it."

"It?" Greg waggled his eyebrows. "Don't you mean *her*?"

Aurora.

He'd be lying if he said he was interested in all exhibits equally. Exhibit Aurora had always baffled him and he had been itching to get on to the research team for years. He just knew her mystery could be solved, and he could very well be the one to solve it.

"You know I could wake her up."

Greg rolled his eyes and pocketed his vape. "I'm not getting into this with you again. Have fun cleaning all the kid fingerprints off the glass." With a pat on the back, he headed towards the parking deck.

Greg wasn't kidding about the fingerprints. Dez mumbled to himself as he scrubbed at the grubby streaks. "Aren't these kids like twelve? Who still presses up against glass at that age?"

He looked at the Sasquatch plaster cast through the foaming cleaner. "What a bunch of bullshit."

He always had a feeling archaeologists had somehow uncovered a Gigantopithecus Blacki footprint, but had forced the Bigfoot storyline due to the museum's reputation. A different team would have asked the right questions: Was this footprint recently made, or did it survive exposure to the elements for 200,000 years? Both options were super intriguing; either there had been an enormous primate still running around within the last decade, or there was more information to be learned about artifacts preserving themselves.

But no, it was Bigfoot.

The "mythology" aspects were his only issue with the museum. Undocumented apes running around? Giant swimming lake lizards? It was offensive. There was concrete evidence of the existence of dinosaurs, mammoths and saber-tooth tigers. If these cryptids really existed, there would be tangible proof. That's all there was to it.

That's how he knew The Sleeping Beauty was very real. The woman had been lying there, unchanged, since the 60s. Multiple teams consisting of archaeologists, scientists, engineers and doctors had confirmed and reconfirmed that she was asleep. For years, the media consistently featured publications about her sleep state. For a while, the museum would include an "Exhibit Aurora Progress Report" in their quarterly newsletters. They hadn't issued one since they hired the new lead two years ago. He couldn't blame the woman for discontinuing updates; everything had remained unchanged.

Proof. Evidence. Research. It was all there for Dez to see, so he believed. What he couldn't believe was how nobody, not even the researchers, had woken her.

He stared at the now spotless glass with the hysterical footprint behind it. He snorted one more time before grabbing his cleaning supplies. Checking his watch, he grinned at his progress. He always saved Exhibit Aurora for last and he'd get a considerable amount of time with her tonight.

"Evening, Your Highness."

He peered at the pristine dome covering the bed; people rarely got super close to the princess, treating her like the priceless goods she was. He usually only had to mop the floors in the space, allowing him to use the remainder of his shifts to ponder the princess's case. He rested his chin on his mop handle, staring at the woman.

"Any other situation, I'd be a creep."

Dez always spoke to Aurora, even if he wasn't sure if she was aware of him. People compared her state to a coma, and research showed that familiar voices sometimes helped such patients. Maybe if she ever woke up, his voice might be the most recognizable.

He wondered if anyone had considered the possible aftermath of her waking. Her estimated birth year was sometime in the fourteenth century. Any family she would have had was long gone. If she woke, she'd be stepping into a completely new world, alone. The thought made Dez's heart ache.

"Someone would help you," he assured. "We've been here for you for so long already."

He wasn't sure if he was trying to comfort himself at this point.

CHAPTER 3

2025, The Museum of Historical Mysteries

"Dammit, that custodian's still hanging around again."

Dr. Kyra Ellison, the lead engineer on Aurora's preservation team, glared at the live camera footage currently in front of her. The sad puppy dog of a man had been spending more and more of his shifts in the exhibit, just staring at The Sleeping Beauty. At first, she had been able to do some off-the-clock, private work in the evenings without issue. It's not that her team wasn't capable—they were brilliant—but there were some things she needed to do on her own. Ever since Desmond (she was pretty sure that was his name) had been hired as a custodian, she hadn't been able to do her one-on-ones with the princess.

Honestly, she was amazed the obsessed young man hadn't yet attempted to kiss her. He just... looked at her. It wasn't like he was doing anything wrong, it was just peculiar.

It could definitely be worse; he could post social media statuses insisting that Aurora was his future wife, like that one socialite patron's loser of a son. What had the paps called him, the Mongoose? That was an insult to mongooses. They were actually intelligent. Although they were also resistant to cobra venom. That would explain how he continuously got out of sticky situations.

She couldn't fault the custodian for just wanting to look at her, and he did keep the museum exceptionally clean compared to their previous employee. She tapped her nails on her keyboard, glancing at the clock. No point in waiting for him to leave; he never cut out early before the end of his shift. She wouldn't lose sleep over what really was a pointless case. She sighed when she remembered there wasn't anything she could do.

"It's not your fault, it's not your fault, it's not your fault." Her therapist would be so pissed off at her right now. They'd spent so long working through her feelings of guilt, only for one moment to derail everything.

Kyra rolled her eyes at the man still gazing at the princess before shutting her laptop. She gathered it, her car keys and her lunchbox before shutting the rest of her equipment down and exiting the lab. She breathed in the fresh air as she started walking towards the parking deck. The difference between the sterile environment of the museum and the real world always jarred her. She adored her workspace, but consistently longed for natural light. She had once suggested installing a sunroof, only to be shot down due to concerns over contamination and environmental control.

She still craved the sun.

As she climbed into her car, she caught a glimpse of herself in the rear-view mirror. The dark circles under her eyes had deepened into a grayish purple. She groaned, craving a good night's sleep even more.

She hated her car. She hated the size, hated paying for gas, and just really hated driving in general. She could have easily teleported herself to and from work, but that wasn't the human way. "You just had to go full on human, didn't you Kyra?" she mumbled to herself as she merged onto the highway.

Magic wasn't safe in this realm anymore. She'd witnessed the horrors of the witch trials: countless innocent women tortured and executed, victims of blind hatred. She'd watched con men peddle fake cures, offering false hope to the desperately sick, only for them to be left penniless and still suffering. And she had seen bumbling illusionists turn her craft into a cheap spectacle. That part hadn't been so bad. She'd even considered joining the entertainment business for a while, effortlessly pulling rabbits and doves from hats. But no matter how careful she could try to be, the risk of getting caught was always there. She couldn't be the spark that ignited a new Salem.

But it would have been so nice to summon sunlight in her lab. To glamour away her sleepy under eyes. To peer into that custodian's mind and figure out why he was so damn obsessed with the princess.

Humans were annoying. Long ago, she thought of them as amusing, endearing even. Things were so much easier when the magical world was not only acknowledged, but respected. She longed for the days of flitting about in glamorous dresses, blessing babies, and protecting those she took a liking to.

Like Aurora.

That beautiful rose. She'd once been so full of life and fire—wanting to learn and improve herself continuously, fearing for her individuality being lost as she approached marrying age. Overall, she'd always been kind. Honest to a fault, but kind. Now she was sleeping under a glass dome, just waiting for someone to wake her, and Kyra couldn't do anything but watch— painfully trying everything in her power to reverse what had happened.

"It's not your fault, it's not your fault, it's not your fault…"

But wasn't it? How had she thought True Love's Kiss was a good idea? True Love existed, but it wasn't instantaneous. It required time, depth, and connection. Aurora had never been given the chance to experience any of it. Men of her time considered her too headstrong. She'd never known romance, especially not the type of romance to break the curse.

Kyra rested her head on her steering wheel after pulling into her driveway. She was tired. Tired of playing human. Tired of nosy custodians. Tired of watching over a forever sleeping woman she couldn't save.

A single, glittering tear rolled down her cheek. She had never cried over Aurora. Not once. But now, the floodgates opened. A second tear joined the first, then another, and another. Seeing the sparkling tears clouding her vision was morbidly hysterical. She wiped her face, catching another glimpse of her reflection in the mirror. A crazed laugh escaped her.

Her tears had healed the dark circles under her eyes.

CHAPTER 4

14th Century, Voltav Castle

The Good Fairy stared helplessly at the young woman in the grand bed. Her breathing was deep and controlled. She looked completely at peace. It was a far cry from the scowl she had been sporting just hours ago, after being forced to dance with every eligible man throughout the entire kingdom. The Fairy managed a slight giggle at the memory, having always been amused by the princess's bullheadedness.

Aurora was perfectly content with continuing life as an unmarried woman, but always knew that wouldn't be possible. She graciously accepted the feast, entertainment, and suitors presented to her, but couldn't hide her displeasure as the night wore on.

One moment, Aurora had been celebrating her birthday. The next, she was in a deep, cursed sleep. Her parents had done everything in their power to protect their daughter from this fate, but it hadn't been enough. Needing some time to get her bearings, the princess had slipped away from the party, noticed by nobody but the fairy, who had thought little of it. She pitied the girl for having so many changes pushed on her in a matter of hours. Perhaps she should have run after her.

Somehow, Aurora had ended up in an abandoned part of the castle, in the only room still holding a spinning wheel. How the spinning wheel had escaped being burned and outlawed with all the others was a mystery. By the time the fairy went to collect Aurora, she had pricked her finger on the spindle, apparently out of curiosity. She'd found her collapsed on the cold stone floor, hair strewn across her face, her tiara cracked from the apparent impact. The fairy had fought tears as she levitated the princess to her bedroom, needing to do something. If she couldn't wake her up, she could at least make sure she was comfortable. She placed her gently on her beautiful bed and repaired the glistening tiara.

She tapped her foot, positive that Carabosse had played some part in Aurora's escape attempt. She had seen nothing out of the ordinary at the party, but that didn't mean The Wicked Fairy hadn't drawn the princess away from her protection. Carabosse, while dark and hateful, still maintained her alluring magic. Her powers of manipulation were unmatched. She could have easily captured Aurora within a trance, taking advantage of her lack of knowledge on spinning wheels to lure the young woman in. It was more likely, though, that she'd entranced the young woman, giving her no choice but to enter the room.

"Where is my daughter?!"

The fairy looked up to see King Florestan and Queen Matilda rushing into the princess's bedroom. Her throat tightened as Matilda collapsed at her daughter's bedside.

"She's gone," she whined between sobs.

"Majesty, do you recall my blessing?"

The queen stared the fairy down, pain raging through her face.

"What good is your blessing now?!"

The fairy shrunk into herself. She'd tried.

Florestan made his way to the bed to comfort his wife.

"Tilda," he nearly whispered, "she's only asleep."

Matilda buried her head in the princess's blanket.

"She might as well be gone! True Love's Kiss, Florestan? How will that even happen?"

The king stroked his wife's back, for once, not knowing what to say. The powerful ruler had been reduced to a grieving father in a split second. He choked back a sob and glanced at the fairy. "Is there anything you can do?"

Helpless, she swallowed hard. She squeezed her eyes shut, remembering the day she initially saved Aurora from death at her christening. She impulsively chose the first blessing she thought of; love. While yes, Aurora was only asleep, she almost agreed with the queen that she might as well be gone. Who knew how long it would take for a True Love to save the day with the fateful kiss? Were her parents and the rest of the kingdom forced to age, perhaps even die, waiting for their princess to wake once again?

The fairy's eyes shot open. Yes, there was something she could do. She faced the king, raising her hand and summoning the magic. "Majesty, I apologize. But it's the best I can do."

With a blast of light, a powerful sleep spell poured from her fingertips, overtaking Aurora's parents before flooding out of the bedroom. Florestan and Matilda sunk to the floor in a deep slumber, and the fairy heard soft thumps in the hallway as servants joined their rulers. The spell stretched past the castle, past the moat, all the way to even the wildlife in the forests. An eerie silence overtook the entire kingdom.

The last of the magic left the fairy's body as she herself almost collapsed from exhaustion. She steadied herself on a banister and gazed at the sleeping king and queen. They looked far more peaceful, no longer having to stare helplessly at their cursed daughter. They'd wake when Aurora would wake, being able to live as though no time had passed at all. She managed to crack a small smile.

"One hundred years should be more than enough time."

CHAPTER 5

1967, Somewhere in Europe

"This is disgusting," Dr. Henry Pach grumbled, shoving thick vines out of his way. "What even is this stuff?"

"Haven't a clue! But remind me to collect a sample on the way back," his father, Dr. Otto Pach, called over his shoulder.

"Can't we just cut through?"

"Absolutely not! What if they're an endangered species?"

Henry sighed. He was pretty sure it was just a type of Greenbrier, but what Otto said went. So he continued to have his arms torn apart by the thorns. None of this had been part of the original plan, so he wasn't remotely dressed for a forest expedition. Meanwhile, his father charged ahead, moving with unbelievable energy, completely oblivious to Henry's struggles. You'd never know the man was in his sixties.

This was supposed to be a vacation. A much needed European trip away from their work at The Museum of Historical Mysteries. The place had become even more popular after acquiring what they believed to be one of the Loch Ness Monster's scales. Henry had begged Otto to step away for a bit, reassuring him that their team of archaeologists and researchers could handle things in their absence. Otto had only agreed when Henry promised they'd go on a nature hike.

He hadn't expected said hike to turn into a three hour historical exploration.

"Dad?" The old loon had been moving so quickly, that he was now out of sight. "DAD?"

"Henry! Hurry!"

Hurry. Of course. He'd get right on that.

As he attempted to follow his father's voice in the distance, his foot snagged on a tangle of vines. After furiously pulling for a moment, to no avail, he yanked out a pocketknife. "Sorry, Dad," he muttered as he easily sliced through the greenery. An awful stench of rotting meat wafted up from the remnants. Henry grimaced. Definitely Greenbrier.

When Henry finally caught up, Otto was standing with his hands on his hips, stoically gazing at something in the distance. Henry sighed, assuming there was a bird or some rare moss. He wandered closer and tapped his father on the shoulder, who turned and faced him with twinkling eyes.

"Henry, look." He pointed to the distance.

"What?"

Otto simply pointed again and Henry squinted, shielding his eyes from the sun. Trees, trees, more trees… Wait, what was that? He swore he saw a glimmer of rainbow light flashing through the leaves.

"I do believe," Otto pulled out a pair of binoculars, "we may have discovered some historic architecture."

"*You* did, Dad," Henry replied.

"No no," Otto corrected, handing Henry the binoculars. "We did. You indulged me in this hike."

Henry peered into the binoculars and couldn't help but grin. He clearly saw a stained glass window at the peak of a high stone tower. Years ago, people abandoned the area they'd been exploring because nobody wanted to brave the overgrown nature. They really weren't sure when humankind had last been there, as absolutely nothing was documented.

"What do you think?" Otto asked mischievously.

Henry smiled wider. "I think we need to check it out."

The path to the tower was thankfully far less treacherous than the rest of their adventure had been. Oddly enough, the deeper they traveled, the more the forest seemed to open up. Otto and Henry were enjoying the sights as a vast castle across a bridge came into view. They froze in complete disbelief.

"Good heavens," Otto whispered.

After gawking for a few moments, the men tentatively approached the bridge. They both automatically tested it, checking for rotting wood.

Somehow, despite what had to be years of exposure, the structure held firm. After crossing, they stood at the castle's enormous doors, exchanging glances.

"Dad?"

"Henry?"

"I thought this area was a wasteland."

"As did I." Otto pressed a palm against the heavy doors. To their astonishment, they swung open without resistance. "But it would appear we were mistaken."

They walked into a large throne room. A thick layer of dust covered every visible surface, the air thick and still. Moth holes riddled the once-beautiful tapestries. At least three of the enormous windows were shattered. Time and neglect had scuffed and rusted the twin thrones, once symbols of royalty.

All things considered, the castle's structure was still in remarkable condition, seeming to resist time itself. Henry swore he saw a glint of light out of the corner of his eye, but found nothing when he glanced around.

"Oh ho! What is this?" Otto wandered to a wall, stooping to look at an object. "Henry, come take a look."

Henry approached and found a medieval shield lying on the floor. Its front bore a welded crest; a diamond intertwined with a briar. He arched an eyebrow—why did that symbol look familiar?

Otto scratched his head. "Late thirteenth, early fourteenth century, definitely."

Henry nodded, and then realization struck. "Dad, that's the d'Ambray crest."

Otto's eyes widened. "My stars, you're right!" He reached for the shield, but stopped himself. "Bollocks, I didn't bring gloves."

"We need to get the team out here. This is incredible."

Otto nodded vigorously. "Perhaps there's more upstairs."

As they ascended the grand staircase, something caught Henry's eye. He stopped short.

A human skull.

His stomach lurched.

"Well then," Otto proclaimed, eyes darting over the remains. "I wonder how long that poor sap has been here." Without hesitation, he grabbed

Henry's arm. "Come on, nothing we can do for him now."

Henry averted his gaze as they stepped over more skeletal remains on the way up.

The upper level was as eerily silent as the lower. Long hallways stretched before them, doors lining the walls. Otto gestured ahead. "Pick a room, any room."

Henry could barely hear him. A sudden, overwhelming scent of roses had filled his nose. His feet moved on instinct, leading him to a particular door. Something about it felt…wrong.

He pressed a hand against the wood and gently pushed it open.

His breath caught.

"Dad?"

Otto was by his side in an instant, peering in, equally dumbfounded. Unlike the rest of the castle, this room was immaculate. The rug was vibrant, without a speck of dust in sight. The bed and nightstand looked newly crafted. And high above them, a pristine stained glass window bathed the room in soft, colorful light.   They stepped inside cautiously, taking in every untouched detail.

"H-how…?" Otto asked.

Henry had no answers.

"This is unbelievable!" Otto clapped Henry on the back. "This might be our most amazing discovery yet!" Unable to contain himself, he pulled his son into a hug and spun him around.

"Oof!" Henry wheezed.

And then he saw her.

He kicked his legs, breaking free from his father's grasp, and shakily pointed towards the bed. Otto turned. There was definitely someone beneath the blankets.

"What…?"

"Hello?" Otto called out to no response.

Slowly, they moved closer, their eyes fixed on the figure before them. A young woman lay in the bed, in just as perfect condition as the rest of the room. Her blonde hair gleamed as if freshly brushed, her skin fresh and untouched by time, and her clothing was rich and regal.

Henry scratched his chin. "Do… do you think she's somehow perfectly preserved?"

Otto didn't reply.

Before Henry could stop him, he'd bent down and placed two fingers at the young woman's throat.   He sucked in a sharp breath.

"Henry… she's asleep."

CHAPTER 6

15th century, Voltav Castle

Prince Philip dug his heels into his horse, Righteous, urging him forward. Time was running out. The thorny vines were growing quickly, threatening to hide the land forever. The weight of an entire kingdom was resting on his shoulders, but he couldn't let it flatten him. He could do this. He was Philip Monjurse XV, son of Philip Monjurse XIV the Mighty. Like all men in his family, he was destined for great things. Since his youth, instructors had trained him in horse riding, sword fighting, and Magical History, hopefully preparing him to fulfill this great prophecy.

The Good Fairy followed closely behind Philip, magicking away any obstacles that he might not have seen. He had thought he was dreaming when she had materialized in his library. She was everything he'd imagined a fairy to be; tall, kind, and glowing ever so slightly. While magic and its history were still studied, the beautiful fairies who practiced the art form were rarely seen after the Disappearing Kingdom incident.

Nearly one hundred years prior, Voltav, ruled by House d'Ambray, had been the most prosperous of the Seven Kingdoms. Under King Florestan, its people thrived in agriculture, knighthood, and education. But instead of using their power to control the neighboring lands, they insisted on living in harmony. They consistently sent their best farmers, commanders, and scholars across the realms to share their wisdom. Though never official, people acknowledged Voltav as the heart of the kingdoms.

Overnight, the kingdom had vanished. Trade ceased. Letters went unanswered. Travelers heading there would find themselves lost, unable to explain the disorientation that had caused them to turn back. All the neighboring kingdoms sent search parties, but none succeeded. After multiple failed search attempts, the kingdom sadly faded into a mere memory within history books.

But Philip never forgot. He had thought of Voltav since he'd first learned about the land at age ten. For the following eleven years, he'd had the same dream. He'd find himself surrounded by fog, standing at a bridge over a large river. The only visible thing across the bridge was of tower of prickly thorns. If he looked hard enough, he could see a glimmer of a stained glass window, peering out from the very top. Something was calling to him from behind that window, but no matter how hard he tried, his feet wouldn't move.

"Highness, look out!"

Philip yanked Righteous out of the way right as a falling branch smashed into the ground. He glanced back at the Fairy and nodded a quick thanks. She'd been serving as his protector since first appearing to him. He'd been coincidentally reading up on magical history when the ethereal being materialized in the room. She'd smiled as she explained she'd been watching over him for a while and had an inkling he was the key to bringing Voltav back. Gifting him with a magical sword, shield, and horseshoes, she'd guided him on the once frequently traveled path to the forgotten kingdom.

"Philip, just keep going! It's there, I promise!"

He had been feeling the disorientation and confusion the past crusaders had explained as he drew closer. His eyes watered and a painful headache blurred his vision, but he pushed Righteous on. The new horseshoes seemed to encourage the steed to keep thundering on until they had crossed the bridge. Philip pulled the horse to a stop before they crashed into the giant tower of thorny branches. He squinted as he gazed upwards, seeing the slight glimmer of stained glass. It was real. His dream was real.

Furiously, he slashed at the branches with the fairy's gifted sword, thankfully slicing through the obstacles as if just air. He was close to exhaustion, but his need to see inside the tower at last drove him to keep going. Suddenly, a crackling roar filled the air, so loud Philip felt it in his bones. He turned to find a large, black dragon flying towards the tower. His eyes widened; dragons had gone extinct, where had this one come from? The fairy flitted next to him, her brows creasing.

"It's Carabosse."

Philip had heard stories of The Wicked Fairy. While most fairies found humans amusing, Carabosse had treated them as her playthings, intercepting their lives and torturing them for her own sick pleasure. He had a feeling she had been behind the Disappearing Kingdom, having been notorious for her powers of manipulation. Philip gazed at The Good Fairy, nearly begging for help as he frantically worked to discern his next move. She seemed to read his mind and shook her head.

"I can't destroy her or her magic. I can only offer blessings to help humans." She pointed to the sword. "I made that more powerful than any normal sword. You just have to use it correctly."

Philip gripped the hilt harder, turning to face the great beast once more as it flew closer. Another roar escaped her mouth, along with a stream of green fire. Philip defended himself and Righteous with the magical shield, still feeling the insane heat threatening to reduce the metal to liquid. He used a break in the fire stream to peer out from behind the shield, seeing how close Carabosse now was.

"Her heart! Aim for the heart!"

Looking at the dragon's chest, he saw a faint green glow within. Was that her heart? This was his only chance. With the last bit of his strength, the prince focused on that glowing center and threw his sword straight towards it. He heaved a sigh of relief as he saw the iron plunge deep into the monster; the flame being snuffed out immediately. Carabosse attempted to roar once more, but a strangled gasp came out instead. Her great body, as well as the thorn tower, disintegrated into ash and sludge.

"Quick, Philip, go to her!"

The fairy waved away some remnants of the dark magic, revealing a door once covered by vines. Philip sprinted inside, past the grand throne room, through endless corridors, and up a spiraling staircase. Bodies were scattered throughout the castle halls, eerily still. Somehow, he knew they weren't dead, just asleep. His legs burned, but he pushed forward until reaching the tower's top.
This was it.

He opened the last remaining door to find a beautiful bedroom, bathed in colorful light, the scent of fresh roses hanging in the air. He turned his focus to the plush bed in the center of the room. And there, he found the most beautiful woman he'd ever seen, sound asleep.

His breath hitched. Her skin was creamy and flushed peach, her golden hair cascaded across her silk pillows and her plump, pink mouth was slightly parted. He slowly walked towards the bed, feeling that familiar pull that had haunted his dreams for so long. But she was no longer out of sight.

"I've never met you, but I feel as though I've known you my whole life," he whispered, bending over her.

And then, without thinking, he pressed his lips to hers.

CHAPTER 7

2025, Kyra's House

Kyra's eyes shot open, escaping the nightmare. She took in some shaky breaths, trying to calm her racing heartbeat. The memories of her failure continued to haunt her when she slept, just waiting for those moments when her guard was down. She rubbed her eyes, glanced at the alarm clock on her side table and groaned—4 A.M. No point in trying to go back to sleep. She swung her legs out from under the sheets, bumping into a warm, furry lump that had been next to her. A sharp yowl, accompanied by claws sinking into her thigh in protest, followed.

"You just had to take a cat form this life cycle, didn't you?"

Unlike witches' familiars, fairy familiars were immortal beings like their masters. Every five hundred years, they would shapeshift into a new animal of their choosing, taking on the characteristics of said animal. Until now, her own familiar, Sigmund, had consistently formed as various reptiles. Kyra had liked that. He had been quiet, low-maintenance, and was perfectly content to be wrapped around her bicep as a snake, or perched on her shoulder as a little gecko.

For some ungodly reason, what once had been an adorable salamander had transformed into an obnoxiously fluffy white cat this time around. He had given himself large blue eyes, a squishy belly, and a massive attitude. If Kyra hadn't witnessed the shift herself, she would have sworn someone had swapped her familiar for a new one. Thankfully, Sigmund had maintained his fierce loyalty towards his fairy, but he bordered on being obsessively needy.

Kyra pried his claws out of her pajama shorts, earning another disgruntled yowl.

"Sig, stop. I'd pay you more attention if you weren't so friggin annoying."

The cat sniffed the air before glaring at his fairy. She rolled her eyes, slipped into her fuzzy booties, and made her way to the bathroom. Sure enough, Sigmund followed close behind, his tail straight up in the air as if he'd never been offended. Flicking on the light, she leaned over the sink and examined her reflection. Another deranged laugh escaped her.

"Mommy should cry more often. Still no eye bags."

Sigmund headbutted her shin before sauntering off to the kitchen, no doubt expecting an early breakfast. Kyra clicked her tongue. Despite her inner turmoil, she looked...good. Probably the best she'd looked in a while. Maybe she could finally muster up the courage to flirt with a cute barista or something. It'd been forever since she had a romp in a flower field with a sweaty, muscular farmhand. She giggled at the thought, before gripping the sink as a different type of flashback passed through her head. It was a continuation of the nightmare she thought she had escaped.

No matter how much time passed, it felt as though it all had happened yesterday. Carabosse had caught on to her sleep scheme and retaliated by placing disorienting charms around Voltav. Kyra had done her best to help the wannabe rescue parties find the sleeping kingdom, but it hadn't been enough. The Wicked Fairy would just keep upping her charms, culminating in the tower of thorns and vines surrounding the castle. Her "more than enough" hundred years was approaching the deadline, so around year seventy-eight, she took matters into her own hands.

She'd attended Phillip's christening disguised as a nun, as fairy invitations had become sparse once we'd all but gone into hiding after the incident. With morale down since Aurora had pricked her finger, and Voltav just seemed to die, a majority of her kind had ventured back to live full time in their home realm. With less and less fairies around, the idea of them simply being imaginary was close to becoming the norm. Kyra had tried hard to continue living among the humans, but her presence became almost intimidating to them.

She thought the baby prince had been like Aurora—special. And maybe he was, but not the kind of special she needed. If she had known that

sooner, she wouldn't have dedicated the next twenty-one years to prepping the young man for True Love's Kiss. She had transported him into an illusion of the castle through his dreams, keeping the princess just out of reach. She had made sure Voltav had stayed part of the history books, knowing Philip's curiosity would be insatiable. She had finally appeared to him when he came of age, gifting him all the materials to rescue The Sleeping Beauty.
And yet, she had still failed.

All she could do after that was maintain the castle's structure and Aurora's room. The rest of the castle, however, had to be left to decay. The magic required to preserve it all was far too draining for Kyra. Thankfully, the Paches had spotted the stained glass window during their fateful hike in the 60s. She had to smile; almost the entire Pach family possessed a curiosity akin only to elves. If not for Henry and Otto's relentless persistence, she and Aurora would likely still be trapped within the castle's walls.
Sigmund singing the song of his people brought Kyra back to reality. The stupid cat was screaming in the kitchen to be fed. She looked at herself one more time in the mirror, taking in the little bit of goodness in her eyes looking awake for the first time in a while. Sulking towards the kitchen, the cat's screams grew louder.

"Alright already, you act like you're starved!"

***

"Are you sure you're okay?"

Kyra massaged her right temple and held back from sighing into her cell. After two years of working nonstop on Aurora's case, she had called in one of her many accumulated work from home days.

"Lila, the fact that you're flabbergasted I'm not coming in just further proves how much I need a break. And I'm not fully taking the day off. You have access to me if you need anything." She drummed her fingers on her dining room table, horrified when two nails popped off. How long had it been since she had the set put on?

"I'm not saying you don't need a break. This is just so unlike you." Dr. Lila Killenger was the Watson to Kyra's Sherlock. Always supportive, she delved into the intense research constantly assigned to her, maintaining a lighthearted atmosphere in the lab.

"I won't bother you," she promised. "Please try to give the old noggin some time off. Aurora's not going anywhere."

"That's why I don't feel as bad."

Lila sighed. She was ecstatic when they received the EEG machine last month, hoping to finally make more progress with the princess. Kyra had known from the start that it would only show what she already knew: Aurora was asleep. Just asleep. Lila had been hoping beyond hope that they would learn something new, if only for Kyra's sake. But, like for the last year and a half, everything remained the same. What a waste of benefactor funding. It could have gone to proving that the Sasquatch footprint was actually legit.

"I'll let you go. Don't let Aurora get into any trouble."

To Kyra's relief, Lila giggled.

"She's pretty well behaved. I think we'll be okay."

Kyra downed her third cup of coffee after hanging up. Sigmund hopped into her lap and nuzzled under her chin. His clinginess could be too much, but he still comforted her when she needed it. She scratched under his chin, pleased when a rumbling purr started in response.

Why did she still continue on? She had already failed, having watched King Florestan, Queen Matilda, the knights, the civilians, and all of Voltav age and pass away in their sleep—the one hundred year blessing no longer protecting them.

Kyra had stayed by Aurora's side.

Century after century, she had stayed.

Because she was a disappointment, a failure, and couldn't bear to leave the princess truly alone. Tears pricked at her eyes, shimmering like liquid starlight. Another borderline psychotic laugh left her, and Sigmund glared.

She was losing it.

But she would look damn good as she did.

CHAPTER 8

*September 2025, Wellington Bits,
Lizzie's Life Lessons by Elizabeth
Hildegrant*

Riddle me this: When you and I, and all other citizens of Wellington, go to bed at night, are we still considered human beings? Of course we are. We still have the right to privacy, the right to equality and freedom from torture. Those who cannot advocate for themselves (children, the elderly, the disabled, the sick) are to be protected by others. While I have been critical of our government's flaws, overall, they recognize basic human dignity.

So tell me why, after half a millennium and a full-blown pandemic, a twenty-one-year-old woman is still being put on public display while in a coma-like state of consciousness?

This woman has no right to privacy; she is placed in a glass display, available for anyone to look at, whenever they want to.

This woman has no right to equality. While yes, she is well cared for, she is being treated as a project, not a person.

This woman is not free from torture; it was only recently that random people off the street could kiss the princess without consequence. It's insane that it took a deadly virus, and yours truly, to finally have the concept of consent taken seriously.

Princess Aurora d'Ambray is a living, breathing, human woman. She once had a life, a family, and a future. Now, she has become part of a complete spectacle. For the fifty-plus years since she arrived at The Museum of Historical Mysteries, Exhibit Aurora has been their most popular attraction. The museum has used said popularity to collect funding for their supposed research into her sleep state. I repeat; it has been over fifty years. Why is she still asleep? How is she still alive and kept only as a display piece?

I believe it is finally time for the museum to make some very important decisions regarding Princess Aurora's care. If all attempts to wake her, by what I admit is an incredible research team, have failed, any further attempts should not be made. Keep the young woman somewhere safe and private with medical monitoring. Use the funding to make the other exhibits even better. If she finally wakes, then use the opportunity to learn from her history.

More than anything, it's time we do right by Aurora. We need to protect her.

CHAPTER 9

2025, The Museum of Historical Mysteries

Dez's eyes nearly rolled out of his head as he read Lizzie's "article" on his phone. It was better than most of the crap she wrote, but still.

"Investigative journalist, my ass." More like a wannabe do gooder trying to change the world through social media. Lizzie hadn't changed much from school, constantly needing to voice her very loud opinions. Like Dez, she had always been dead set on achieving new heights with her chosen career path; hers being journalism. But unlike Dez, the talent and knowledge didn't come as easily. Denied by multiple writing programs, she had scraped her way through a year of community college before finally securing a spot at a tiny university.

Her professional career started because of sheer luck. A viral think piece on women's underwear launched her into social media stardom. Rebranding as a digital journalist, she would post quick bits catered towards phone addicts with short attention spans. She ended up going into business with a guy who had originally been a fan, creating the *Wellington Bits*. The website and coinciding app was all over social media feeds, whether people wanted to see their "news writing" or not.

Dez had to admit that Lizzie had a point. He had questioned why the museum continued to keep Exhibit Aurora open, instead of whisking her away to a private facility and really focusing on waking her up. The princess deserved to experience life again, and it didn't feel like that was the goal anymore.

It probably had to do with funding. Typical.

The day had been unusually slow for the museum, meaning Dez had little to deep clean. He had been hanging out with the princess when Greg texted him the *Wellington Bits* link. Although he usually avoided Lizzie's nonsense, he was unfortunately drawn to anything related to Exhibit Aurora. He always felt that if he could just find something—anything—that others had missed, he could finally wake the princess. Become her real life knight in shining armor.

The click clacking of heels pulled him from his thoughts. Dr. Killenger, his former professor, had apparently just locked the lab and was heading home. That was strange.

"You're here a little late tonight, Doc."

She smiled at him. Her smile had always been kind and inviting. "Dr. Ellison didn't come in today, so it took me little more time to do double the work."

Ah, the elusive Dr. Ellison. The head engineer was rarely seen roaming the museum halls, choosing instead to spend all her time around Exhibit Aurora. The woman was supposed to be the most brilliant mind in the biomedical engineering field, so why hadn't any actual progress been made? Maybe that's why she avoided people-fewer questions to answer.

"Have you made any progress with your finds, Dr. Desmond?" Killinger teased.

Dez cringed. "I don't even know if I'm going to go for my doctorate yet. I'd need to get another full scholarship to do it."

She waved a hand dismissively. "Don't be modest. You know there are tons of programs who'd kill to have you."

"Except this one."

"Get over it." Dez couldn't hold back the laugh as Killenger rolled her eyes. "That little intern doesn't even get to do anything. She's a glorified paper pusher. And besides, I couldn't deal with two Aurora obsessed team members."

Dez raised an eyebrow. "Obsessed?"

"Do you know how much time Kyra invests into Exhibit Aurora?" She gestured at the exhibit. "This is the first day off she's taken since she started working here. And thank god, because that woman is so burnt out it's not even funny."

Dez looked at Aurora again. He felt bad for being so quick to judge Dr. Ellison. Apparently, they had a lot in common. Killenger dug her car keys out of her purse. "I'm heading out. Have fun on your date."

Dez snorted and packed up his supplies. He gave the princess one more glance before heading towards the janitorial closet. He'd never say it out loud, but she really was beautiful. She had blonde hair, perfect skin and, he guessed her eyes were blue. Amazingly, nothing about her eye color had ever been published. Somebody had to have known, but he doubted that was very high on the list when it came to importance. Along with being a pretty face, she had an athletic build. Members of the medical team would whisk her away every Friday for her aquatic therapy sessions. The changes were subtle, but her muscle tone had definitely improved since the 60s.

As he pondered the treatments, something caught his eye.

The lab door was wide open. That wasn't right. Security required a key code, a swipe card and a fingerprint in order to access the lab. Was it a glitch? Dr. Killenger wasn't careless in the slightest, so this had to be a mistake. He hesitated before moving closer. With shaking hands, he pressed the reset button, relieved when the welcome screen appeared. Just a glitch. He turned to phone a member of the security team, then stopped.

The lab was right there. *The* lab. Computers, books, equipment, all right there…

Nope. Bad idea. He needed to get out of here. If he ever wanted a real chance at working here, he couldn't get caught basically breaking in.

But then he saw it.

In the corner sat the state-of-the-art EEG machine in all its glory. It had been modified for Aurora, utilizing her pillow as a sensor instead of the usual cap. The exhibit designers had hidden the wires, integrating them into the lavish tapestries on either side of the domed bed.

Dez stared at the machine. It was prepped, and all he had to do was roll it into Aurora's room, plug it in, and—

Nope. *Bad idea.*

He knew he had to leave, but his feet wouldn't move. His heart was racing so fast that he could hear his pulse in his ears. Today, of all days, the security system had glitched. Dr. Ellison, the only person who could stop him, had not come in today. This had to be fate.

Fuck it.

If he was going to lose his job, he'd go out with a bang. He unlocked the brakes on the machine and began rolling it towards the princess. He powered it on as he walked, scrolling through past scans. Typical sleep patterns, epilepsy tests, and an absolutely bizarre check for narcolepsy. They had performed the last scan, comparing REM cycles, four months ago. What the hell had they been doing since then?

He rolled up to Aurora's bedside and found the hidden wire ports. He gazed at the princess as he plugged everything in, hands still shaking. Electronic waves danced across the monitor, signaling everything was working properly. His fingers flew over the keyboard as he pulled up buried code. Taking one more deep breath, he hit enter.

"Well, princess, let's see if we can finally wake you up."

CHAPTER 10

Aurora's Dreams

Aurora inhaled deeply, enjoying the fragrant wildflowers surrounding her. It was one thing she could still take pleasure in. While a large book sat in her lap, she learned long ago she wouldn't be able to read it. Ever since she arrived there—wherever there was—reading hadn't been possible. The words were there, but her mind failed to process what she read. She couldn't explain why. The letters became foreign, or blurred, or shifted around.

Although this place she'd called home for… How long had it been? Time didn't seem to exist here, so she was never sure. But the little world had still offered other pastimes and entertainment. Birds danced in the sky above, their songs filling the air. Fireflies and crickets would lull her to rest at night, never completely unconscious, just drifting. Regularly, waves from the nearby seaside would sweep her away. Typically, one would fear being pulled under a burst of water. But she discovered she could still breathe, even when completely submerged. She'd float right under the surface for a while, enjoying the ripples massaging her muscles. Another wave would gently wash her up on shore after a bit, leaving her completely rejuvenated.

She never went hungry. She simply imagined an item of food she wanted and it would materialize in front of her. She'd sampled various meals she'd once only seen pictures of. Everything tasted wonderful, yet...off, as though something necessary was missing.
She hadn't been poisoned yet, so she continued to accept the food and drink.

Aurora lay back in the field, the long grass tickling her cheek. She was bored and had been for a long time. The small birds and bugs seemed to be the only other signs of life in this world. She'd once been known for her need for independence. Now, the thing she craved most was human interaction. What she'd give to ask how someone else's day had been, what they had for breakfast, what they thought of the weather. Mundane conversations that she hadn't been privy to for so long.

She stared at the clouds, trying to form them into shapes. A rabbit, a fairy, her mother…*Mother*. What had become of her parents? She often tried to remember what had occurred after her birthday party escape, but always drew a blank. The memories just weren't there. She just knew one moment, she had gotten lost in the hallways, and the next, she was here.

Aurora sat back up and opened the large book still in her lap. She knew she wouldn't be able to read it, but she always tried anyway, hopeful that at some point, the words would make sense again. Her eyes widened as she flipped through the pages.

"What on earth?"

The pages were blank.

"Well then…"

This was new. And she had no clue what to think about it. The book always contained beautiful calligraphy. Had the words simply flown off the page?

H

She threw the book off her legs as the singular letter appeared on a page. What had caused that? She frantically looked at her surroundings, half expecting a wisp to appear. Surely it was a ghostly spirit messing with her.

But wait.

She had been able to determine the letter was an H. She slowly crawled towards the book, gingerly opening it again to the only page with writing now on it.

Hello?

Hello. She could read it. It wasn't blurry; it wasn't shifting about; it was clearly Hello. She held the book closer to her face. "Hello?" she whispered the reply into the paper. Nothing else happened. No new words. The book couldn't hear her.

A quill, she needed a quill.

Aurora squeezed her eyes shut, imagining a pheasant's feather quill and a pot of black ink. She had only done this for food, so desperately hoped it would work for other objects. She released the breath she'd been holding as she opened her eyes to the writing materials sitting next to her.

Carefully loading the quill, she once again opened the book to the Hello page. She trembled slightly as she pressed the tip to the paper. She hadn't written in so long. Hopefully it wasn't something else she could no longer do.

Hello?

Hello there.

She could still write.

***

2025, The Museum of Historical Mysteries

Dez's eyes widened as the reply appeared on the monitor.

Hello there.

He raced back to the keyboard, excitement humming through his fingers as he typed back.

Am I speaking to Princess Aurora d'Ambray?

A slight pause.

That would be me.

Dez laughed. The museum had spent so many wasted years researching and studying, attempting to make some sort of contact with Aurora. And he had done it in a matter of minutes. More words appeared on the monitor.

With whom am I writing to?

Writing. She was somehow writing, and it was getting converted into type through the EEG. God, he was brilliant.

I'm Desmond. You can call me Dez.

What a strange name. Are you foreign?

He ran a hand through his hair, astonished. He was having a conversation with Aurora.

Most likely foreign to you.

Most likely? You're either foreign or not.

Sassy one, wasn't she?

Apologies, this is the first human...you are a human, right? The first human interaction I've had in a very long time..

I was a human the last time I checked, yes.

You're certainly a peculiar one, Dez.

Peculiar good, or peculiar bad?

I honestly do not care currently. I'm just glad to be speaking with someone.

He laughed again. He couldn't help it. She was blunt, and he liked it.

*Apologies again, but may I ask **how** I'm speaking with you?*

It's a long story....

I obviously have time.

Dez crossed his arms and pondered. Should he really be explaining that she was asleep, had been asleep for centuries, and he was communicating with her through a piece of technology she definitely wasn't familiar with? There had to be some ethics issues involved.

His phone buzzed. "Crap," he muttered as he pulled it out. It was from his boss.

Are you okay? You haven't clocked out yet and you're a half hour past your shift.

Shit.

Shoot, sorry, I forgot to clock out. I'm home.

No problem, I'll clock you out and deduct the extra time. That's not normal for you. Just wanted to make sure everything was fine.

All good! Night!

He shoved his cell back in his pocket and turned back to the keyboard.

I'm so sorry, but I have to go.

Another pause.

What? No, please, I haven't spoken with anyone else in so long.

He gnawed the inside of his mouth, feeling guilty now. He had started this and now he was letting her down.

I'll be back tomorrow, I promise.

Time doesn't exist here. I'll just keep an eye on the book then.... I'd be lying if I didn't say I'm a bit sad.

I'm really sorry. I'm kind of... not supposed to be doing this. I'm going to be more careful from now on.

A rebel? I can appreciate that. Go ahead and collect yourself. I'll be eagerly awaiting our next conversation.

That was a relief. He'd be more careful from now on. He reached for the power switch, but hesitated. He needed to erase the scan from the system, but didn't want to lose this. Grinning, he pulled a thumb drive he always carried from his pocket and plugged it into the machine. As the data transferred, he leaned back with a satisfied hum.

"Being a nerd for the win."

CHAPTER 11

2025, The Museum of Historical Mysteries

"UNHAND me, you heathen!"

Greg snickered as the Dalton wannabe flailed in his grip. "Heathen? Pretty sure that's you."

"How dare you?!" It was almost comical how the guy's feet barely touched the ground as Greg dragged him out by his collar.

"Sir, I'm doing my job."

"I have every right to be here!"

Greg laughed harder. "And I have every right as an employee to remove any patron who doesn't follow the rules. Attempting to tamper with an exhibit is most definitely breaking the rules." He plopped the loser down once they were a decent distance from the museum entrance.

"I wasn't tampering! And how was I supposed to know that? It's the literal Sleeping Beauty!"

Greg could have punched the guy, but he didn't want to get sued. "Any patron who enters the museum is required to follow the rules and protocols clearly posted at the entrance, available at our information hub, and on our website. I'm assuming you're going to tell me you don't know how to read?"

The guy straightened his jacket and smoothed down his hair. "Do you know who I am? How much money my family has given to this establishment?"

Greg stood firm. "I know exactly who you are, Mr. Mongoose."

"It's MONJURSE!" He nearly stamped his foot like a two-year-old.

Greg bit back a grin. "Well, Mr. Monty *Mongoose,* yes, I'm very familiar with your antics. Has your family seen your most recent paparazzi photo yet?" Monty turned green. "Have *you* even seen it yet? It's hysterical. Nice boxers, man."

Monty's face now turned beet red. "Fine. You win, for now. But you'll be—"

"Hearing from your mother. Yes, I'm sure I will be."

Monty turned on his heel and stomped off. Greg couldn't resist one last jab. "You know, people would take you more seriously if you didn't continue to wear boat shoes after you very publicly lost your boating license!"

Who got a DUI while boating anyway?

Greg wandered back into the museum, straightening his tie. Encounters like that were thankfully rare, but it was still insane. He'd caught Monty trying, and failing, to pick the locks on Aurora's bed. Who knew what could've happened if Greg hadn't stopped him? The Monjurse heir had a reputation for being an entitled little prick, constantly touching and taking things that didn't belong to him, only to have his family nonchalantly bail him out.

Thankfully, Greg was pretty sure he could start the paperwork to have the Mongoose permanently banned from the museum. Really, it should have happened ages ago, especially after the fossil incident at the Cryptid Gala last year.

"You serving as bodyguard now too?"

Greg looked up to see another of his least favorite people leaning up against a pillar. "Lizzie, why are you here?"

She crossed her arms. "Research."

He scowled. "You *just* released something on Aurora. Find something else to bitch about."

Lizzie mockingly clutched her chest. "Bitch? I never bitch. I simply say what needs to be said."

Greg rolled his eyes. "Yeah, sure." He turned to head towards the main office to file the Mongoose complaint. Lizzie trailed behind.

"I mean this with full offense—go away."

"I want to hear about what just happened. You're kind of a hero."

"I'm just doing my job. I'm no hero."

Lizzie pulled out her phone. "At least let me snap a picture of you for the site. The people will love it."

Greg whipped around, his hand instinctively reaching out to swat the phone away. "Lizzie, you know damn well we have a photo policy here. Put your phone away and get out of here before I escort you out, too."

She smirked. "Is that a threat?"

He clenched his jaw. Maybe he could get her banned as well while he was at it. "I'm simply telling you the ramifications of ignoring the museum policy." He stood up to his full height, towering over her. "Now, either make your way out of here or you can join the Chupacabra exhibit. I'm sure you'd fit in perfectly."

Lizzie scrunched her already upturned nose, making her look even more pig like. "I have a business meeting I have to make anyway, so fine." She started heading for the exit. "Go ahead and be unappreciated by the public. The museum's reputation can continue to suffer."

Greg scoffed. "It must be nice to live in delulu land! You know our patron numbers have increased exponentially since COVID, right? Oh wait, you weren't invited to the press party, so you wouldn't know."   He swore he heard her hold back a sob. He was being ruder than necessary, but the woman was a leech. "Have fun in your 'business meeting' with that partner of yours. He prints your work and pimps you out—hell of a partnership."

There was no mistaking the soft sniffle that followed that time.

Greg shook his head as he continued to head office. As he passed Exhibit Aurora, he glanced inside. The princess still looked peaceful, even though Monty had attempted to break through the glass. He wondered if she had been the diplomatic type of royal who gave everyone a chance. Would she have heard Monty and Lizzie out, allowing them to plead their case?

Dez had said he always tried to talk to her. Something about familiar voices aiding coma patients. Greg figured he might as well give it a shot. He cupped his hand to his mouth and called into the exhibit.

"Your Highness, I'm sure you would've been a great judge of character. But just in case you didn't realize, the Mongoose is an asshole, and the reporter is a sugar baby. Neither are worth your time."

He felt a bit silly, but if Dez was right, maybe she would at least appreciate the gossip.

CHAPTER 12

2025, Dez's Apartment

Dez grinned as he read the transcript of his conversation with Aurora for probably the millionth time. It had been so brief, but he felt he'd made some of the most scientific progress the museum had ever seen. It sucked that he couldn't share it with anyone.

He'd been debating continuing on with the conversations and saving them for the next eight months. By then, he'd have graduated, could quit the custodian job, and then go to Dr. Ellison with his findings. What could she possibly do in that situation? He'd be providing her with everything she'd ever wanted. Surely, she'd hire him on the spot.
Right?

He'd also been racked with guilt. If Dr. Ellison was as involved with Aurora's case as Killenger said, he felt almost obligated to share the information as soon as possible.

Laying back on his bed, Dez smashed a pillow into his face, muffling an exasperated yell. He'd made an outstanding discovery—something he'd always known he was capable of, even if no one else had believed in him. He tossed the pillow to the side, letting out a sigh.

Well, he still hadn't woken her up yet. That was the actual goal. But speaking with her had to be a step in the right direction.

He pulled his laptop up his chest to read the conversation again.

What a strange name. Are you foreign?

The museum had never disclosed the exact location the princess had been found. The last name "d'Ambray" had to place her in Europe somewhere. "Desmond" was Irish, derived from South Munster. The first Earl of Desmond was recorded in the seventeenth century, so it'd make sense for Aurora to not be familiar with it. She had most likely been asleep for a couple hundred years already.

He rubbed his temples—history was absolutely not his thing. He'd been forced to reach out to a former roommate who was now a professor in the field. Dez didn't have a problem with the guy, but he tended to ramble before finally getting to the point. He pitied his students. After ten minutes of dodging coffee invitations, he'd managed to get the information on name origins and Earls.

You're certainly a peculiar one, Dez.

That wasn't the first time a word like that had been used to describe him.

Weird.

Odd.

Interesting.

She hadn't said peculiar good or peculiar bad, though. Heck, she had continued to talk to him.

A rebel? I can appreciate that.

Now that was different…he'd never been described in such a way. He always followed the rules to the T. He had to in order to get all the scholarships he'd received. Currently, he'd been consistently terrified at the idea of getting caught. But he couldn't deny the thrill of keeping such a big secret.

I'll be eagerly awaiting our next conversation.

He closed his laptop.

He'd keep it a secret for just a little while longer. He wanted to get to know her more as the princess, not the project. This would be something he'd keep close to his chest for a long time, and he was going to enjoy it when he could.

***

Aurora's Dreams

Aurora had been checking the book constantly since first writing to Dez. When nothing new appeared, she would simply reread their initial conversation. She hadn't realized how isolated she had felt. Even the brief conversation they shared had ignited something in her. It had been so long since there was another person in her life. She had found herself smiling randomly, looking forward to having new words appear.

Speaking of which.

She checked the book for probably the millionth time, pouting when there still wasn't anything new. How long had it been? Surely a full day by now. She'd already had two meals, sea time and had decided to even try painting. Granted, she didn't know what his situation was. He didn't know hers. She'd make sure to discuss all that this evening.

Wait…evening.

There were clearly evenings here. So time somehow existed, she just didn't have any way to record it. Sunrises and sunsets didn't exist here, it was either night or day, no in between. But Dez might be in a different point in time altogether. The sun had been high when they first spoke.

She anxiously opened the book again and squealed when she saw new words had appeared.

Aurora?

She eagerly grabbed her quill.

I'm here.

How are you?

Truthfully, I've been anxiously awaiting another message from you.

I'm sorry, I would have been here sooner, but got tied up with work.

What role do you currently hold?

There was a long pause.

I… clean.

She tilted her head, confused. Was he ashamed of that?

It would appear you're not thrilled with your position of servitude.

Servants had always been so much kinder than the nobles she had interacted with. Having to work for what they had made them humbler.

It's temporary. I'm studying to be an engineer.

Engineer? Building military equipment?

Sorry, that probably means something different to you. I'm working towards being in an applied science field.

She frowned. That was one area she had struggled with during her schooling.

That's fascinating.

You don't sound super enthusiastic.

I didn't mean to sound unenthusiastic. It's more so I don't understand science that well. I enjoy philosophy and math, though.

She held her breath as she waited for his response.

You'd be surprised. The type of science I'm studying uses a lot of math. And I'm guessing your philosophy studies are more similar to my science studies than you think.

She released the breath with a relieved huff.

That's interesting. Actually, it relates to something I wanted to talk about. We seem to be... different in certain ways. Are you in a separate realm than I am?

Another long pause.

It might be better to explain that face to face.

CHAPTER 13

2025, The Museum of Historical Mysteries

"You look fantastic."

Kyra had called off yesterday as well. Even with the guilt she'd been feeling, she had still been too drained to return. Most of the two days had been spent crying and snuggling with Sigmund.

"You needed the days off. Amazing what some extra rest and relaxation can do for the body, huh?"

She just continued to smile and nod. She couldn't tell Lila that she had, in fact, not gotten any extra rest or relaxation. If anything, she was more stressed out than before, just completely out of tears. And she definitely couldn't mention the real reason for her fresh face. *Well, I'm actually a fairy and haven't really cried over some past trauma until two days ago, and my tears have healing properties.*

Yeah, that would go over well.

"Seeing that you didn't call me yesterday, I'm assuming business as usual with the princess?"

"Yup, she's been good." Lila pulled her keycard from her pocket and headed for the lab. "I'm guessing you're going to check in on her first?"

"Of course, she was without me for two whole days."

"Good morning, Your Highness."

Even after all this time, Kyra couldn't break the habit of addressing Aurora formally. She took a deep breath, always hoping the scent of roses would return. She initially tried to use the fragrance as a form of enticement, but it had faded away with the rest of her blessing long ago.

Nothing but the sterile, lemony scent of floor cleaner now.

She crossed her arms and stared at the Sleeping Beauty. She had cried so much the past two days that now, she just felt numb.

"Highness, surely you wouldn't blame me if I just wanted to…"

Stop.

She just wanted to stop.

Turn in her resignation. Leave Lila in charge. Pack up Sigmund and retreat to her home realm. Even though she'd hardly slept the past two days, not having to do anything Aurora related had been nice. She'd been able to schedule a last-minute e-visit with her therapist, Maura, to discuss her downward spiral.

Kyra, you've been at this, and only this, for two years. Of course you're going to want some you time.

Maura was the only human who knew Kyra's secret. When she'd first started therapy, she thought she could continue to play human. After just one session, it became apparent that Maura was going to have to know the whole truth. Even though she had been living as a human for centuries now, it had still been difficult to understand mental health. If she wanted real help, she needed to be honest. She hadn't cast a memory-wiping spell for quite some time, so wasn't sure what would happen if her therapist had freaked out. Amazingly, Maura had done little more than blink at the confession. After a short moment, she had muttered, "Well, that makes more sense."

Kyra peered at Aurora once more before heading off to the lab, ready to lose herself in data that never changed.

And then she saw it.

Her heart nearly stopped. She blinked, leaning closer until her nose was almost touching the glass.   "Lila?" she called, afraid to look away. "LILA!"

The click clack of the high heels echoed through the hall before Lila burst in. She was soon at Kyra's side, face flushed pink. "What? What happened?"

"Look!" Kyra pointed towards the glass with a trembling hand. "Her... her head. It moved."

Lila moved closer and squinted. "Kyra, come on. You're tired. They probably just positioned her weird after aquatic therapy."

"Her. Head. Moved." Kyra snapped. "I know her face, I know every detail. Her head moved."

Lila began to argue, but a soft moan silenced her.

The two women turned back to Aurora, eyes widening as her head did indeed move. It was slow and subtle, but unmistakable. Her face turned towards them as if she were trying to listen. Almost as if she were aware.

"Oh my god," Lila whispered, "She... she did move."

Although Kyra felt completely drained, she could have cried tears of joy at that moment. She only held them back because she couldn't explain glittering fairy tears at the moment.

Lila shook her head, almost in a daze. "She's not in a REM cycle, you can't move during that. But she's not in that coma like state either. This... this is new."

"Shit, I need to write this down." Kyra's hands fumbled as she pulled a notebook from her bag. "Lila, I don't know what to do."

Lila's laughter was borderline hysterical. "You and me both. No one expected this. Not in the two years since you've worked here, not ever." She pulled her phone out, fingers just as shaky as Kyra's. "I'll call the medical team."

Kyra could only nod. She peered back at the girl she had been watching over for centuries. As Lila rapidly chattered into her phone, she felt a warm, fuzzy feeling spread through her.

Hope.

For the first time in so long, she felt hope.

CHAPTER 14

2025, Dez's Apartment

"Oh COME ON."

Dez nearly threw the secondhand tablet across the room, only resisting when he thought of the fifty bucks he'd forked over for it. It was cheap, but it added up when one was a graduate student.

It had been three weeks. Three weeks since he and Aurora had connected. And nearly three weeks since he'd promised to explain her situation better if they could actually see each other. After tapping into Aurora's mind so quickly, he'd been riding the "I'm a genius" high. Good ole Dez, always so smart, so successful, so much better than everyone else…

He was also fantastic at putting his foot in his mouth.

After initial contact, he'd tried connecting his phone, laptop, and even an old webcam to the EEG to no avail. He'd even messed with wiring a hotspot into her head, which in hindsight, was a really stupid idea. He was currently trying to clone the code onto the tablet and build a makeshift FaceTime app, but it was failing spectacularly.

Dez set the device on his end table, then flopped face-first on his bed. Why hadn't the lab door been left open in June? The thought of spending the summer with Aurora was so appealing. But now, between being up to his eyeballs in research for his midterm project and the exhibit, his head was about ready to implode.

He needed to come clean with her—his plans proved to be more difficult than he initially thought. She'd be disappointed, but they could at least continue talking. He smiled into the mattress. Their conversations had become the highlight of his evenings.

She was smart, charming, and funny as hell. They'd bonded over being dedicated to knowledge and their love of math. Although he had advanced technology on his side, Aurora was quicker with advanced equations as she only had her mind. She'd make a hell of a robotics engineer if she were born in this era.

His phone buzzed. He peeked at the screen without moving his face from the mattress. Another text from his boss.

FYI, don't bother cleaning Exhibit Aurora if her team is still there tonight. They're trying some new fancy schmancy electrode or something.

Dez frowned. They had the whole day during regular hours to test out new equipment. Besides, for some reason they'd limited the public hours recently, allowing more research time. Why did they need to stay late?

Then again, he was definitely breaking all sorts of rules, so he couldn't think about "playing fair."

Sounds good.

He tossed the phone next to the tablet and shoved his face back into the mattress. Maybe it *was* time to tell Dr. Ellison everything. They wouldn't have to use any new equipment if he did. The shame of using his hacking skills to completely bypass the security system was eating at him as well.

He snorted, imagining how Aurora would react. She'd give him a lecture on virtue ethics or something. He'd been way off when he said her philosophy studies were like his engineering studies. She was obviously the most familiar with the philosophers pre-fifteenth century. Similar to history, philosophy had never been his thing, but he could read Aurora's notes on Marguerite Porete forever.

Theologians and other clerks,
You won't understand this book,
— However bright your wits —
If you do not meet it humbly,
And in this way, Love and Faith
Make you surmount Reason, for

Come on, that was brilliant. Before Aurora, he'd never once would have touched something titled *The Mirror of Simple Souls*. He'd checked it out from the library soon after she wrote him that quote.

Aurora was passionate about knowledge and made things interesting—even fun to learn about. She'd be an amazing college professor too, come to think about it.

His phone started ringing. He sent it straight to voicemail; who the heck *called* people nowadays?

Another ring, another redirect to voicemail.

Yet another ring, a *FaceTime request* this time? Dez snarled as he rolled over and answered.

"WHAT?"

His mother's face appeared on the screen, her mouth dropping open in shock. "Desmond Cathal Buckley, how dare you?"

He scrambled to sit up. "Mom! I'm so sorry!"

"You'd better be sorry," she said, her eyes squinting before turning into an amused roll. "I'm just trying to be a good mother and check in on my hardworking son."

If there was one thing Sloane Buckley was good at, it was guilt tripping.

"I'm under a lot of stress, okay? Answering my phone has been the last thing on my mind."

She sniffed, "I suppose it's midterm season, isn't it? Still, I know you didn't even look to see who was calling you."

"Guilty," he threw his hand up in surrender, "but you've got my attention now. What's up?"

She rolled her eyes again before cracking a smile. "I figured you'd want to know about your father's current project."

Dez groaned. "I thought he was retiring."

"That man is never going to retire and you know it. Now do you want to hear about it, or not?"

He'd inherited his love of science and technology from his father; Dr. Cormac Buckley, a renowned neurologist.

"Is he at least only working part time?"

"Thankfully, yes. It's barely part time, but he's home before 4 P.M. now. Anyway, I figured you'd be interested in this thing because it involves lucid dreaming."

Dez's ears perked up. "Go on."

"So, in September of last year, some researchers claimed they had two people able to communicate through lucid dreams. It was just a simple message, but they say it worked."

He slumped. He'd heard about the project when it first happened, but the announcement had been brief. There wasn't any concrete proof either, with the only thing released being a video of computer generated mannequins participating in the experiment.

"Mom, that didn't go anywhere."

She clicked her tongue. "No no no, *they* couldn't get it to go anywhere. So they gave the whole program to your father."

He shot up in bed. "WHAT?!"

"He doesn't have the time to play with it, so he's giving it to you."

Dez was gobsmacked. This could be the key to actually seeing Aurora, and it was just being given to him? "Seriously?"

She smirked. "Well, *I'm* really giving it to you. He promised he'd take me on a cruise and I'm not letting him get distracted by a new shiny plaything. It's all packed up in the garage. Come grab it whenever."

He grinned. "I'll try to swing by before work."

"Oh yes, how is your girlfriend?"

"MOM!"

She'd been referring to Aurora as his girlfriend ever since his obsession with the exhibit became apparent. Her eyes twinkled with mischief. "You know, you're actually older than her now, right? It'd be cool having a princess as a daughter-in-law."

"Goodbye, Mother."

He hung up before she could say anything else.

Aurora might have the chance to see him. A real chance. And he was definitely going to take it.

CHAPTER 15

2025, The Museum of Historical Mysteries

Communication disconnected

The EEG blinked red as it failed to connect to their new piece of equipment; a makeshift polygraph machine.

Lila sighed. "It was worth a shot."

Kyra's lips tightened. "Polygraphs are all pseudoscience quackery anyway."

"Hun, there's still hope. Her moving and making sound is still a great sign."

Lila, always the optimist, made a good point. During the entire time Kyra had kept watch, the princess had never moved on her own or made the usual sleep sounds. Since that day she returned to work, Aurora had been doing both consistently.

"You're right. I just really want to understand why it's happening now."

Lila rubbed her shoulder. "I know, I do too, but we should take today as a win. Any progress is good."

That was also true. Kyra looked at her coworker, who had undoubtedly become her best friend in this human life. Friends didn't keep secrets. Maybe if Lila knew she was a fairy, even more progress could be made.

But what if she reacted negatively? It was one thing to study the supernatural from an academic standpoint and another thing entirely to be confronted with it. Would Lila think she was some kind of imposter? A fraud who had inserted herself into the field under false pretenses? Or worse, what if Lila saw her as a freak show to be studied? She'd be a brand new exhibit herself: The Real Life Tinkerbell.

Kyra swallowed and took a breath. "Lila I—"

A crashing sound cut her off. They turned to find a bottle of window cleaner rolling towards them. Lila stopped it with her heel, rolling her eyes.

"Clumsy, that one." She looked out into the hallway. "Dr. Desmond?"

Dr. Desmond? Had the museum hired someone new without Kyra's knowledge? She straightened her lab coat to introduce herself, only to see the lovestruck custodian awkwardly enter the room.

"I'm so sorry, Dr. Killenger. I was told you might still be working, so I wanted to check before cleaning up. Leaned on my cart and…gravity happened."

Kyra frowned in sharp contrast to Lila's bright smile. Why had he even bothered coming to the exhibit if he knew they might still be here? Had he been eavesdropping?

"Kyra, don't scare the poor boy away." Lila gestured towards him, "Dr. Kyra Ellison, this is Desmond Buckley."

Buckley? As in Dr. Cormac Buckley?

He tentatively extended his hand, "You can call me Dez."

Kyra shook his hand with a firm grip. "Charmed."

He didn't flinch, despite the pressure of her grasp. That earned him a few points.

Lila suddenly started tugging Kyra towards the hallway. "We're actually done, so go ahead and mop the floors."

Kyra and Dez gave a simultaneous "What?"

Lila smirked. "Remember, progress? You don't need another sleepless night."

Kyra twisted out of her grip. "Maybe, but we still need to put the equipment away." She held up a finger as Lila went to protest. "Protocol. And I'm using my boss card."

Lila huffed. "Fine." Then her eyes twinkled. "Dez can help."

A yelp escaped the custodian. "Dr. Killenger, I really shouldn't be touching anything."

"Yeah, what he said," Kyra echoed, "Lila, what's gotten into you?"

Lila yanked her in close, her voice barely a whisper. "Look, the kid is just as obsessed with Exhibit Aurora as you are. He was in a bunch of my classes and is crazy brilliant. I was hoping you'd hire him once he graduated, so don't go all mean Dr. Ellison on him."

"I am *not* mean," Kyra hissed.

"Yeah, sure," Lila retorted. "Dez, come help us out, it's okay. Nothing you're not familiar with."

He stepped closer, barely holding his excitement back. "You sure?"

Lila jammed her elbow into Kyra's ribs.

"Of course," she forced out, "Dr. Killenger speaks very highly of you."

CHAPTER 16

2025, The Museum of Historical Mysteries

"Just curious, are you related to Dr. Buckley?"

Dez smiled. He rarely mentioned his dad, fearful people would think he'd helped him along with everything. And seeing that he referred to the museum's current intern as a nepo baby, he'd definitely be called a hypocrite. His parents had always made sure his achievements were his own; he put himself through school, was rewarded with scholarships and got published with no outside help.

"Yeah, he's my dad."

Dr. Ellison blinked in astonishment. "I've been trying to get him on the team since I started here."

"You're not the only one." He chuckled, wrapping up some wires. "Dad's not a fan of sleep studies, focuses more on epilepsy research. That and Mom has been trying to get him to travel the world with her. He doesn't believe in rest."

"Who does that sound like?" Dr. Killenger teased.

"I haven't a clue what you're talking about," Dr. Ellison sniffed. "Tell your father the offer's always on the table."

"Don't count on it," Dez chuffed, "but I'll let him know."

What he should do was tell her that a lucid dreaming program and all its equipment was hiding in his janitorial cart. If they worked together, they could make a breakthrough. And she'd still get to work with a Buckley.

But what if she just took the equipment, shooed him out and got him banned from the museum? It was that "what if" that kept him biting his tongue. She seemed reasonable, but she also seemed like someone who followed strict rules. Rules that he was currently breaking.

"How long have you worked here now? Since summer, right?" He nodded. Dr. Ellison counted some bolts before packing them up. "What made you want to work here?"

Killinger snorted. "Girl, he's basically been here longer than our entire team has."

Dez blushed. "My class came here on a field trip when I was twelve, I just fell in love with the place." He glanced at Aurora. "It's just a custodial job, but I get to be around my favorite things, so it works out."

He swore she cracked a smile. "Twelve huh? And you're how old now?"

"Twenty-five."

She hummed. "About to graduate?"

"In May."

She smiled; a small one, but it was there. "I'll keep that in mind."

Dez couldn't help but grin as he plugged in the EEG wires. Once her tough exterior had been chipped away, Dr. Ellison was downright lovely. She had genuinely cared about his education and had even offered some book recommendations. Killinger had reminded him to send his resume again before the women left. "You can thank me later," she whispered.

It had been a good day. A great day even. He couldn't wait to tell Aurora about it.

He typed a quick Hello as he began plugging in the lucid dreaming equipment.

Where have you been?!

Ah crud, she was all about punctuality. It wasn't that late, was it? He checked the time.

Shit.

Apologies, Your Highness."

By God's bones, Dez, I told you not to call me that.

He laughed. Medieval cursing was something else.

I have a very good excuse.

Fine, present your case.

Time to add "judge" to her growing list of potential careers.

I think I figured out a way for you to actually see me.

Wait, really?

Ah, he was in her good graces again.

Completely serious.

Well? Get on with it then. And don't ramble about details like you can sometimes.

He chuckled as he pulled out the dreaming cap. She was just as eager as he was.

I do not ramble.

You do too. Now move along.

Placing the cap on his head, he powered the main program up on the tablet. He took a deep breath—Ideally, he'd induce REM sleep for both of them, start lucid dreaming, and then trigger the video calling setup he'd finally perfected.

Simple, right?

He grimaced. He hadn't been able to fully test everything, so was flying by the seat of his pants. If something went wrong, there was no one to bail him out.

But it would be worth it. He knew it would be.

Taking one more deep breath, he lay back on the bench he'd dragged in and powered everything up.

"Sweet dreams."

CHAPTER 17

Aurora's Dreams

Aurora crossed her arms and glared at the book.

First, the man had been late, and now he was futzing about with whatever this solution was. She'd given Dez a lot of grace, but had a feeling he was struggling. He was obviously brilliant, but she assumed speaking face to face would be difficult to figure out.

She squeezed her eyes shut and imagined an encrusted goblet with blood-red liquid swirling inside. Wine had always been readily available to her in the castle, but she'd hardly drunk any. She needed it now.

Opening her eyes, she grinned as the goblet sat in front of her. Swirling the cup before taking a sip, she checked the book again. Still nothing new. How was this going to work anyway? She half expected a miniature Dez to appear in the pages like a real life storybook. That would be fun. She took another sip as she tried to conjure up an image of what the mystery man looked like. What color was his hair? His eyes? His skin?

What did his voice sound like?

What would he think about her?

She scoffed. As if that mattered. She was beautiful and loved how she looked, it didn't matter what any man thought. And she was skilled with a bow and arrow if any man dared to believe he could have an opinion on the matter.

What sounded like a wind chime blew through with a gentle breeze. That was new, she quite liked it. Closing her eyes, she let the melody float around her, feeling the sun warm her face. A goblet of wine, gentle sunbeams, and calming music. How lovely.

Then a loud snapping sound ruined it.

Aurora's eyes popped open, and she glanced around, trying to find the source of the noise. Not too far away, she spotted something hanging from a chestnut tree. Whatever it was kicked its legs and let out a yell.

"UM, A LITTLE HELP?!"

Oh.

OH.

Aurora picked up her long skirts and ran towards the tree, the figure becoming clearer the closer she got. It was a man wearing strange gray clothing that looked like a tunic and chausses sewn together, with an odd folded section at the neck. She shielded her eyes from the sun, gazing up.

"Dez...?"

"AURORA?"

She almost curtsied out of old habit, but thankfully thought better of it. "Hang on, I'll get you down."

"Hanging on is all I really can do right now!"

She giggled and closed her eyes, imagining a large, sturdy ladder. A gasp from Dez signaled it had appeared. She went to climb it, only to have her dress snag on the bottom. Curses.

Wait a second.

She hadn't tried this yet, but it was worth a shot. Closing her eyes again, she imagined she was wearing a pair of bloomers and stays. It wasn't exactly ladylike, but it was the first thing she thought of. She opened her eyes and grinned at her new outfit before clambering up the ladder.

"Here!" She reached her hand out, "Swing over here!"

Dez's eyes widened. "I'm pretty sure I told you how NOT athletic I am."

She groaned. "You want to hang there all day? At least attempt it, I'll catch you."

"And if I miss?"

"You can't get hurt here, I promise you."

Well, she couldn't get hurt here. She wasn't sure about others. He looked down, gulped, and then began to swing. After gaining enough momentum, he let go and came barreling towards Aurora with a screech. She managed to grab him around the waist as he made it halfway onto the ladder.

"See, you're fine."

He fumbled to get himself completely steady. "You are *far* too calm about this."

She began heading down. "You are overreacting *far* too much."

Once they both were safely on the ground and Aurora had materialized her dress back, they finally got the chance to look at each other.

He was handsome.

Tall, lanky and definitely not athletic, but he was handsome. He had fair skin with freckles scattered across his cheeks. His hair was, funnily enough, a chestnut shade of brown and he had striking green eyes.

"Uh, Aurora?"

She'd been staring. "Sorry, I'm honestly in disbelief that you're here. How are you here exactly?"

He ruffled his hair. "Okay, yeah, it's… a lot."

"Again, I'm obviously not going anywhere. We have plenty of time."

"You do, I don't know how long this is going to last."

Her eyes narrowed. "Is this a spell? I know those usually have limited time."

"Something like that."

She put her hands on her hips, cocking an eyebrow. "Well, then start talking. I waited a decent amount of time already and just rescued you from a tree. I think I deserve an explanation."

Before he could speak again, he flickered like a flame in the wind. His eyes widened. "Shit, the connection's unstable."

More terms she didn't understand again. "Can I do anything to help?"

He flickered again. "Maybe if I ground somehow."

"Ground?"

"Like...focus harder? Acknowledge I'm really here."

"Oh, here," she grabbed both his hands, "close your eyes and just listen to me. You're finally here, I'm here, we're finally meeting. We're in…my own little realm. We're under a chestnut tree, you can probably hear waves from the seaside in the distance, you might smell some of the wine I had on my breath—apologies."

He chortled and opened his eyes again. The flickering had stopped, so Aurora figured the grounding had been successful. She noticed he was staring straight at her face.

His grin widened. "Your eyes are blue. I knew it."

CHAPTER 18

Aurora's Dreams

"Is this supposed to taste like this?"

Aurora had materialized a drink for Dez to further calm his nerves. She shrugged. "Honestly, I couldn't tell you what it's supposed to taste like. Usually just the knights drank it."

Dez wrinkled his nose. No wonder mead wasn't as popular now.

Aurora smirked. "Would you like something else?"

He placed the cup on the ground. "No, it's alright. I should probably keep my mind sharp anyway."

"Alright," she folded her hands in her lap, her posture impossibly regal. "Now, explain yourself."

"Has anyone ever told you how direct you are?"

"Many times. It's simpler not to flit about in certain situations. Besides," she tucked a strand of hair behind her ear, "great leaders don't have the time for fluff."

He couldn't help but admire her. She always had a point. He knew she would have been in the history books, whether she'd been in an eternal sleep or not. He rolled his shoulders and groaned. Time to explain everything.

"You have to promise me that you won't freak out."

Her eyes twinkled. "I won't promise anything of the sort. I can promise that I'll remain as calm as I can."

Oh boy.

"Aurora, when were you born?"

"September 26th, 1420. Why?"

He chewed his lip. Hearing her say it out loud made it all the more real. Here went nothing. "I was born in the year 2000."

She blinked, furrowed her brows, then blinked again. "Pardon?"

"I was born in the year 2000, I'm currently living in the year 2025… and so are you."

He expected her to scream, cry, or at the very least, kick him out of her head. But she continued to sit there, hands still in her lap, staring at him. Finally, she spoke.

"Am...am I dead?"

He immediately shock his head.

"You're sure I'm not a ghost?"

"I'm positive."

She took a deep breath. "If it's 2025, how am I alive?"

"You're asleep."

Her eyes narrowed. "Poppycock."

"Aurora," he used a firmer tone this time, "you're asleep. Archaeologists found you in an abandoned castle in the 1960s. You've been kept safe in a museum since then. You haven't aged, you're perfectly healthy and this," he waved his hand, "is your dream."

She was quiet again, searching his face for any sign of a lie. He wanted to reach out and grab her hand, but worried the gesture would be unwelcome.

"What's a museum?"

The question baffled him. He'd dropped a bomb on her, and she was still curious about what was unknown to her. "I don't think that really became a thing until the Renaissance. It's a place where scholars can display their discoveries. People visit to look and learn about objects from the past."

She nodded slowly. "Similar to a library?"

He had to smile. "Exactly like a library."

"So I'm… a discovery now? On display?"

"Yes."

"And I'm asleep."

"Yes."

"And this is all a dream."

"Yes."

She blinked a few more times before falling back into the grass. "By Christ's fingernails."

Dez let her lie there, giving her time to process everything. All things considered, she was reacting way better than he expected. She had closed her eyes and was taking long, deep breaths.

He gazed around at her dream world; it was beautiful. Because dreams mainly stem from pre-existing knowledge, he assumed Aurora lived a wonderful life before she slept. Various fruit trees swayed in the breeze, plush grass and wildflowers carpeted the ground, and a gorgeous seaside stretched into the distance.

"Dez?"

He turned to find her still sprawled out, looking up at the sky. "Yes?"

"What did you mean when you said you knew my eyes were blue?"

His face went hot. "Uh…"

"If I'm actually asleep," she propped herself up on her elbows, "and this is the first time seeing me in a somewhat awake state, how did you know?"

"Genetics," he answered. "With your hair color and complexion, science would predict blue eyes. They suit you, real pretty."

Had that just slipped out?

Luckily, she smiled. "Well, thank you. You're an absolute charmer."

He grinned. "Aurora, I promise you that you're safe. So many people have been trying to wake you up since you were discovered. For over fifty years now. People care about you."

"What happened to my family?"

He slumped. He couldn't answer that. No records of the d'Ambray lineage existed past the late 14th century. As he went to tell her he just didn't know, he felt the flickering sensation return.

"Shit."

She raised an eyebrow at him before her eyes widened. She went to grasp his hand in an apparent grounding attempt, but it was too late.

"Dez, wait—"

The dream shattered.

***

2025, The Museum of Historical Mysteries

Dez shielded his eyes from the florescent lighting as he woke. The hardness of the bench became extremely apparent.

"Goddammit."

He sat up, took the cap off and gazed at the machinery.

Disconnected.

"Goddammit again."

He began powering down everything, trying not to get upset. Any progress was good, right? Dr. Killenger had always said that. The fact that he'd been able to enter Aurora's dream world and have a conversation with her was huge. He'd just have to figure out a way to make the lucid dreaming, EEG, and his own brainwave connections more stable. He shouldn't have been surprised by the instability of the setup, given its high power consumption. That was part of engineering; figuring out what worked and finding ways to make it better.

He stupidly packed everything up when it hit him; He hadn't checked on Aurora.

"Shit."

He dashed over to the dome, nearly slipping on the floor he had just cleaned.

His heart sank.

She was still asleep, but had turned completely onto her side. Her arms and legs were curled in, her body folded into a fetal position. She was self-soothing. In a rush, he powered the EEG machine back on and typed a message.

Aurora?

Nothing.

Aurora? Please, I didn't do that!

Still nothing.

He fell to his knees and pressed up against the glass, screw the smudges. Maybe there was a chance she could hear him.

"I'm sorry. I'm so sorry."

CHAPTER 19

October 2025, Wellington Bits,
Lizzie's Life Lessons by Elizabeth
Hildegrant

What is The Museum of Historical Mysteries hiding?

For the past five weeks, Exhibit Aurora has only been open three days a week. This is the first time something like this has happened since I was in middle school over a decade ago. One would think that if the reduced hours were due to research, Dr. Kyra Ellison would have released a statement to the public by now. If you ask me, the limited access has to do with security issues.

I've been keeping this information under wraps, but I witnessed an alarming situation back in September. I saw one of the museum's tour guides kicking Monty Monjurse out of the building. I can't confirm it, but I'd bet good money that the Mongoose was causing trouble in Exhibit Aurora. Just the night before—actually, in the wee hours of that same morning—someone caught the Monjurse heir in a park fountain wearing only his boxers, ranting about being related to Prince Charming and "kissing himself a wife."

After the Mongoose's removal from the museum, I attempted to get an interview with the tour guide who had escorted him from the premises, but they refused to talk. The very next day, an announcement declared Monty permanently banned from The Museum of Historical Mysteries. Whatever he did must have been extremely serious, seeing that Mommy and Daddy

Mongoose have managed to sweep all of his past antics under the rug without issue.

Digging further into the Monjurse family, I discovered that their lineage stretches back to the 15th century, and possibly even earlier. Monty is, in fact, a direct descendant of the renowned King Philip Monjurse XV. Furthermore, Monty hadn't turned twenty-one by the time the kissing ban was instated, meaning he never could "shoot his shot," so to speak. Could it be that the Mongoose believes it's his destiny to wake the princess?

So what exactly happened between Monty and Princess Aurora that day? Was she harmed in some way? We may never truly know, but I'd say all signs point to yes. I believe it's time for the museum to address the public regarding the situation, as it relates to their most beloved exhibit. So many people care about Aurora d'Ambray, and we deserve to know what's going on.

CHAPTER 20

2025, Kyra's House

"Oh I HATE that little RAT."

Sigmund chirped at the mention of rodents.

"No Sig, not an actual rat. But maybe I could turn her into one…"

Transforming annoying reporters into rats probably didn't fit into the White Magic category, but Kyra could definitely spin it as being for the greater good.

"I don't know, bud. She probably wouldn't taste that great, even if she were a rodent." Sigmund trotted off to his water dish. As if he'd care about taste, he'd probably just gleefully bat Lizzie around before finally putting her out of her misery. She could turn Monty into an actual Mongoose while she was at it. How that imbecile was related to Philip, she would never understand.

"I'm a good fairy, I swear," Kyra muttered to herself.

Stupid wannabe reporter, constantly sticking her big nose into everything. First, she demanded respect for Aurora's privacy. Now, she wanted each and every detail on the princess released.

"By Queen Mab, that girl needs to find a new hobby." Sigmund yowled from the kitchen, clearly judging her. "Oh shut up, I haven't sworn the fairy way in eons. Sometimes the usual bullshit doesn't cut it."
Her phone buzzed, and she grimaced when she saw the message from the big boss.

I scheduled you for a video interview tonight to clarify everything. Do your thing.

Bloody hell.

Geri, you know I hate doing those stupid things.

Well, you're so good at them, and you have all the information. We need to shut the social media darling up. So suck it up, buttercup.

Of course she was good at interviews—she'd been a TV reporter before she took on the Kyra persona, and a government official before that. Both positions had allowed her to stay connected to Aurora. When she realized being part of the research team would get her as close as possible since the archaeologists had discovered the princess, she applied for a biomedical engineering program. A bachelor's, master's and PhD later, Geraldine Pach, Otto's great-granddaughter and Henry's granddaughter, had personally offered her the lead position.

Kyra leaned back in her chair, eyes drifting to the giant chest in the corner of her home office. It held all the degrees she'd earned throughout the centuries. Some were for Denise, others for Jaclyn, and a few for Madeline. Different personas she'd carefully crafted.

Kyra had to admit that living so many human lives had been an outstanding experience. She'd been a duchess, a rancher, a musician, and so much more. Her image had been different with each new persona—it was like sampling every flavor of her favorite candy. She chuckled when she thought of the giant hair that Ashley, her TV reporter persona, had sported in the late 80s.

"OOF." Sigmund had landed on her chest with a loud trill. She scratched behind his ears, earning a deep purr.

"Are you going to crash my interview like you did last time?"

She swore the cat was smiling. So that was a yes. "At least people love cats nowadays."

***

"This is Deandre Wallace with *Channel 9 Thursday Evening News Report*. A Mongoose, a social media star and a biomedical expert; what do these three things all have in common?"

Kyra smirked. Thank god Deandre hadn't called Lizzie a journalist.

"We are all familiar with Princess Aurora d'Ambray by now. She's been a staple at The Museum of Historical Mysteries for over fifty years. So why has access to her exhibit suddenly become limited? Here to answer that very question is Dr. Kyra Ellison, the team lead for Exhibit Aurora."

Kyra took a deep breath, double checked her mic once more, and turned on her webcam. Showtime.

"Dr. Ellison, welcome. Thank you for joining us tonight."

She flashed her most dazzling smile. "Thank you, Deandre. The pleasure is mine."

"I know you're incredibly busy, so I'll get straight to the point. Why the suddenly limited access to Exhibit Aurora?"

She took a quick breath. "I can confirm that Monty Monjurse caused a disturbance in the exhibit this past September. One of our senior tour guides, acting very professionally, had to escort him off the premises. We have now permanently banned him from the museum."

"So the *Wellington Bits* article was accurate?"

Deandre hated Lizzie just as much as she did. He refused to mention her by name.

"Yes," Kyra confirmed.

"Has the museum limited hours to improve security?"

"Absolutely not; our security is top-notch and frequently updated. Mr. Monjurse never posed an actual threat to the exhibit. Aurora was completely safe. We banned him as a precaution. And if anyone recalls the Crypid Gala last year, this isn't the first time his actions have caused problems for the museum."

"I applaud the museum for taking action against such a notable family."

"Thank you, Deandre. Now, regarding the limited hours, we needed some time before we released this information to the public, but I can also confirm that Princess Aurora has displayed movement in her sleep."

Deandre's eyes widened. "If I'm not mistaken, the princess hasn't moved on her own since she was first placed in the museum, correct?"

"You're absolutely right. This is an incredible breakthrough, and we needed time to adjust to this new reality. We've been trying to determine why she's moving and whether it's because of external factors. We unfortunately had to limit the exhibit hours to establish a baseline sleep state. We don't want to move her for fear of messing anything because of a new location."

"This is incredible news. Congratulations, Dr. Ellison."

"Thank you, Deandre. I'm pleased to announce that Exhibit Aurora will resume normal hours in November. We're making adjustments to her bedding situation to ensure her comfort and it's taking up some time."

"Well, wonderful. Aurora is clearly in capable hands. Thank you again for joining us, Dr. Ellison. I'll let you get some rest now."

"Thank you, Deandre. I appreciate your time."

As soon as the call ended, Kyra dropped her smile and massaged her cheeks. She might be a pro at interviews, but keeping up that grin was exhausting.

"BRRP."

Sigmund was screaming for a second dinner. Kyra rolled her eyes and headed for the kitchen.

"You didn't interrupt, so I guess you deserve some tuna."

Sigmund's triumphant yowl echoed through the house.

CHAPTER 21

2025, Dez's Apartment

Dez smiled as Dr. Ellison and Deandre signed off. That woman had verbally smacked Lizzie and Monty down in the most intelligent way, and he had loved every second. His respect for her grew by the day. The interview gave him hope that the so-called lab rats of the world wouldn't let themselves to be walked all over.

He closed his laptop and cracked the oven to check his cookies. He had used his mom's tried-and-true raspberry thumbprint recipe. They'd been a long-time favorite of both him and his dad.

Dez had pulled a Dr. Ellison and taken his first sick day since elementary school. Aurora needed time to process everything, and he knew he wouldn't be able to resist checking on her if he went into the museum. So, he'd done something he hadn't done in quite a while: he'd invited his father over for a late-night snack.

While Dez had always felt supported by his parents, he could never shake the thought that he'd disappointed his dad by not going into the medical field. He excelled in all the necessary subjects, except for one—he was terrified of of emotions. The thought of telling a parent that their child was possibly going to die made him sick to his stomach.

Dez had been amazed at how easily Greg had taken him in as a friend; something about an extrovert picking an introvert and just adopting them. The fact that Greg worked in the museum's education department while Dez was a janitor was absolutely hysterical. But Greg had also given him the confidence to stand up to Lizzie at last, and now Dez was one of the only people who could actually make her shut her trap.

The doorbell rang.

"It's unlocked," Dez called.

Dr. Buckley stepped into the kitchen. "You really shouldn't leave your door open, Dez."

Dez shrugged. "Don't worry, I only left it unlocked because I knew you were coming."

His dad frowned. "Still, anyone could just wander in."

Dez smiled. "Alright, alright, I'll be more careful."

His dad sniffed the air. "Oh, do I smell raspberry thumbprints?"

Dez chuckled as his father practically floated toward the oven. The cookies were his one true weakness.

"Mom sent me the recipe," Dez said. "Hopefully they're okay."

"They look good so far." His dad leaned on the island. "What's the special occasion?"

"Can't a guy invite his dear old dad over for some quality time?"

Dr. Buckley laughed. "Of course. You just don't even bother calling your parents, so this is out of the norm."

He'd been taking guilt trip lessons from his mother.

"Mom's dragging you off on a cruise soon," Dez said. "I wanted to talk to you before you guys head off."

"Uh oh. What'd you do?"

"Shut up."

His dad smirked as he reached for some oven mitts.

"There's still two more minutes," Dez pointed out.

"I know," Dr. Buckley said, pulling the tray out anyway. "I like them a little under."

Dez gave him a look. "Why don't you tell mom that?"

His dad rolled his eyes. "Dez, love makes you do crazy things. Like not telling your wife you preferred it when she got the baking time wrong on her prize winning cookies."

"Good to know," Dez muttered. "Now, speaking of love…"

His dad blew on a cookie. "You have a lady in your life that your mother somehow doesn't know about?"

"Kind of?"

Dr. Buckley raised an eyebrow. "Kind of. Well, that's better than nothing."

"I've been busy, okay?"

His dad took a bite of a cookie and grinned. "Well done. And you know I'm just messing with you. Seeing as I didn't ask your mother out until I finished residency, I'm not one to talk."

Ah, the romantic lives of medical professionals—they were either sleeping with everyone in the hospital or completely alone.

Dez poured them some milk. "Basically, there's this girl I've known for a while, and I'm starting to think about her differently."

"Dreaming about her?"

"Something like that." Dez chugged some milk. "I just don't know what to do."

"Oh, that's easy." His dad finished his third cookie. "Ask her out."

"That doesn't sound easy, Dad."

"Then just keep talking to her. Learn more about her life, her aspirations, her hobbies. Normal stuff. If she feels the same way, there will be signs."

Apparently, it *was* that easy.

"Thanks, Dad."

"No problem. Now, what's this about your mom giving you that lucid dreaming equipment?"

"What? No clue what you're talking about," Dez said, playing dumb.

Dr. Buckley groaned. "I guess I have to resign myself to floating around the Bahamas for a month."

The cookies were long gone by the time his dad left. Not that Dez minded, less cleanup.

His phone buzzed. Probably Greg.

Aye, THE Dez Buckley took a night off?

I took a… what do you call it… a mental health day? Just needed a night in. Dad came over, we ate cookies.

Sounds like a romping roaring good time.

Raspberry thumbprints and milk.

Your mom's recipe??? Why wasn't I invited?

You said you had a date.

I got played. It ended up being an ex that's kinda obsessed with me. Would have preferred cookies.

I feel like I should be concerned about that.

Nah, it's cool. I called her mom to come get her.

Not making me any less concerned.

I'm fine. Anywho, I'm betting your work wife missed you.

Work wife?

Aurora.

So we're married now?

Duh. Just checking in! Invite me the next time you bake.

Roger that.

Dez flopped onto his sofa. Hopefully, he hadn't made a mistake by skipping work. Knowing Aurora, she'd be pissed. But was letting her cool off the best idea?

Of course it was. It had to be.

His phone buzzed again. He sighed. "When did I become so popular?"

It was his mom.

Thank you for spending time with your father, he said the cookies were good. Also, what's this about a girl?

He groaned. Married people really told each other everything.

CHAPTER 22

2025, The Lab

Something had been different with Aurora this past week. She was behaving almost like a petulant teenager, refusing to get out of bed. She had continued to move in her sleep, but now with visible frustration; thrashing, slamming a hand into the mattress and kicking her blankets off. It had gotten so bad that the medical team couldn't take her to aquatic therapy. She'd practically clung to the bed, refusing to be moved from the exhibit.

The soft murmurs of sleep had turned into aggravated grunts. Something in her head was making her angry, and the team just couldn't figure it out.

Kyra had spent the entire day hunched over the Exhibit Aurora archives, trying to find anything that could explain the changes. As always, nothing helped. Otto and Henry had primarily documented how little Aurora changed over time. Even when they had started physical therapy in the 80s, her sleep state had remained consistent.

What had caused such a drastic turn?

"Hey," Lila tapped Kyra's shoulder, "you staying late?"

Kyra nodded. "Yeah. Something's not right."

Lila sighed. "You know, we were so happy when she started moving. Now she's beating me up."

"I know. I can't figure it out." Kyra closed the 1989 file with a little more force than necessary. It was just as helpful as the others—completely useless.

"Oh look at that," Lila held up her wrist, showing off a deep bruise. "She's got a heck of an arm."

Kyra smirked. "I guess we know her therapy's working?"

"Maybe too well."

Aurora had always been skilled at hand-to-hand combat. Kyra remembered the time she had punched a knight who dared to grope her. She'd hit him so hard, she'd knocked two teeth loose. The man had actually had the audacity to go to King Florestan to complain. The king had first laughed in his face, then taken Aurora to the training grounds to teach the rest of the knights the proper way to throw a punch.

Florestan had been so proud of his daughter.

"Yoohoo, paging Dr. Ellison?"

Kyra snapped out of her thoughts as Lila waved a hand in front of her face.

"Sorry, zoned out."

"It's okay. It's been a long week. Anyway, I'm going to head out. I think Dez is in—I wanted to ask if he's noticed anything in the exhibit."

"That's… that's a good idea."

"I am a doctor, after all." Lila gave an exaggerated bow before walking away.

Kyra pulled out the 1990 file to see if she could find anything new. She knew she wouldn't, but it was worth a shot anyway. She flipped to a photo of Otto, Henry, Henry's son Noah, and five-year-old Geraldine standing next to Aurora's bed. Four generations of the Pach family in one image—and Aurora had been asleep longer than all their ages combined.

She rested her chin on her hand. What would Otto say now? He had passed away seven years after that photo, never achieving his dream of waking Aurora. Henry, now in his nineties, was rumored to be hanging on purely in the hopes of seeing her wake before he died. Noah, completely disinterested with the museum, had gone into accounting and everyone joked he was the "boring" one. But Geri had thankfully inherited Otto and Henry's love of history.

Sure enough, 1990 was a bust. Kyra finally decided to call it a night; there was no point in staying late just to stare at the same dead ends. She collected her things, locked up the lab, and started toward the exit. On her way out, she peered in on Exhibit Aurora and found Dez in his usual spot. At first, she'd found his constant presence odd. Now, she had to admit; it was kind of sweet.

"Hey," she called.

"Hi, Dr. Ellison," he waved. "You alright?"

"For the most part. It's been a rough week."

"Agreed," he grumbled. "I actually took a page out of your book and called out a couple nights ago."

She chuckled. "Hey, don't let anyone question your work ethic. Good night, Dez."

"Good night, Dr. Ellison, drive safe."

Kyra slid into her car, expecting to feel frustration, but she didn't. Instead, she found herself once again studying her reflection. The faint purple tinge under her eyes had returned, but she didn't care. It meant the endless crying had finally stopped.

Sure, they had made no new progress. Sure, Aurora was acting strangely. But Kyra couldn't help but feel like something incredible was about to happen. It had most likely just been a rough week for everyone. Heck, even Dez had called out from his simple custodial job.

Wait.

What day had Dez called out?

Kyra squeezed her eyes shut, thinking hard. If he hadn't mentioned it, she would have sworn he'd been there all week. Had anyone said anything? Lila? Greg?

I'm sitting there waiting for a redhead to show up, and my crazy ex girlfriend suddenly appears. I could have been at Dez's eating cookies with him and his dad.

Greg had no luck with women.

I literally had to call her mom to come pick her up! I felt horrible. The woman's a teacher. She was coming to get her kid on a school night. What is my life?

Dez had been home. It had been a weeknight… but which one?

Were you at least able to see Dr. Ellison on the news?

No! I heard it was epic though…

Kyra's eyes popped open. Thursday. It had happened on Thursday. Aurora had started behaving aggressively over the weekend. Kyra drummed her fingers on her steering wheel. Coincidence? Or did Dez have something to do with it?

Come to think of it… hadn't Aurora started moving after Kyra returned to work? And hadn't Dez been lingering around the exhibit more just before that? She rubbed her temples; she was just more confused now. There had to be a way to sort it all out.

She sighed. There was a way. A simple one. And it would tell her everything she needed to know.

Kyra hesitated for a moment, then stepped out of her car. She glanced around to make sure no one was watching, double-checked, and then climbed back in.

"It's been so long…"

She took a couple of deep breaths, focusing on the magic she hadn't used in centuries. A familiar buzz hummed in the pit of her stomach and sparks flickered under her fingernails.

"Rappel de localisation. Présentez-vous."

Fairies didn't need incantations, but the words helped focus the magic when one was out of practice.

Miraculously, a steady stream of blue mist flowed from her fingertips. She smiled, gathered it in her hands, and blew.

A hazy image of Exhibit Aurora appeared within the swirling cloud. A glowing blue silhouette lay at the center—Aurora. A second figure, this one pink, hovered near her—Dez.

The spell could only clearly recall past events if the caster had witnessed them firsthand. This was just the leftover energy.

Kyra frowned and blew on the cloud again, shuffling through the past six weeks. Every night, except last Thursday, Dez's pink silhouette appeared, lingering far later than his shift required.

Something fishy was going on.

Kyra blinked the cloud away and collapsed back into her car seat. Magic was like riding a bike; she hadn't forgotten how, but after centuries of being out of practice, it was exhausting. Sweat trickled down her neck. She had to figure out what was going on.

Mustering up what little energy she had left, she forced herself out of the car and started back toward the museum.

"I'm gonna catch you, Dez. Whatever it is you're doing."

CHAPTER 23

Aurora's Dreams

"Aurora?"

Aurora pressed her mouth into a tight, thin line. She hadn't said a word to Dez from the moment he'd entered her dream state that day. It'd been a week since she'd even allowed him in, which was something she hadn't realized she could do. This time, she'd had to rescue him from the sea; he'd ended up a tangled mess of limbs and seaweed. Clumsy idiot. Instead of materializing a towel to dry him off, she'd conjured a gale-force wind. He was now looking at her, hair blown wild, eyes wide with shock.

"Aurora."

He took a serious tone. She tensed at his directness.

"I know you saw my notes. I didn't cause the disconnection intentionally; I was just so excited to see you I didn't make it as stable as I should have. It's fixed now, I promise."

Aurora crossed her arms and huffed. Dez frowned.

"Okay, you know what—" He took her by the shoulders and pulled her closer. "I've been wanting to meet you, actually meet you, since I first saw you when I was twelve. I begged my parents to take me on museum trips. I read every piece of information about you. I even took a crappy custodial job just so I could be around you. Why would I poof away on purpose after finally meeting you face to face?"

She relaxed in his grip. No, he was right. She was letting her stubbornness ruin things.

"I suppose not." She placed her hands on his forearms, "I... I apologize."

He gave her a small smile. "Apology accepted. Now," he let her go, "why'd you finally let me in?"

She reached for his hand, already missing his touch, and started leading him away from the seaside. "I read all the notes you sent. They made me realize that I've been lucid dreaming this whole time that I've... been here."

He nodded. "Given what you're able to do, that makes sense. Although…"

"Although?"

"I don't think I've explained REM sleep to you yet, but basically, we go through different cycles when we sleep. You can lucid dream during a REM cycle, but I don't know about the coma-like state you've typically been in."

"Coma?"

"Prolonged state of unconsciousness. Coma patients don't usually respond normally to outside stimulants."

She nodded slowly. "Have I been treated like someone in a coma? Just… lying there?" She wasn't sure how she felt about people just staring at her lifeless body.

"Pretty much. But recently, you actually started moving."

She chewed her lip. "How recently?"

His lips curled into a smirk. "Since we started talking."

She couldn't help but burst into a wide grin. "I suppose you're taking credit for my progress?"

"Well, evidence would lead to that conclusion, wouldn't it, Your Highness?"

She yanked her hand from his and smacked his shoulder.

"Um, ow."

"Don't call me that."

***

"Whoa."

Dez gazed up at the enormous castle Aurora had led him to.

"So… what's this?"

Aurora approached the large double doors and pushed them open. "It's my home." She walked in while Dez hurried after.

"Your home?"

She nodded as they entered the throne room. "Voltav Castle, House of d'Ambray, where I was born, raised… and apparently found." She stopped in front of two jewel encrusted thrones. "My memory has always been precise. I was able to recreate the whole thing." She took a seat on one throne and patted the other. "Sit."

Dez did as he was told. "Your ruler side is showing."

She crossed her legs, resting her chin on her hand. "Can you believe I was expected to get married to some incompetent buffoon and let him rule *my* kingdom? All my education, training, hard work, it would have meant nothing."

"You would have found a way to rule. You know it."

She shook her head again. "I wasn't about to be a dictator, Dez. My father is the…well, *was* one of the best rulers The Seven Kingdoms had ever seen."

Her chest tightened. She'd been avoiding thinking about that. Father… Mother… What had become of them? She pictured them standing before her, as if she had never been separated from them. Her mother's olive skin, warm brown eyes, jet black hair… Her father's golden hair, fair skin, piercing blue eyes—she'd really been a splitting image of him.

The sound of footsteps pulled her back to the present… or the dream version of it. Dez's mouth fell open. "Uh, who's that?"

Aurora looked up to see none other than her parents entering the throne room. They looked just like they always had; her mother, the epitome of grace, and her father, firm yet gentle. They passed through, hand in hand, just gazing into each other's eyes. They'd always been so in love. Aurora's breath quickened.   "Those are my parents."

Dez grabbed her hand and squeezed. "Did you do that?"

Her voice trembled. "I might have. I'm not positive."

The king and queen wandered right past the thrones and disappeared into the stone wall. Dez and Aurora sat in silence, stunned.

"I don't think they could hear us," Dez finally whispered.

Aurora wanted to cry. "Maybe this is my coma state? Before, I couldn't create another living creature. Now that I can, I guess I can't interact with them?" She didn't want to be solving mysteries right now.

Dez rubbed her arm. "One of my favorite professors always said any progress is good. You're figuring out the extent of your abilities."

She managed a smile. He was right.

"Look, why don't you show me around the castle? That'll take your mind off…everything."

She sucked in a breath, preventing any tears from falling.

"Perhaps the library?"

He grinned mischievously. "Lead the way, Your Majesty."

"Call me that again and I'll have you beheaded."

CHAPTER 24

Aurora's Dreams

The library ended up being a bust.

Although books filled the many shelves from floor to ceiling, neither Aurora nor Dez could read any of them. The words shifted and warped, making deciphering anything impossible.

"Well, that's annoying." Dez squinted at a page as the letters turned themselves into nonsense.

"Imagine dealing with that for centuries," Aurora muttered, crossing her arms.

"If you want, I could send you some modern day books through our written conversations. Then you could have one book full of stuff if you get bored."

She looked at him, eyes glimmering with hope. "Won't that take a while? Monks devote their whole lives to transcribing the Bible."

He held back a smile. Years of coding had made him a skilled typist. "I'm way faster than a monk. It'll be okay, promise."

Her hug was instant and almost suffocated him. "Thank you thank you thank you!" She let him go so he could breathe. "Now, let's go find a different room to explore."

She decided on the grand ballroom. Dez's mouth dropped open the moment they stepped inside. Polished stone floors gleamed beneath the windows that stretched up to an intricately decorated ceiling. Ornate candelabras sparkled, reflecting light throughout the space. "Why was the architecture so much more impressive before we had modern building technology?" he muttered to himself.

"Technology?" she asked.

"Don't worry about it. No more real world stuff today."

"Understood." She lifted a corner of her dress and looked at him slyly. "Do you dance?"

Oh no.

"Absolutely not."

"I'll teach you." Before he could protest, she grabbed his arm and pulled him to the center of the ballroom.

"Aurora, there's no music." Ge hoped the sad excuse would work. She simply closed her eyes and summoned a self playing harp.

"I fear you're getting way too good at that," Dez grumbled.

"I fear you talk too much. Now, put your hand on my waist."

When he didn't move quickly enough, she forcefully placed his hand on her waist and gripped the other in hers. "Just listen to the music, sway a bit, and don't step on my foot."

The harp plucked a waltz as Aurora gently guided him through the movements. He relaxed a little. It wasn't too hard, and being close to her was nice. "When was the last time you did this?"

She chuckled. "My twenty-first birthday celebration. Also known as my marriage market."

"Marriage market?"

"I was of marrying age. My parents invited every eligible man they could find—and I do mean *every*. It was horrid."

They were swaying more comfortably now. Dez was actually enjoying himself. "I thought royals got married off as soon as possible."

"Typically, yes. I'm my parents' only child and they had me very young. Father was the most amazing king, and he wanted Voltav to continue thriving under his rule. He used the opportunity of having a longer reign to make sure I received the same quality of education a son would have."

The king would definitely be championing women's rights if he were around today. Dez appreciated that. "I'm assuming you didn't find your Prince Charming?"

She rolled her eyes. "No. And I hate to think of who I would have ended up with if I hadn't been able to choose."

Dez realized they had stopped dancing and were simply holding each other. "Is that the last thing you remember before here?"

"Yes. I remember slipping away from the celebration to find my bearings. Then, nothing. Just darkness."

His mind started racing. "You were born in 1420, so you turned twenty-one in 1441. That means you fell asleep that year."

She nodded. "But what caused it?"

"I don't know." His thumb absentmindedly traced circles on her lower back. "But maybe figuring that out can help me research."

Aurora's cheeks flushed and she slowly pulled away. "You should probably go."

"What? Why?"

"You're not supposed to be doing… whatever it is that you're doing to visit me, correct?"

He grimaced. "Correct."

"You've been here a while, haven't you?"

He nodded, reluctantly. "You're right."

Her expression softened. "I really enjoyed spending time with you."

"Same." He smiled.

"Hopefully you don't end up in more seaweed," she giggled.

With a flash of light, the ballroom, and Aurora, melted away.

***

2025, The Museum of Historical Mysteries

That florescent light really was harsh. Dez rubbed his eyes as he sat up. This time, he'd thought ahead and brought a pillow for his lower back, so the bench wasn't as bad. He pulled off the cap and couldn't help but smile. Aurora was incredible. She was intelligent, sharp-witted, and funny. And she was so beautiful.

He put his face in his hands. He had a crush on her. He had a crush on the Sleeping Beauty, whom he'd spent a good majority of his life fascinated by. Of course.

"Well, what am I gonna do now?" he mumbled to himself.

"I suggest you explain yourself."

Shit. Shit shit shit shit.

He slowly turned to find none other than Dr. Kyra Ellison standing in the exhibit entryway, arms crossed and foot tapping furiously.

"Well?"

Dez swallowed hard. He was done for.

CHAPTER 25

2025, The Museum of Historical Mysteries

"Well?"

Dez stood frozen, looking like a deer caught in headlights.

"I should call the security team on you."

"NO! No no no, please, please…" he basically crawled over, a groveling mess. "Dr. Ellison, please, I was going to tell you, I swear."

She glared angrily over his shoulder. "Tell me you've been messing around with my 100k EEG?"

He covered his face. "I've taken exceptional care of it, I promise."

"I don't care!" Kyra shrieked. "You, a custodian, have been tinkering with a very expensive piece of equipment without permission!" She marched over to the machine, her hands balling into fists. Her eyes passed over unfamiliar wires and gadgets. "What the hell is all this?"

Dez had scrambled over to her. "Just.. just hear me out."

She spun around so hard that a few hairpins flew out of her bun. "This is not okay! You broke so many rules! You put Aurora at risk, put *my job* at risk…" She shoved loose strands of hair behind her ears. "And how the hell did you bypass the security system??" She had just assured the public that the museum's security was state-of-the art. What would people think if this got out?

The custodian hunched his shoulders. "Um…"

"DEZ!"

He flinched. "I'm a hacker as a side job."

Of course he was.

"Getting in was easy."

She swore she felt steam come out of her ears.

"For ME! Getting in was easy for me! It's a fantastic security system! You don't have to worry about some Joe Schmoe breaking in!"

She began to pace. "You better have a damn good reason for this."

"I… Hang on. Can I… Can I show you?"

She felt a migraine coming on. "You know, why the hell not? This is already a dumpster fire." Maura was going to eat this up in their next session.

Dez fumbled with his phone, swiping through frantically before shoving it in her face. "Here, read."

"Gimme that." She yanked it from his grasp and looked at the screen.

Aurora: Hello there
Dez: Am I speaking to Princess Aurora d'Ambray?
Aurora: That would be me.

What? She scrolled more.

Aurora: What? No, please, I haven't spoken with anyone else in so long.
Dez: I'll be back tomorrow, I promise.

Kyra looked back at Dez, who was chewing his lip so hard it had started bleeding.

EEG connection established
REM Sleep activated
User induced lucid dreaming
Video connection established

This… was this what she thought it was? She looked at Dez, anger melting into shock. "Dez…?"

"The lab door glitched one day. I saw the equipment and I…I just couldn't help myself. I'm sorry." The words were tumbling out. "I established a connection with Aurora. At first, it was just through text." He ran a hand through his messy hair. "My dad was given an abandoned lucid dreaming project. My mom gave me everything. It ended up being just what I needed. Everything fell into place." He stared longingly at Aurora. "I got… into her dream, Dr. Ellison. I've been able to talk to her, face to face."

Kyra just stood there. He'd done it. He'd managed to connect with Aurora—something she hadn't managed to do, even with both science and magic on her side. Centuries' worth of degrees, personas, and research, and a custodian was the one who had made the breakthrough.

"I saved everything." Dez continued, "I was going to come to you if the lucid dreaming system worked. I thought we'd be able to work together."

She looked at his phone. "It says here you got it to work a week ago. Why didn't you come to me then?"

He looked ashamed. "She got mad at me."

"She?"

"Aurora." He rubbed the back of his neck. "She's able to control who enters her dream. I told her she was asleep, and I don't know about you, but if I discovered I had been living in the Matrix for centuries, I'd be frustrated too."

Yeah, that sounded like Aurora. "So she's aware of the situation?"

He nodded. "She is."

"Okay." Her palms burned, and she noticed her fists were still balled up. She released them and flexed her fingers. "I mean…"

"I saved everything," he repeated. "I'll give it all to you. Do whatever you want with it. Just please, don't… don't take me away from her."

Kyra's fury evaporated. He was just a kid who'd stumbled into something bigger than himself. A kid who'd made what seemed impossible, possible. And he liked Aurora, that was obvious. Her fairy side squealed with glee. Her human side stayed calm.

"Dez, I can't deny how extraordinary this is. Dr. Killenger said you were brilliant, but I didn't think you were *this* brilliant."

He perked up. "You think I'm brilliant?"

"Desmond."

"Yeah, sorry."

She started pacing again, the gears in her head turning. "What I should do is demand you give me all the information you've collected, confiscate your equipment, involve authorities, and tell your father what you've done."

He cringed.

"But what I'm going to do is let you continue."

His eyes nearly popped out of his head. "You… you will?"

"Yes, but I expect you to follow some guidelines."

He nodded vigorously. "Anything, I'll do anything."

She crossed her arms. "I will be present for all your connections."

"Of course."

"All equipment stays here. I want copies of all the documentation on my desk by tomorrow morning."

"I can print it all tonight and give you a thumb drive as well."

"You will do all my data entry for free."

"Absolutely."

"And…" she sighed. She was really going to do this. "You will conduct your research during normal working hours as your final project for school. I will mentor you, and you will be paid for your time."

He just blinked at her.

"Dez?"

He shook his head, trying to register what he just heard. "Seriously?"

"Seriously." She managed a small smile. "We both have the same end goal. We'll get there sooner if we work together."

The next thing she knew, Dez had swept her up in a massive bear hug, lifting her off her feet.

"Dr. Ellison, you're an angel! I won't let you down!"

She grinned, genuinely. "More like a fairy godmother, but close enough."

CHAPTER 26

January 2026, Wellington Bits,
Lizzie's Life Lessons by Elizabeth
Hildegrant

Hello readers!

Did you miss me?

I took a little break to focus more on my family and friends during the holidays. Speaking of holidays, I hope you all had a wonderful Thanksgiving, Christmas, Hanukkah, Kwanzaa, or whatever it is you celebrate as the year concludes!

I wasn't originally planning on returning to writing until February, but I stumbled upon some juicy intel that I just couldn't keep to myself. Ready for this?

Dr. Kyra Ellison has taken on a mentee.

I know, I was shocked too. Not only has Dr. Ellison never done this, but nobody on the Exhibit Aurora team ever has either. They've been incredibly secretive throughout the entire project.

So who's the lucky student?

Desmond Buckley.

Yes, the guy who just so happens to be the son of the renowned neurologist, Dr. Cormac Buckley. The same Dr. Buckley the museum has been trying to hire forever. And fun fact—Desmond and I went to middle and high school together.

Desmond has always been interested in Exhibit Aurora; his family members are well known VIP patrons of The Museum of Historical Mysteries. But is interest enough to catch the eye of one of the most brilliant minds of our time?

Yes, Desmond has always been smart. He's currently completing his last semester of grad school with an advanced degree in computer engineering. But is he intelligent enough to hold a position that many others—surely some more qualified—were denied? What kind of leg up does this guy have? Does he have access to information nobody else does? Could the museum not get Dr. Buckley, so they settled for his son? And most importantly, are things looking up for Princess Aurora. Stay tuned, everybody. This story is just getting started.

CHAPTER 27

2026, The Museum of Historical Mysteries

"By God's bones, that girl needs to crawl back into whatever hole she was hiding in."

Dez shoved his phone back in his pocket, disgusted by Lizzie's jibber jabber. Kyra cocked an eyebrow.

"By God's bones?"

"Medieval cursing."

"Ah," she nodded, "I'd say you're spending too much time with Aurora, but that's why I hired you."

"Yeah, tell that to Lizzie," he groaned.

Kyra scoffed. "If that woman disappeared off the face of the earth, absolutely nobody would miss her. She has the audacity to say you're not smart enough to work for me, when the only reason she has any semblance of a career is because she's fucking her business partner."

Dez nearly collapsed in a fit of laughter. One of the unexpected perks of working with Kyra—aside from, well, making scientific history—was their shared and unfiltered hatred of Lizzie.

"It's *true*," she added with a smirk.

Dez wheezed. "Oh, it's absolutely true. It's just hilarious hearing you say it."

She shrugged. "Swearing's a sign of intelligence." Clicking out of Lizzie's article on her laptop, she rolled her eyes. "Did you actually go to school with that harpy?"

"Unfortunately, yes."

"Has she always been…like that?" she asked, looking for the right words.

"A loudmouth, pretentious, untalented shrew? Yes."

She nodded approvingly. "Well, seeing that it took her this long to realize you were on the team, I think we're doing fine."

Aside from the absolute terror Kyra had struck in him the night he'd been caught, things had been going swimmingly since he joined the team. It still tickled him he could say that.

He was on the team. He was literally getting paid for school, no longer had to mop floors, and, best of all, he got to spend time with Aurora. He'd learned so much about her in the past three months and just wanted to keep learning.

Having Kyra along for the ride had proven to be extremely beneficial. While working under her supervision had been awkward at first, he soon felt reassured under her watchful eye. She could adjust the unstable connections and pull the kill switch if anything went catastrophically wrong, which, thankfully, hadn't happened.

"What do you two have planned for your date today?" Kyra asked, way too casually.

Dez turned pink. "It's not a date."

She smirked. "It most certainly is. You're crazy about her."

Whelp. Was it that obvious?

"And," she continued, "it sounds like she's pretty crazy about you too."

He scratched his head. "You think?"

She smiled whimsically. "I know."

***

Kyra looked at Dez, fast asleep under the dreaming cap. The boy was being paid to take naps and frolic about with a princess.

Not that she begrudged him for it. He worked unbelievably hard. Whether it was because of guilt or sheer determination, she didn't particularly care. She took jabs at him mainly because he could rest, while her nights were still sleepless or nightmare filled. It seemed the better her current life got, the more her past life tried to haunt her.

But there was no denying they were making progress. Through the conversations with Aurora, they'd further mapped her sleep cycles, deepened their understanding of her sleep state, and gathered an impressive amount of research on lucid dreaming. She'd let Dez keep all that for his own future work, as she had little interest in the subject. "Just give me a shout out in your Nobel Prize speech," she'd joked.

Lila, meanwhile, was delighted to have Dez on the team, going as far as to take credit for it. "I knew you two would get along," she'd boasted, "And he makes a damn good cup of coffee."

Lila obviously hadn't a clue that Dez had been caught hacking their security system, tampering with equipment and doing a whole heck of a lot of unauthorized work. And Kyra was planning on keeping it that way. Nobody needed to know she'd hired, in essence, a criminal.

Dez had been establishing a timeline of Aurora's life leading up to her falling asleep. "If we can figure out the why, we can figure out the how," he'd insisted, furiously typing out notes. She had just smiled and let him work. He had no clue that she had always known the answer to the why.

Honesty had been a recurring topic in her recent sessions with Maura.

I think you're going to have to tell him at some point, Kyra.

I know, I just feel like it would just destroy him.

I said at 'some point,' not 'tomorrow.' And if he likes her as much as you say he does…

That had been the real reason she hadn't told him. Dez and Aurora were building a true, genuine, deep connection. Kyra would often catch him gazing at her on the security footage, making the most ridiculous goo-goo eyes. She'd actually seen Aurora smiling in her sleep during their dream meetings.

This wasn't the Aurora Kyra had known so long ago. The pre-sleep Aurora had been independent, fiercely practical, and preached that no man was worth her time. This Aurora, the dream Aurora, was willingly opening up to Dez. Kyra had been very hands off with the whole situation. She had once thought someone else was "special." She'd thought Philip would save Aurora, in turn saving all of Voltav.

But he didn't.

Sure, he'd gone on to be a beloved ruler, likened to King Florestan himself. But his kiss had been utterly useless.

Was Dez the type of special that would save Aurora? She stared at him now, curled up on the bench, a ridiculous grin on his face even in sleep. "You've got to be the one," she murmured. "You just got to be."

CHAPTER 28

Aurora's Dreams

"Dez, keep up!"

Aurora laughed as he bounced around on the horse like a rag doll.

"I thought you said horseback riding was easy!" he called out, holding on for dear life.

"It is," she flipped her hair, "for the right person."

He managed to get close enough for her to reach out and grab his horse's reins. She eased it to a slower trot so they could ride side by side. "This is why I said we should've shared a horse." He grumbled.

She flashed him a grin. "Why, Sir Desmond, that would be far too scandalous."

He grinned right back. "And who's here to stop us, Your Majesty?"

They were flirting again. And she quite enjoyed it. She'd learned the term from one book Dez had written out for her. She didn't think there was a more perfect word for dancing around the possibility of romance.

When she had first longed for human companionship, she never imagined someone like Dez would show up. He was scholarly, hardworking, and endearing, and he made her laugh harder than anyone ever had. She wouldn't have ever found someone like him at her birthday celebration. In a very small way, she was grateful for her eternal sleep; without it, they would never have crossed paths.

Had she worried that she had grown so attached simply because he was the first human she'd encountered in centuries? Of course. She had kept some walls up, never allowing herself to dig too deeply into her emotions.

But he was so easy to talk to—he had never given her a reason not to trust him.

She'd begun considering their future, whether or not she woke up. She'd learned that arranged marriages had thankfully fallen out of favor in the real world. People were allowed to spend as much time together as they wished before they even had to consider marriage.

Marriage.

She'd be lying if she said she hadn't imagined what having Dez as a husband would be like. He obviously cared for her, and she enjoyed spending time with him. Weren't those two important qualities in a marriage?

She glanced up and caught him staring at her again. She smirked—he had the tendency to do that.

"Yes?"

He blushed. "Sorry."

"No need to apologize. I know I'm beautiful."

He chuckled, and they pulled their horses to a halt. She dismounted before helping him do the same. God forbid he fall off.

"Thank you, m'lady."

He took her hand, and they wandered towards the edge of the cliffside they'd ridden up. The waves of the sea crashed in the distance and she swore she saw large fish jumping through the foam. New wildlife, like the horses, had materialized recently. She wondered if it was because, through Dez, she was connecting somewhat to the world outside her dreams.

The horses that had materialized in the castle stables were carbon copies of the ones she grew up riding. She was thrilled to hear the horses whinnying during her daily walk of the grounds. Horseback riding was another thing she could share with Dez.

"Alright, let's get to work," Dez mused.

Ugh, work. She'd just wanted to spend time with him, but he'd insisted on trying out something new with his studies. They'd compromised—well, Aurora had demanded—on riding the horses first.

"Should I close my eyes?" she asked.

He shrugged. "Up to you. I'm not sure if anything's even gonna come through."

Aurora closed her eyes and enjoyed Dez stroking the backs of her hands with his thumbs. Goodness, that was nice. Maybe studying wasn't so bad if she got to be close to him.

A wind chime sounded in the distance, just like when he'd first appeared in the tree. Was that it? "I hear chimes," she said, almost inquisitively. She opened her eyes to his mischievous smile.

"That's it," he confirmed. "Have you ever heard that before?"

She nodded. "Just once, when you first came here. I thought little of it."

He thrust his fist into the air, something he did whenever they accomplished something. "I had the notification sounds on when I first tried the lucid dreaming equipment," he explained. "I turned them off after that because it can get annoying, but wanted to test a theory I had today."

She smiled, though the intricacies of his technology were still confusing to her.

"Sorry," he chuckled, "Basically, I set a timer to play a sound in the connection that links us. That's what you just heard. It means that you can hear some outside factors."

"Are they really outside factors, though?" she pondered. "If it's only sounds through our connection, just how outside is it?"

"True," he agreed, "But it's something? We realized your sea adventures are concurrent with your aquatic therapy in the real world."

"I suppose." She really didn't want to theorize anymore. "Was that all?"

"Not in the education seeking mood today, are we?"

She shrugged. "To be perfectly honest, no, not at all."

She released his hands and wandered over to a mossy stone to sit. "Aurora?"

"I'm fine. I wanted to spend some time with you, that's all."

"We are?"

Men. She glared at him, and his smile dropped.

"I did something wrong."

She sighed. "Dez, you are so unbelievably intelligent and usually very caring, but sometimes you're utterly oblivious."

He joined her on the rock. "I am sorry. I won't talk about the project anymore."

She couldn't resist reaching out and placing her hand on his. "You're incapable of that."

"I am not."

"Are too."

"I'll prove it to you. We can talk about whatever you want, no more research speak allowed."

She arched an eyebrow. This was an opportunity she couldn't pass up. "Tell me about the first time you met me."

He looked at her, confused. "You… were there?"

"I don't mean that time," she clarified. "I mean when you first saw me at the museum."

Silence.

She knew he was going to be weird about the subject. She didn't know exactly why, but she still wanted to hear the story. He knew almost everything about her life up until she fell asleep; she knew hardly anything about his.

"Does this have to do with the initial age difference?"

He squirmed. Yes, that was it. Children being betrothed from birth had been common practice in her time. In fact, her parents were expected to promise her to a foreign prince, already in his thirties when she was born. Amazingly, King Florestan vehemently refused to go through with the deal, stating a baby's fate being sealed before they could even speak was simply wrong.

Dez continuously mentioned how ahead of his time her father had seemed, and she had to agree. Why *had* they been marrying off children when they had no say? Modern historians believed they did it because people of her time died young, but she knew that wasn't true. Either records had been lost or written incorrectly, because she had known plenty of people who lived past forty; her nurse, a distant cousin, one of those god awful suitors…. She knew now just how fortunate her upbringing had been. Her heart ached for her parents even more.

"Are you okay?" Dez had interlaced his fingers in hers.

"I'll be fine." She turned to face him, "Don't worry about the age difference. You obviously had no romantic feelings towards me until recently, correct?"

He turned bright red. *Adorable.*

"So yes, correct. Since that's the case, just tell me. I'm genuinely curious. I want to learn more about you if we're going to keep—" She was unsure of how to define what they were.

He let out a deep sigh. "No, you're right. Okay, so…"

CHAPTER 29

2012, The Museum of Historical Mysteries

"I can't kiss her? What was the point of bringing us here then?"

Dez rolled his eyes as his classmates sulked away from the exhibit. Hormones were stupid.

"She's twice your age, chill," he called after them.

"Yeah, find someone else to get your dick wet."

Dez groaned. Of course Lizzie had to add her two cents. Her nose was either stuck up in the air, or shoved into everyone else's business.

She sniffed. "I'm allowed to voice my opinion."

"Yeah, just don't get all defensive when nobody wants to listen to you."

"I—"

Dez turned away before she could finish.

"I can't stand you!" she shrieked as she stomped off.

"The feeling's mutual," he mumbled once she was out of sight.

He went back to staring at the woman behind the glass. Why would anyone want to kiss her anyway? Not that she wasn't pretty or anything—she was obviously stunning. But Dez was more interested in what was going on inside her head.

He grunted as Greg suddenly slapped him on the back.

"What'd you say to Lizzie? She's bawling behind the boba serpent exhibit."

Titanoboa. And good, Lizzie was among her own kind—snakes.

"I just told her the truth," Dez shrugged, "that nobody wants to listen to her."

Greg shrugged right back. "Cool."

It wasn't like all of Lizzie's classmates had immediately shunned her. She had some good qualities; she tried to speak up for what was right and tutored elementary school kids. That was about it, though. The rest of her personality was just noise. Opinions she refused to shut up about and a toxic fascination with rumors and gossip. Dez didn't care about Lizzie. He was focused on the exhibit in front of him.

"Didn't they want to hire your dad?" Greg asked.

Dez groaned. "Yup."

"I'm assuming the great Dr. Buckley wants nothing to do with it?"

"Yup."

His dad's absolute disinterest in anything related to Exhibit Aurora (meaning The Museum of Historical Mysteries as a whole), meant this was Dez's first visit. Which was a shame, because it'd been fascinating. He hadn't been super into archaeology and history, but the data and research involved were appealing.

"You think she dreams?" Greg asked.

"I don't know," Dez said. "She doesn't move. Maybe she's brain dead."

"Dark."

He knew that wasn't the case. No working brain meant no breathing, and she wasn't on a ventilator. It was more likely a coma. Greg reached out to tap on the glass, and Dez slapped his hand away.

"Dude! She's not a friggin fish!"

"Owww abuuuse." Greg whined.

"Shut up, Mr. Linebacker. You know that was nothing."

Greg and Dez were the definition of opposites attract; Dez was the equivalent of a string bean with an insanely high IQ, while Greg was the lovable beefcake who graciously accepted the study buddy into his life. Greg wasn't stupid by any means, science just didn't come as easily to him.

"Gotta admit," Greg quipped, "she is pretty hot."

Dez smacked him again.

"Aaahhh, I'm gonna sue youuu."

"Shut up. There's more to her than her looks. She hasn't aged, she doesn't eat, doesn't drink, doesn't move…" he trailed off. The entire case was fascinating. He wondered if there was any research available to the public.

"I don't want to leave."

"Yeah, this seems like your own little nerd heaven. I will admit, the Bigfoot print is pretty cool."

"That's crap."

"Is not."

"Is too, you fool."

"You need to work here someday," Greg said, randomly.

"My dad would be so proud," Dez deadpanned.

Greg smirked. "You know he actually would be. He doesn't have to enjoy it."

Dez stared back at the princess. "I just gotta know how she got here."

Dez slipped away from the rest of the group as the guide led them into the planetarium. Watching a forty-minute show on astrology definitely wasn't his thing—myths, ugh. Without realizing it, he had wandered back into Exhibit Aurora.

The woman looked so peaceful; if he looked hard enough, he could indeed see the slow rise and fall of her chest.

"What happened to you?"

"Well, she fell asleep."

Dez turned abruptly to find an older man in a lab coat standing in front of a tapestry.

"I'm sorry. Am I interfering with research?" Dez asked.

The man wandered over. "Not at all. Just checking on our princess." He held out a hand. "Dr. Henry Pach. And who might you be?"

Pach? Wasn't that the family who founded the museum? He took the man's outstretched hand.   "Desmond."

"Well, Desmond, do you have a last name?"

"Uh…." He always tried to avoid that, even from a young age, "Buckley."

Dr. Pach's eyes glittered. "Don't worry," he said, "I won't try to get you to beg your dad to work here. He's made it very apparent he has no interest in our type of work." He clasped his hands behind his back and strode over so he was gazing down at the princess.

"Your type of work?" Dez asked.

"He doesn't consider it 'real'. Although I can assure you it's very real." He pulled a cloth from his pocket and wiped away a small smudge on the glass. "We have an observation: this young woman has been asleep for a while and somehow hasn't aged. We formed a hypothesis: some outside force has preserved her while she remains alive. And we're testing and experimenting every day to prove what the outside preservation is." He turned to Dez and smiled. "Is that not science?"

Dez nodded. It was undeniably science.

"Are you planning to go into medicine as well, Mr. Buckley?"

"Nah," Dez shook his head, "I'm better with computers than people."

Dr. Pach smirked. "Once you've graduated, consider putting in an application here."

CHAPTER 30

Aurora's Dreams

"What's this about kissing?"

Dez cringed. He'd avoided telling Aurora about the kissing aspect until now, simply because it didn't sit well with him. Honestly, it was gross.

"Okay, so," How would he explain this mess? "Nobody really knows where it originated, but this lore came about that you could only be woken up by a kiss."

Aurora furrowed her brow. "I've lost my family, I'm on display for the public to gawk at, and anyone can stroll up and *kiss me?*" Utter pain crossed her face and Dez could feel his heart crack.

"People were strange when you were first discovered."

She huffed. "People are just strange."

He couldn't help but chuckle, and she managed a small smile.

"If it makes you feel any better, that didn't last long. They made it so they had to be twenty-one to kiss you, and you had to fill out a bunch of paperwork."

"Paperwork?"

"Like a contract. They had to prove they were twenty-one and agree to the rules. They had to show proper hygiene, the kiss couldn't last longer than two seconds, and they kept a record of kissers, so no repeats." The words felt disgusting rolling off his tongue. "The museum could turn anyone away, no questions asked."

She looked up at him. "You're speaking as if this was all in the past."

He realized he left that part out. "Because it's not a thing anymore."

"Oh."

They sat in pure silence for a moment.

"I was really trying not to tell you."

"It's fine. You were just trying to protect my feelings." She sighed. "Who ended up putting a stop to it?"

"Lady Rona."

"I thought nobility was phased out in your country?"

Lord, he was dumb.

"Yeah, it was, sorry. Coping mechanism." She tilted her head. This was going way off track. "Did you learn about the Black Plague?"

"Ugh," she groaned, "Did I. My father had an unhealthy obsession with it and one of my history tutors specialized in the subject."

Good—he wouldn't have to explain the origins of a global virus. He pinched the bridge of his nose; his head was starting to hurt. "Basically, five years ago, we had a modern version of it, worldwide. It was called the Coronavirus, or COVID-19."

She nodded. "Ah. Lady Rona, Corona. It's a joke."

"Yeah… An attempt to distract from a deadly pandemic." He continued, "One way it's spread is through human contact, so no more kissing. Nobody wanted you to get sick."

She smiled. "People care about me that much?"

He couldn't help but grin. "Yes. You mean a lot to many people." He took her hand again. "After that ordeal, they stopped the kissing so you wouldn't get COVID… then Lizzie brought up consent."

"That little stinking brat?"

Wonderful. He knew she'd wake with an existing hatred for Lizzie. "Like I said, she has SOME good ideas; it doesn't happen often. She got people to realize that random strangers kissing you without your permission was pretty wrong."

"I still don't believe I would enjoy Lizzie's company."

He chuckled. "You absolutely wouldn't. She's awful."

"I suppose I feel better that I'm not being kissed anymore." She slyly ran a finger up his arm. "Didn't you want to kiss me?"

"What? No!" She drew her finger away. "No, Aurora, I didn't mean it like that. I didn't know you, I'm not gonna kiss some girl I know nothing about. I was just focused on getting you awake, I still am."

She sighed, her smile returning. "You're a good man, Dez."

"I try."

After a few deep breaths and ocean watching, Aurora and Dez had ridden back to the castle. He dismounted on his own, albeit without an ounce of grace.

"I suppose I should applaud you." Aurora teased.

"I don't think I'll be winning any dressage competitions anytime soon."

She linked arms with him. "Come, I want to show you something before you go."

Another surprise? She led him past the throne room, up a grand staircase, and past the library. This was new. They hadn't ventured in this direction yet.

"Where are you taking me?" he asked.

"To my bedroom."

Dez gulped.

"Is something wrong?"

"Nope, nothing at all." She had said it so offhandedly, so he shouldn't be freaking out.

Aurora pushed open a giant door and lead Dez inside. He gazed around the bedroom. It differed vastly from what he'd already seen. The rest of the castle had been opulent, filled with enormous windows, jewel encrusted furniture and elaborate artwork placed throughout. Aurora's bedroom almost seemed plain in comparison.

A solid blue rug covered most of the stone floor. Simple white bedding draped the plush large bed. A single ottoman sat beside it, their communication book placed on top. There were no grand windows, just a single stained glass one close to the ceiling. The sun streaming in cast rainbow flecks throughout the room. He took a breath-were those roses?

"I know it's not much, but it's how I like it," she said.

He shook his head. "No, I like it. I think you should really only have what you need in your space."

"That definitely was the thought process behind it." She walked over to her bedside and picked up the book. "Before we met, I somehow never thought about why I didn't sleep here. I think it was because I used to read before bed, it relaxed me. I couldn't read, so no relaxation."

She flipped through a few pages. "I still can't sleep, but at least I have a form of comfort back. Thank you, again, for sending me books. I really cherish them." She clutched the book to her chest and smiled. The rainbow light danced across her skin, making her look almost ethereal. Dez couldn't help but stare.

"Make me a promise."

Dez arched an eyebrow. "What kind of promise?"

"I'll keep teaching you about the royal activities and helping with research, if you keep telling me stories about your past."

He wanted to share every portion of his life with her.

"Deal."

She grinned, positively glowing. "I can't wait for our next meeting, Dez."

Before he knew it, he'd blown her a kiss—something he'd never done unironically.

The tinkling of her laughter faded along with the dream.

CHAPTER 31

2026, The Museum of Historical Mysteries

Kyra looked up from her laptop as Dez stirred awake. She checked the time.

"Enjoy your very, very, very long date?" she teased.

"Not a date," he groaned, still half asleep.

"We've gone over this already." She stood and wandered over to power off the machines. "You like her, she likes you, you're spending tons of time together, holding hands. Totally a date."

He rubbed his eyes. "How did you know we hold hands?"

She smirked. "I didn't. I guessed, and you just confirmed it."

"Goddamit, Kyra."

She giggled as she wrapped the cap wires. "You're smart, Dez, but I'll always be smarter with the ways of romance."

He managed to stand up and help to put the equipment away. "She's… she's just something else. Something special."

Kyra knew that far too well. She stared at the princess in her much larger domed bed. Lila had finally convinced the museum to replace it once Aurora started moving around more consistently. She was currently curled on her side, hugging her pillow and smiling in her sleep again. Goodness, Dez made her so happy.

"I had to tell her about the kissing lore this time around."

Kyra froze.

"Why?"

"She wanted to know about the first time I saw the exhibit. Kind of hard to avoid that any longer."

Kyra huffed. "Did she take it well?"

"It was definitely a shock initially," he said, "but she was okay after I told her it wasn't allowed anymore."

She nodded. "Well, not ideal, but as long as she's not super upset."

Aurora had been shielded from both Carabosse's curse and Kyra's blessing during her entire upbringing. It felt as though if the king and queen kept her blissfully unaware, her destiny somehow wouldn't be fulfilled. Kyra could have easily told her herself, but she wanted to allow her as normal a life as possible.

That'd been another source of her guilt that she'd worked through with Maura. Kyra had wondered if making Aurora aware of her fate could have led her to seek a romantic connection, one that would blossom into True Love. She would have helped whoever the True Love was defeat Carabosse, and they would have planted a smooch on Aurora almost immediately, and everyone would have lived happily ever after so much faster.

Maura had thankfully brought her to her senses. In reality, if Aurora had known her fate, any romantic connection she formed could have felt forced. That and with her stubbornness, she most definitely would have been insanely picky. Kyra could just picture her pricking herself on purpose rather than settling. Even if she had found someone, there was absolutely no guarantee the kiss would have worked.

Kyra knew she couldn't keep dwelling on the what ifs. She, Dez, and Aurora had shared incredible experiences throughout this endless journey. While Kyra had cried, lost sleep, and spiraled, she also loved so much about the different personas she had lived as.

She peered over at Dez, who had finished packing up and was now gazing longingly at Aurora.

Oh, he had it bad.

"Get a room."

He scowled. "Let me have this small bit of joy, please."

"Have you never been in a relationship before?" she asked.

The now familiar flush crawled up his neck. "I have. It's just been a while." He grabbed a nearby water bottle and took a sip to cool off. "I don't have much time for wining and dining when I'm coding or researching."

"I guess having your girlfriend at your workplace is perfect then."

"Okay," he crossed his arms, "she's not my girlfriend. She doesn't even know the term yet. Yes, we flirt, we hold hands, and I'll admit, I have really strong feelings for her. But," he looked back at Aurora, "I haven't even kissed her. Courting didn't even start until after her time, so I don't want to confuse her."

Kyra's heart skipped a beat. That was one of the cutest things she'd ever heard. He *had* to be the one. Her Good fairy instincts were showing again. "I'm sorry. I know it doesn't seem like it, but I love love. And," she patted his shoulder, "I happen to be quite fond of you. I tease those I'm closest to."

He groaned, but managed a smile. "Not love yet, but thanks."

Yet. Not love yet. She had to continue to stay out of it. Matchmaking, especially fairy matchmaking, never seemed to have good results.

Dez started rolling the equipment back to the lab. "I'll get all this locked up, then I'm gonna write my field notes."

She rolled her eyes. "Again, they're not called field notes just because you two spend so much time outside. Just call it journaling."

"But that's not as fun."

"Then call them The Aurora Files, or something."

"Hey, that's a good idea!"

She just had to open her big mouth.

***

Sigmund actually seemed stunned when Kyra arrived home from work early. She caught him in the middle of bunny kicking a catnip turtle.

"Mommy actually gets work done when she hires super helpful people."

He slow blinked at her, and her heart melted again.

"Come here." She scooped the floof up and rubbed his belly. "We can have some quality cuddling time."

Sigmund started purring as she carried him over to the couch. It'd been so long since she hadn't stayed late at the lab or brought work home. What did humans do when they had actual downtime? What was she to do when she wasn't currently a ball of pure stress?

"I don't know, bud. Should we finally try watching that reality TV everyone seems to be obsessed with?"

Sigmund trilled. She was going to take that as a yes. She was ready to turn her brain off and not think about how Dez and Aurora were undeniably perfect for each other. And how she would decorate for their wedding. And what cute babies they would make.

She grabbed her smart TV remote and randomly chose a streaming service.

The entire suggestions feed was filled with dating, wedding, and extravagant matchmaking shows.

Nope, back to true crime.

CHAPTER 32

2026, The Museum of Historical Mysteries

Dez peered out from behind a clay bust of Osiris. He scanned the area, searching for any flashes of the familiar platinum blonde hair. He nearly jumped out of his skin as a hand grabbed his shoulder.

"Dude, it's me."

He heaved a sigh of relief as Greg rubbed his arm. "Woof, you're tense."

"My job isn't all sunshine and rainbows, Greg."

"No, you look like you're being chased."

Dez looked around the display again. "Because I am."

"Oh shit." Greg hunched down as much as his tall frame allowed. "What'd you do?"

"Why do people always think I did something?"

"Because goody-goody Dez never does anything bad. If someone's after you, you must have majorly pissed them off."

Dez snorted. "I was coming back from my lunch break and friggin Lizzie was waiting for me at the museum entrance."

Greg swore again. "Why the hell would she show her face around here? I thought she quit being a pain after Dr. Ellison destroyed her."

"She's been trying to contact me for weeks now. Something about 'learning the truth' or whatever. I've been ignoring her, so apparently she showed up in person. I slipped in through the back, but I'm pretty sure she's still trying to hunt me down."

"For Christ's sake." Greg stood. "I'll find her."

Normally Dez didn't let Greg handle his problems, but he was especially tired after spending the previous night mapping out more of Aurora's family history. Right now, Greg's imposing six-foot-plus figure seemed like a great asset.

"Okay. I last saw her around the Nessie exhibit."

"We're off to catch a lizard," Greg sang off-key as he strode away.

Dez sank to the floor behind the display. This was not how he was supposed to be spending his afternoon. Aurora was going to teach him how to use a bow and arrow, and he didn't want to keep her waiting.

He'd kept his word, sharing stories from his childhood; about his parents, school, and things he had told no one aside from Greg. Now Aurora knew some of his deepest secrets.

Your father sounds amazing, Dez.

He is.

Why would you worry about not going into medicine?

Because it's one of the most highly respected fields. I want him and Mom to be proud of me.

Dez, what are you currently doing?

Speaking with you…?

How?

Through a lucid dreaming program.

Who was responsible for setting that up?

Well…me.

You not only reached a goal you set for yourself as a child, you did something that nobody else had been able to do in over fifty years. If your parents aren't proud of you, they're not worth your time.

Again, she'd been her normal direct self, but she was right. That night, he'd went home and called his parents. They were still somewhere north of Cuba, and the connection had been spotty, but he'd told them he loved them.

Dez craned his head around the bust again. Surely, Greg had gotten rid of Lizzie by now. Right?

Crawling away from the new Egyptian exhibit, he stood and hurried toward the planetarium. Nobody would ever expect him to be in there. One of the scheduled films was playing, allowing him to slip easily into a seat at the back. He was safe.

Until his phone rang. Patrons shot him dirty looks, shushing loudly. He scrambled for his phone, apologizing profusely as he stumbled out of the theatre.

"Hello?" he hissed.

"Where are you???"

Kyra.

"Long story short, Lizzie's out to get me."

"Shit, can you make it to the archival entrance?"

Dez pictured the museum's layout in his head. He'd need to go through the reptile exhibit, but it was doable.

"I'll try."

"I'll meet you there."

***

"Ow, ow, ow."

When he said he'd have to go through the reptile exhibit, he hadn't meant literally through the vegetation. He'd heard Greg and Lizzie arguing in the distance; she was apparently putting up a fight this time. Narrowly avoiding stepping on a bearded dragon, he'd stayed hidden among the greenery and logs. Whose bright idea was it to incorporate live animals into the display? He'd thankfully avoided their handler, who was answering boa constrictor questions from a very chatty five-year-old.

After tripping over a branch, he finally spotted the archival entrance. The door swung open and Kyra's hand waved him forward. He made a mad dash for it.

"Got you!"

Dez yelped as someone grabbed his sleeve, sending him straight to the floor. The harsh florescent lights buzzed overhead, and when he looked up, a pig nose and near-white hair greeted him.

"Dez!" Greg was kneeling at his side in an instant. "Lizzie, you psycho!"

Lizzie attempted to crouch next to them, but Greg blocked her with an outstretched arm.

"I expect answers, and I'm not leaving until I get them." She crossed her arms. "I have a duty to the public."

"Oh shut up," Greg grumbled, trying to cradle Dez's head, but Dez stopped him.

"... No," he moaned, "you don't want to move me if I have a head injury or something."

"Nerd."

"Hush your mouth. I might have a concussion. Call a medic."

"That won't be necessary." Kyra's warm voice cut through the chaos. She placed her hands over Dez's eyes. "Greg, could you escort Ms. Hildegrant to the exit?"

"Oh trust me, I've been trying."

Lizzie stomped her foot. "I am NOT leaving until I get an interview with Dez!"

Kyra ignored the tantrum and removed her hands. Dez blinked at her worried hazel eyes.

She smiled. "Your pupils are dilating. I think you're okay."

With her and Greg's help, Dez sat up. His head throbbed and his ears were ringing.

"Wonderful. Now we can talk."

Dez, Greg, and Kyra all shot daggers in Lizzie's direction.

"Lizzie," Dez grunted, "Go. Away."

"But the people—"

"Oh WHAT people?" Greg snapped. "Lizzie, take your failed journalist self out of here right now. Nobody cares about your social media followers."

Lizzie turned bright red. "Failed? Failed?! Do you know how hard I've worked to get where I am today?" She stalked closer. "You want to talk failure? What about him?" She jabbed a finger at Dez. "I'm sure his father is real proud of him! The man has a thriving medical career while his son is pissing his life away in a museum!"

Dez gripped onto Greg and Kyra. "My parents *are* proud of me. Shut up, Lizzie."

"Well, how about—"

Lizzie froze suddenly. Her nose scrunched, arms mid flail, mouth agape. Her eyes glowed an icy blue.

"... What?" Dez gasped.

Dude," Greg muttered, his eyes wide.

They looked at Kyra, now speechless.

Her hand was outstretched, a matching blue glow sparking at her fingertips.

CHAPTER 33

2026, The Museum of Historical Mysteries

Spontaneous magic happened often with newly materialized fairies. Kyra had experienced it frequently when she was younger; many a flower field and bonfire had formed when her emotions got the best of her. It was very similar to puberty in humans; messy, unpredictable, and impossible to control completely. Older, more experienced fairies learned to control their powers, but spontaneity could still occur. Particularly when protecting someone they cared about. It was like an adrenaline rush. Magic could flare to life in ways a fairy never thought possible in moments of distress.

Oops.

Yay for forming good human relationships?

Dez and Greg just gawked at Kyra, having witnessed her freeze Lizzie mid screech. Her arm outstretched, hand in a fist, apparently attempting to punch something.

Kyra shot a stream of blue mist at the woman, wrapping her into a cocoon of sorts. The museum lights reflected off of her, giving an eerie glow. Kyra wiped the sweat from her brow. At least the spell hadn't drained her this time. She turned to face Greg and Dez; the two were holding on to each other like schoolchildren. She took a breath.

"Okay, look—"

Greg clutched at Dez's arm, his expression a mix of horror and awe. "Witch! She's a witch!"

"No such thing!" Dez shrieked back.

"Then how do you explain that???" Greg pointed at Lizzie's suspended form.

Dez shuddered. "Um… there's… there's gotta be an explanation…"

"Bro, now is not the time to be all Dr. Desmond!"

"Quiet!" Kyra ordered.

The two were immediately silent, just blinking at her. She took a deep breath, trying to calm the magic still fluttering in her stomach.

Greg shifted to his knees and clasped his hands together. "Please, Dr. Ellison! Don't turn me into a frog!"

Kyra scowled. How demeaning.

"First of all," she snapped her fingers and Lizzie shifted slightly in the air, "we should probably move this to the lab." She turned and began walking, Lizzie's frozen body floating close behind. Dez and Greg gave each other a confused look.

"Well?" she called over her shoulder. "Come on!"

The two scrambled to catch up, Dez running to her side.

"Kyra, I—"

She held her hand up, cutting him off.

"Please, just wait until we get to the lab. I'll explain everything, but I have to sit down."

The rest of the walk was in complete silence. Thankfully, Lila had been sent out to search for a medieval text Aurora had mentioned and the medical team had finished their work earlier. Kyra didn't need anyone else having an existential crisis today.

Once inside, she snapped her fingers again. Lizzie crumpled onto the floor as the mist cocoon evaporated. Kyra narrowed her eyes. She hoped that'd leave a mark. Vile woman insulting Dez's intelligence right in front of her. How dare she?

"Did you kill her???" Greg asked fearfully.

"Of course not. I don't do dark magic."

Greg grabbed Lizzie's wrist, apparently checking for a pulse. Finding one, he let her arm carelessly drop back to the floor. "So you are a witch?"

Dez groaned, "Again, no such thing."

"Uh, yes, there is."

Dez blinked at her. The poor guy was going to explode.

"There are plenty of witches," Kyra clarified, "but I'm not one of them." She wandered over to her office chair and sank into it. "I'm a fairy."

It came out a lot easier this time around. Maybe she trusted these two more than she thought.

"Fairy?!"

She simply nodded.

"Kyra, I…just…are you feeling okay?" Dez hesitantly wandered closer. If there was one thing that Kyra had learned about Dez, it was that he was purely logical. He wasn't necessarily close-minded, just believed in scientific methods, research, and evidence.

"Dez, I'm a fairy. I have magic powers. I'm immortal. My cat is my familiar and can shapeshift."

"Shapeshifting cat? Sweet."

Greg, on the other hand, was apparently far more open to magic.

Kyra continued. "I was there when Aurora was born. I was there when she fell asleep. And I've stayed by her side ever since."

Dez was stunned. "That's not possible."

Kyra let her head fall onto her desk. "It is. I'm living proof."

Lizzie moaned and stirred. Without thinking, Kyra shot out a hand. A green spark exploded from her fingers, darting across the room and hitting Lizzie square in the forehead. The woman slumped back into unconsciousness.

"Sorry, that one should last for a few hours."

Dez slid down her desk to the floor. "Kyra—"

"Dez," she interrupted, "I know you don't believe in any of it, but magic is real. I'm a fairy, I swear by Queen Mab herself."

Dez ran a shaky hand through his hair. "Queen Mab?"

Greg rested a hand on Kyra's shoulder. "Dr. Ellison, you know he needs evidence. That little spell you just did is obviously enough for me." He looked at Lizzie in a messy heap on the floor. "Do you have anything… more concrete? Like a book or a photo or something?"

"For the love of…" Kyra shut her eyes and focused. This was going to be hard.

"Just hang on. Grab my hand."

Greg gripped her hand and she touched the top of Dez's head. He was sweating so much it was like he had just come out of a pool.

"Maison. Moi-même. Deux hommes. Transport," she muttered. With a flash, she, Greg, and Dez disappeared from the lab.

CHAPTER 34

2026, Kyra's House

A flash of light and the sensation of spinning made Dez nauseous. The moment he felt solid ground, he opened his eyes, stood, and immediately hurled.

"Dude gross!" Greg moaned.

Kyra wrinkled her nose. "You're cleaning that up. I just got that rug."

"Can't you just magic it away?" Greg asked.

"Sure I can," she quipped, "but I don't want to."

A yowl sounded out of nowhere.

"Shit," Kyra cursed as she magicked the mess away. "Don't need Sig trying to eat that. And I guess I'm already taking advantage of my powers again." She sighed. "My therapist will not be pleased with this regression."

"Therapist???" Greg said, flabbergasted.

The biggest, fluffiest white cat that Dez had ever seen leapt into his lap. It looked at him with big blue eyes and started kneading his legs.

"Ow! Kyra, control your beast!"

Kyra snorted. "I couldn't control Sigmund if I tried. He's making biscuits, it means he likes you. Part of his job is to make sure I always have company and am comforted. He must realize I care a lot about you."

Greg bent over and reached out a hand for Sigmund to sniff. The cat apparently approved, allowing himself to be scritched behind the ears. "What a beautiful boy! Aren't you just the best little familiar?"

"Don't inflate his ego even more." Kyra started walking down a hallway. "Make yourselves at home."

Dez stared at Greg. "How are you being so cool about this?"

Greg scooped the cat off of Dez and snuggled him close. "I don't know."

"You don't know what?"

Greg shrugged and scratched under Sigmund's chin. "I mean, it seems pretty self-explanatory. She froze Lizzie, knocked her unconscious, teleported us here, and just made your puke disappear. Maybe it's just me, but that seems like magic."

Dez chewed his lip. Greg was right, but he just couldn't comprehend magic actually existing. Sigmund headbutted Greg's cheek. "Well, aren't you just the sweetest thing?"

"He's playing with you," Kyra said as she wandered back in, lugging a giant, intricate chest along with her. "He just wants you to feed him."

Sigmund chirped, apparently confirming his grand plan.

Greg nuzzled him. "You can manipulate me all you want, buddy. You're adorable. Dr. Ellison, let me know if you ever need a cat sitter."

Kyra giggled. "I'll keep that in mind. He seems to like you a lot." She gestured for Dez to come closer as she bent to open the chest. He hesitantly stepped toward her.

"I am sorry for acting kinda like an asshat."

She smiled, having calmed down. "It's alright. I wasn't expecting you to understand right away."

She began pulling out degrees, photos, and books. Dez saw a law degree, an English degree, a media degree—all from different schools.

"Kyra, I thought you went to Johns Hopkins?"

"I did," she replied, "But Ashley went to Kent, Sherri went to Tulsa, and Julie went to Cambridge." She handed him a stack of photos. Dez flipped through. They were all pictures of various women throughout the years, dating as far back as the 1920s. Looking closer, he realized they all had the same eyes. Kyra's eyes. Even in the black and white photos, they were unmistakable. Greg leaned over Dez's shoulder, still holding Sigmund to his chest. The cat was purring so hard, he was rumbling.

"Dr. Ellison, is this your fairy family?"

Kyra smirked. "Something like that. Here," she finally dug out a thick, leather-bound book. "Here we are. And there's plenty more where that came from."

Dez took the book in his hands; it was a deep brown leather with gold designs embossed on the front. A glow seemed to emit from it.

"What's this?" he asked.

"*The Fairy Chronicles, Book I.*" Kyra answered. "It details fairy history, our laws, our abilities, our connection to the human realm. A lot of it was in old dialect, but I think I translated most of it."

Greg gazed at the book. "That thing looks ancient."

"Because it is," Kyra mused. "I copied everything over myself centuries ago."

"Impressive," Dez replied as he flipped through the pages.

He furrowed his brow as he skimmed over the beautiful script. There were diagrams, explanations of spells, anatomical sketches of fairies, and historical records of notable beings. It was unbelievable, yet the pieces were starting to fit.

"Oh, that's me," Kyra pointed at a paragraph in the records section. Dez and Greg stared at the symbols almost floating on the page. They couldn't read them.

"Humans can't read certain fairy symbols. I was basically just referred to as The Good Fairy."

"THE Good Fairy? That sounds awfully important," Greg said as he glanced over to her.

"Not to toot my own horn, but I was." She placed another, much smaller book into Dez's hands. He ran a hand over the front and read the title.

"*The Sleeping Beauty.*"

He arched an eyebrow.

"Just read the beginning of it."

Dez cleared his throat and began reading.

Once upon a time, there lived King Florestan and Queen Matilda. The king was one of the greatest to have lived, and the queen was one of the kindest. The couple were beloved throughout their entire kingdom of Voltav.

When Queen Matilda gave birth to their first and only child, the entire kingdom celebrated. Nobility, the clergy, and every fairy who lived among the Voltav citizens were invited to the baby girl's christening. Her name: Princess Aurora d'Ambray.

The fairies offered various blessings to the baby; she was gifted with kindness, intelligence, athleticism and creativity. As the last fairy, the esteemed Good Fairy, was about to gift her blessing, a wind blew through the ballroom.

The Wicked Fairy, Carabosse, materialized in front of the bassinet. Furious that Florestan and Matilda had not invited her, she waved a finger over baby Aurora, announcing she also had a gift. "Yes, the princess will have all the qualities gifted to her. But on the evening of her twenty-first birthday, she will prick her finger on the spindle of a spinning wheel and die!"

Matilda cradled her baby and cried as Florestan drew his sword, but Carabosse disappeared in a puff of smoke. The princess was doomed.

But The Good Fairy stepped forward, reminding the King and Queen that she had yet to give her blessing. While she could not remove Carabosse's curse, she could counteract it.

"Sweet Princess. She will prick her finger on her twenty-first birthday. But she will not die, she will simply sleep. She will not wake from this sleep until she has a True Love's Kiss."

For True Love is the most powerful earthly thing.

The trio sat in silence for a while.

"It's a fairy tale," Dez finally said.

"It's very real," Kyra replied.

"It's insane, is what it is," Greg added.

Kyra turned to Dez. "It sounds preposterous, but you have to believe. You've dedicated most of your life to figuring out why she wouldn't wake up. How she was under the care of the most brilliant team of experts from around the world, yourself included, yet nothing worked."

Dez gnawed at his lip.

"Dez," Kyra continued, "you got into her dreams using science, yes. But dreams themselves are influenced by magic, you've had to of realized that. The two have always existed together. Magic just got forgotten when the fairies started leaving…" she sighed. "Morale went down, and fairies didn't feel that living among humans was worth it anymore. I'm the only one left on earth."

Greg wrapped his arm around Dez's shoulders. "You can talk to Aurora?"

Dez nodded. "I'll tell you about it later. I'm assuming I'm allowed to now, Kyra?"

"Yeah, this whole mess has thrown any type of ethics out the window."

Greg pulled Dez closer. "Dude, it's crazy, but I think there's enough here for you to believe Dr. Ellison."

Dez thought for a moment. Text, photos, demonstrations—the evidence was clear. Somehow.

"Okay." He scratched his head. "I'm still a bit confused, but I'm on board."

"Do we get fairy perks now???"

"Greg."

"Sorry."

CHAPTER 35

Aurora's Dreams

Aurora was resisting the urge to rage. Dez was late. Very late.

He hadn't been late since the first time they met face to face, and even then, it had only been a short while. Was he bored with her?

No, he couldn't be. They had formed a bond. A relationship. He wouldn't just abandon her.

What if something had gone horribly wrong in the real world? What if he was hurt, or sick, or… dead? She shook her head, forcing the terrible thoughts from her mind.

She heard a noise behind her and smiled with relief. There he was. She turned, expecting bright green eyes to meet hers, only to find a dark, shadowy figure.

She froze.

The figure had the shape of a person, but had no distinguishable features. No eyes, no nose, no mouth…just gray. It didn't move either, simply standing there. Mustering up some courage, she addressed it. "H-hello?"

Nothing.

"Hello?"

Still nothing. Aurora slowly began to back away. She had a bad feeling about this.

Suddenly, the creature rushed forward, pressing a hand to her chest. A heavy suffocating pressure spread through her as she collapsed to the ground. The creature lingered right above her, its weight pinning her down. She tried to scream, but nothing came out. A sense of dread filled the air, and despair crept into her mind. Tears pricked in the corners of her eyes as it almost felt the creature was sucking her breath away.

"Hey! Get off of her!"

Dez seemed to appear out of nowhere. He dove headfirst into the figure, knocking Aurora free from its grasp. She clutched her chest and gasped for air, trying to steady her breath. Rolling onto her side, she saw Dez grappling with the figure; a mix of man and shadows rolling in the grass. Then, just as suddenly as it had appeared, the shadow vanished.

Aurora crawled over to Dez, who had also ended up on the ground. She rested her head on his chest.

"Are you alright?"

He kissed the top of her head. That was new.

"I'm fine, you?"

"I... I think so."

"Aurora, what was that thing?"

She took another deep breath. "I have no idea."

She thought she was safe here. She'd been in complete control over the dream and was only getting better day by day. How had something like that materialized? And why had it tried to hurt her?

"I'm sorry I was late," Dez muttered.

"Don't worry about that. I knew you'd come." She turned so she could see his face. "I'm really glad you showed up when you did.".

"Ow."

"That can't hurt. Be quiet."

"You have a beautiful, heart-shaped face with a lovely pointed chin. It hurts more than you think."

She smiled. "Why were you late?"

"You said not to worry about that."

"I can't help but worry. What happened?"

He groaned. "Lizzie, of all people, showed up at the museum and was literally chasing me down."

Aurora frowned. "Why?"

"She wants to know more about you."

"Me?" She sat up. "What about me?"

"She seems to think she has to know everything. I'm assuming she knows I was hired because something new was happening with you."

"Well, according to you, tons of progress has been made."

"Yeah, but Lizzie doesn't need to know that. We'll get more work done if the press isn't breathing down our necks."

She nodded. "Fair point." She patted his chest. "Now, I know we planned on archery, but I have a feeling neither of us is in the shape for that now."

He groaned. "I concur."

After they had both managed to stand, they linked arms and walked toward the seaside. They leaned on each other, still shaken from the encounter with the shadow figure.

"Did you fish at all?" Dez asked.

"That was one 'manly' thing I refused to do," she replied. "I'll gladly enjoy a fish dinner after it's been gutted, prepared and fully cooked, but having to kill the animal myself... no thank you." She looked at him. "I know, hypocritical. I love so many dishes with fish and meat."

Dez shrugged. "I see nothing wrong with it. There's a difference between taking a life and it being completely out of sight." He pointed to the waves. "Speaking of fish."

Dolphins danced in the water, clicking and singing happily to each other.

"That's pretty accurate."

Aurora laughed. "There were dolphins local to us when I was awake. I'm actually familiar with them."

Dez hummed. "I know, you're going to keep that in the back of your mind to figure out Voltav's location."

It was Dez's turn to laugh. "You know me too well, Your Highness."

"Perhaps you're too easy to read, Sir Desmond."

The two watched the dolphins for a while, knowing Dez couldn't stay as long as they usually liked.

"I really don't want to leave you."

"I know."

"Especially with that... thing attacking you."

"I'll be alright." She wasn't sure if she completely believed her own words, but she had to try. Dez pulled her close and kissed the top of her head again.

She beamed. "Don't you want to kiss somewhere else?"

He blushed. So cute. He was still nervous.

"Good night, Dez. Hopefully Lizzie doesn't try to get you again."
And with that, the dream faded away.

CHAPTER 36

February 2026, Wellington Bits, Lizzie's Life Lessons by Elizabeth Hildegrant

I have never been so disrespected in my life.

This past week, I visited The Museum of Historical Mysteries, intending to interview Exhibit Aurora's newest team member, Desmond Buckley.

Imagine my horror when I was treated like Monty Monjurse; I was met with absolute rudeness from a tour guide, Dr. Ellison and Desmond himself, only to be asked to leave.

When I calmly explained that I was simply doing my job, Dr. Ellison practically flew into a rage. I don't even recall everything she said. Her words were so sharp, so dismissive, and cut deeper than I care to admit.

It wasn't just what she said, but how she said it, Like I was some pest being swatted away, not a professional seeking the truth. I've dealt with condescension before, but this was different. This felt personal.

I am a journalist. I have a duty to the people to keep them informed. Something sinister is going on with Exhibit Aurora, and we deserve to know!

Ever since I was a child, I've had to fight ten times harder than those around me to make it in this industry. I have so much working against me; I'm a woman, I'm young, and I don't have a bunch of fancy degrees. I am constantly treated as "less than," and written off as a "just social media star who got lucky." I'm left out of press events and forgotten when it comes to

Wellington industry parties. Just two years ago, I was conveniently the only writer in this city who was not invited to the museum's grand re-opening party after the height of the pandemic. How is that fair? Why is every other press writer and their mother handed everything on a silver platter?

But even with so much going against me, I refuse to give up. I'm a writer of the little people, the forgotten, the underestimated. And I'm still here. I will continue my research, my fieldwork, and my devotion to the *Wellington Bits*.

Mark my words, something is up with Princess Aurora, and I'll be the one to figure it out.

CHAPTER 37

2026, The Museum of Historical Mysteries

Lizzie had gone too far this time.

While the museum's regular patrons and benefactors remained loyal, the internet was another story. Trolls and Lizzie's fangirls flooded the museum's social media pages, slamming them relentlessly.

@User3004: Who treats someone like that? She's just doing her job.

@crashing09: The museum needs to fix this, Lizzie is owed an apology.

@MeteoRite45: Justice for Lizzie!

@mothmanlives: #LetLizzieIn

She had always been an annoyance, but now Greg, along with the rest of the staff, realized just how much influence she could have.

"So, what's going on with the princess?"

Greg sighed. It was his first field trip tour of the semester and this group had been a special kind of stupid since they arrived.

"I'm happy to report that Aurora is still consistently moving in her sleep, hence the new, larger bed," he said, hoping to steer them back to the usual script.

"We know that, you dork," a girl sneered. "We mean, what are you hiding?"

Her classmates murmured in agreement. Greg had already held back so many groans of frustration that day. The kids had been pestering him about Aurora nonstop since the beginning of the tour. Now that they were in the exhibit, they were being snot-nosed little shits.

"I think you should bring the kissing back," a boy suggested smugly.

His classmates erupted into chaos. Some laughed, others shrieked in disgust, and some girls smacked the boys in protest. As usual, their teacher stood by doing nothing.

Greg put on his best gym coach voice. "Hey!"

Silence.

He still had it. He just needed to keep it going.

"I'm going to assume you all follow *The Wellington Bits* to some extent?"

"Yeah! Lizzie's hot!"

Another smack. Greg snapped his fingers to regain control.

"Listen up. I'm going off script, but I think it's for the greater good. You all know Lizzie went to school with Desmond Buckley, right? I was there too. And Desmond—Dez—has been my best friend since fourth grade."

That kept their attention. Even their teacher looked interested now.

Greg continued. "Lizzie wants you to think she cares sooo much about Aurora, but she doesn't. Not really. She cares about Lizzie. She hops on whatever bandwagon can get her the most attention. So no, we at The Museum of Historical Mysteries have no respect for someone like her. If she wants to be invited to our press events, she needs to behave like a professional, not some TMZ wannabe."

Some kids nodded. *"Good, progress,"* Greg thought.

"If you want to talk passion, talk to Dez. He was introduced to Exhibit Aurora on our middle school field trip, just like you guys. I joke, but he became obsessed. He made it his life's goal to get on the team one day and be the one to wake her up. He studied every article, every text, every tiny detail about the princess."

He looked at Aurora and smiled. She was resting on her side comfortably, snuggling into a new fleece blanket Dez had gotten her for Valentine's Day.

"Valedictorian. Full ride scholarships. Currently, the top of his class in grad school. He got rejected from the museum's internship program, so he worked harder and got hired outright by Dr. Ellison herself while working as a janitor for the museum."

The group was completely silent, hanging on to his every word. He had them.

"Because of Dez, more progress has been made over the last few weeks than in the over fifty years since Aurora first came to the museum. It's his work. No one handed him anything. It's just Dez putting in the effort to achieve his goals. So if he wants to turn down interviews to focus purely on his work, he's earned the right. He doesn't want fame. He's smart, and he's humble."

He nodded, showing the end of his speech.

"Well, when you put it like that…" one kid muttered.

"Lizzie's not that hot anyway," the former fanboy added.

"Her hair's a mess. It got fried during her last session."

Greg rolled his eyes. "So, Bigfoot exhibit?"

***

"That's him!"

A swarm of pre-teen girls ran up to Dez, eyes wide with excitement and phones in hand.

"Can I get a picture?!"

"You're awesome!"

"Are you in love with Aurora?"

"Uh…" Dez backed up into the welcome sign. What the heck was going on?

"Hey, girls, back up!" Greg pushed through the crowd, positioning himself in front of Dez.

"What did I just say about letting him do his work?"

The girls immediately looked guilty. "Sorry, Mr. Greg."

"I'm not the one to apologize to." He stepped aside and gestured to Dez.

They sheepishly turned to him. "Sorry, Mr. Buckley. We just think what you're doing is great."

Dez unclenched his jaw. "Uh, thank you?"

"Could we still get a group photo? Please?"

Greg smirked. "That's better. What do you think, Dez? They asked nicely."

"Sure," Dez answered, still not sure what was happening. The girls cheered, posed for a quick picture, then ran off to their bus. They giggled as they shared the photo in their group chat.

Dez turned to Greg, still baffled. "What on earth was that?"

Greg held his hands up, looking smug. "I fear I made you very popular with the younger demographic."

Dez groaned. "The hell."

Greg's phone dinged in his pocket. He pulled it out, scrolled for a minute, then grinned.

"Oh, you are going to love this."

"Greg, what'd you do?"

He handed Dez the phone. The most recent *Lizzie's Life Lessons* was pulled up.

@OLIVIA2025: Lizzie needs to back off.

@User1402: My class was just at The Museum of Historical Mysteries for a field trip today. They're doing everything they can to take care of Aurora, nothing's wrong. And the tour guide Greg is an absolute legend.

@Smash4TheLikes: If Lizzie wants to be invited to those little parties so bad, maybe she should quit acting like a jerk. It's giving mean girl energy.

@effly: #LizzieThePickMe

Dez exhaled sharply. "Jesus, kids are harsh."

"Yeah, but she needed to hear it," Greg said, tucking his phone away. "They have the guts to say what we're all thinking."

Dez smiled. "I don't have a clue what you did, but thanks."

Greg clapped him on the back. "No problem. Now," he started tugging him to Exhibit Aurora, "you know Aurora hates it when you're late."

CHAPTER 38

2026, The Museum of Historical Mysteries

Kyra couldn't help but laugh as she refreshed Lizzie's article again. More and more comments flooded in, and she hadn't seen one in support of the witch. Not witch, that was offensive to witches. They were all lovely. Hag. Shrew. Harpy. Those were much better.

"What on earth are you cackling about?" Lila asked.

Kyra looked up from her laptop. "Oh, just karma."

Lila hummed. "Lizzie related karma?"

"Possibly."

"I figured. Whatever makes you happy." Lila slipped on a pair of headphones and hunched over her own laptop. She'd been assigned more historical research after Dez learned that dolphins had once been native to Voltav.

"Thanks again for doing that," Kyra said. "I know it's not necessarily your main specialty."

Lila waved a hand dismissively. "One of my undergrad's in history, it's totally cool." She looked up at the clock. "Now close that horrid article and get to the exhibit. It's research time."

Lila still didn't know the full extent of Dez's program, and she didn't ask. She just knew that Kyra was less stressed, Dez was thriving, and Aurora was making incredible progress. That's all that mattered.

Kyra shut her computer, kissed Lila on the cheek, and made her way to the exhibit. Dez and Greg were already there, finishing the setup.

"You know," she said, "I was wary about dragging Greg into this, but he's a good listener."

Greg grinned. "You two are good teachers."

Dez plugged in a wire. "I'm really glad you didn't mind wipe him too."

"Oh, ditto," Kyra huffed. "That's particularly exhausting."

The day everything went down, they'd teleported back to the lab and had to decide what to do with Lizzie. They figured their best option was to wipe the tail end of her rant from her memory, plant a false recollection of Greg escorting her out, and leave her outside to wake up.

They'd stood over her, still completely unconscious, on the park bench they'd chosen as her drop off spot.

"You sure you don't want to wipe my mind too?" Greg had asked. "I feel like I'm intruding…"

"Absolutely not," Kyra insisted. "You've proven to be very useful. And Sigmund adores you. Traitor."

"Greg's the Barbarian," Dez remarked.

Both Greg and Kyra blinked at him.

"D&D?" Dez prompted.

"Nerd," Greg and Kyra said in unison.

According to Dez, Greg was the Barbarian, Kyra the Ranger, and himself the Wizard. Apparently, that made for a good team. Neither Greg nor Kyra completely understood it, but they worked extremely well together.

Greg powered on the equipment. "Okie dokie, naptime for you, Dez."

Dez placed the cap on his head and stretched out on the bench. "Why haven't we invested in something more comfortable for me yet?"

Kyra rolled her eyes. "Who's the princess? Go to sleep."

And with that, he dozed off.

***

"Dr. Ellison?"

Kyra looked up from the physics book she'd been reading. "Greg, I told you, call me Kyra."

"Nope. You earned that title."

She grinned. "What's up?"

Greg glanced at Dez. "Do you… Do you think he's gonna wake her up?"

She closed her book. "I have faith."

He smirked. "Faith in the science, or faith in the magic?"

Greg had figured it out.

She sighed. "Honestly, I don't know at this point. Humans had to adapt to a lot once my kind left. They've done incredible things with science and medicine, things I never thought possible. Heck, I've done amazing things myself without using my magic in more recent years."

Greg's gaze shifted to Aurora. "But nothing's been able to wake her up yet."

"I know. But the reason I have faith now is that Dez has gotten closer than anyone else."

Greg frowned. "From the way you talk about magic, it doesn't sound like anything can break the spell but that kiss."

Kyra bit her lip. Deep down, she knew Greg was right. Carabosse's original curse had been powerful and dark. Kyra had used an ancient blessing to counteract it as much as possible, but ultimately, the only thing that could wake Aurora was appeasing the magic still consuming her. True Love's Kiss.

"Uh, Dr. Ellison? I don't think that's supposed to be happening…"

Kyra looked at the EEG monitor to see the brainwaves dancing erratically.

She squinted. "I mean, it's different, but I don't think it's cau—"

The monitor flashed red and started beeping.

"Yeah, that's not good."

She ran over to the keyboard, somehow maintaining her composure.

"Greg, try to wake him up."

"But you said—"

"I don't care what I said before. He's in non-REM. He'll be fine."

Greg shook Dez's shoulders. "Dez? Dez! Wake up!" He lightly slapped his face. "Dr. Ellison, I'd really prefer *not* to have Dez as a new exhibit!"

Kyra groaned. Nothing was working. She typed in the emergency shutdown command.

Program session aborted.

As soon as the machinery flickered off, Dez bolted upright.

"Aurora? Aurora! Help!"

Greg held him in place. "Dez, you're awake! Breathe!"

Kyra crouched in front of him, gently taking his face in her hands. "Dez, breathe, you're okay."

"AURORA!"

Tears streamed down his face. Kyra and Greg exchanged a panicked look. Neither of them had any idea what to do. They did the only thing they could and wrapped Dez in a hug until his breathing slowed.

CHAPTER 39

?

Dez opened his eyes to nothing but gray.

"What?"

He sat up, blinking rapidly, trying to adjust to the dim surroundings. His head pounded in sync with a faint beeping in the distance.

"Hello?"

His voice barely carried. He pressed his hands to the floor, which was smooth and cool, like tile. Crawling forward, he reached out blindly, searching for something, anything, to hold on to. His fingers brushed up against a wall. As he leaned fully into it, the surrounding space lit up.

"Shit." He flinched, shielding his eyes from the sudden brightness.

The walls appeared to be the inside of a machine, pulsing with glowing data streams. Brainwaves flickered across the wall opposite him, the same patterns he'd seen countless times on the EEG monitor. The beeping grew louder. His temples throbbed. This was very wrong.

"Aurora?" he called out.

Silence.

"Aurora?!"

A small, circular window appeared to his left, embedded in a sealed metal door. Pulse fluttering, Dez stumbled toward it. The door was ice cold beneath his fingers. He pressed his face against the glass, peering into the thick gray smog swirling on the other side. The mist shifted, revealing a brief glimpse of the field he'd come to know behind Voltav Castle.

"What..."

His stomach dropped. Aurora lay in the grass, completely still. And the shadow figure was above her once again. Its hand was pressed on her chest, the rest of its form hovering inches from her face.

"No…"

Was she still breathing?

"NO!"

Nobody could hear him. He slammed his hands against the glass and metal, screaming out Aurora's name and begging the creature to stop.

"Aurora!"

He was hitting the door so hard, his palms were bleeding. He didn't care. Again and again, he banged, leaving dark red handprints with every blow. The room erupted into chaos. The brainwave streams on the walls flickered wildly. The beeping accelerated into an ear-splitting alarm. A strobe light flashed red, casting the space in an eerie, pulsing glow.

"HEY!" he roared. "Let go of her!"

In one final attempt, he threw his entire weight against the window. A sharp crack formed across the glass. The shadow froze. Slowly, it turned its faceless head toward him. It was in front of the window in an instant. It had no eyes, but Dez could feel it watching him. It reached out a cloudy hand, which twisted like smoke as it forced its way into the room. Dez hit the floor hard, scrambling back as the figure re-materialized in the room. The beeping had turned into a frantic siren. The red strobe pulsed, casting eerie, shifting shadows across the space. Dez's head was swimming. The creature was suddenly in front of him.

"No—"

Dez barely got the word out before it pressed a hand to his chest. He was on his back immediately, his body becoming completely paralyzed. He couldn't move, couldn't scream, couldn't blink, the creature just floated above him. And then he felt it. His breath was being pulled from his lungs. His chest was tight, his face felt numb, and he couldn't even tell if his heart was still beating. This was how Aurora had looked. Was she still even alive? Was he about to meet the same fate? The edges of his vision darkened. His mind slipped further, sinking into darkness.

And then everything went black.

CHAPTER 40

2026, The Museum of Historical Mysteries

Dez bolted upright, gasping for air. He could move again.
"Aurora? Aurora! Help!"

Greg was there, holding onto his shoulders. "Dez, you're awake! Breathe!"

Then, warm hands cradled his head. He blinked rapidly before locking eyes with Kyra's hazel ones. "Dez, breathe, you're okay."

He was definitely not okay.

"AURORA!"

His cry was raw and desperate. Tears began to fall, he couldn't stop them. He felt so tired, so hurt, so confused. Kyra and Greg had wrapped their arms around him, holding him tightly.

Dez sobbed uncontrollably. Greg pressed their foreheads together. "Dez... what happened?"

He sucked in shuddering breaths, still unable to speak.

Kyra gave Greg a worried look. "Get him some water."

Greg nodded and started toward the lab, but Dez grabbed him. "Is... is Aurora okay? Please tell me she's okay."

"She's fine. I promise."

Dez wouldn't believe that unless he saw it for himself. He pushed himself onto his unsteady legs, muscles screaming in protest. Greg caught him before he collapsed.

"Careful," Greg muttered, guiding him toward the bed.

Dez leaned against the glass and peered in. Aurora lay there, arms at her sides, mouth parted slightly. A bead of sweat clung right above her eyebrow.

"She's… She's not okay." He wriggled out of Greg's hold and pressed up closer against the glass. She was thankfully still breathing, but she looked… sick. Unnaturally pale.

"Kyra?" She stood next to him. "Kyra, unlock this."

"What?"

"Unlock. The. Dome."

"I— oh my god, Greg, get the first aid kit."

Dez stared at the glass around Aurora and was horrified by the bloody handprints smeared on top. He flipped his hands over and looked at his palms. It was his blood. The injuries had crossed over. Somehow, the damage from the dream had become real. And then the pain hit. It seared across his hands like daggers and spread like fire up his forearms. He felt like he'd been scraped raw against pavement, only worse. So much worse.

"Kyra," he gasped, "it hurts...it hurts so bad."

Kyra took his hands without hesitation, blood and all.

"Shh," she soothed, "I'll fix it."

A soft, yellow light emitted between their clasped hands. Dez felt a cooling sensation throughout his veins, numbing the pain. A light vibration rippled over his skin, knitting it back together. The glow faded, and Kyra let go. They were completely healed. Greg stood behind her, mouth wide open.

"Yo, the fact that you haven't been using magic all this time is wild."

"Wasn't worth the risk before," Kyra scoffed. She unhooked her work lanyard and tossed it at him. "Here, unlock the bed."

Greg fumbled with the keys. "Wha—"

"Greg, unlock the bed."

Kyra continued to soothe Dez as Greg cautiously used a series of keys and codes to unlock Aurora's bed. The glass dome hissed as it lifted.

They all just stared for a moment. Kyra finally broke the eerie silence.

"Go ahead, Dez," she whispered.

Dez leaned over Aurora once again. She was still alive, but was so still; her skin had a gray tinge to it. He reached out and gently brushed a finger down her cheek. Their first real touch. He wiped the sweat from her forehead. What had that…that thing done to her?

"Aurora…."

Tears welled in his eyes again. He cupped the side of her head, gently running his fingers through her hair. Her body had no reaction, not even a flinch. He couldn't stop the tears from falling now. A large, fat droplet rolled off his nose and landed on her pale cheek.

Light exploded out from the fallen tear, shimmering as it mixed with the overhead lights, dancing like golden dust. Dez stepped back, covering his eyes. As it finally dissipated, Kyra and Greg rushed to his side.

"Queen Mab…" Kyra muttered.

The sickly gray color had disappeared from Aurora's skin. Her cheeks flushed the familiar peachy color as her breathing once again steadied. She turned her head slightly, lightly moaning, as if she was settling back into sleep.

"Did… did I do that?" Dez asked.

Kyra's eyes narrowed. "I think so?" She took his chin and studied his eyes. A crazed laugh escaped her.

Greg's hands clamped around Dez's face. "Does Dez have powers now?!"

Kyra grinned. "No, I think when I healed you, some of my magic transferred. My tears heal, so yours healed Aurora."

Greg pouted. "So no superpowers?"

Kyra chuckled. "No, it's probably worn off now." She looked at Aurora. "I'm just glad she's okay."

Dez barely heard them. He had gone back to running his fingers through her hair. He didn't know what he would have done if he'd lost her. She was so perfect.

Greg smirked. "You got it bad."

Dez just nodded. He didn't care if they teased. It was true.

Kyra squeezed his shoulder. "We have to close her back up."

"I know. Just… Just one second."

He leaned over and placed a soft kiss on her cheek. As he moved away, an aching feeling sank in his chest. For a split second, he'd hoped that would work.

CHAPTER 41

Aurora's Dreams

Aurora opened her eyes. Night had fallen, and the fireflies danced above her.

She reached up, touching her cheek. She could have sworn she felt the lightest brush of lips there. But that couldn't be. She was still alone. That thing had appeared out of nowhere again, catching her completely off guard. It'd pushed her into the grass with just its palm, paralyzing her instantly. Unable to move, she could do nothing but lie there, eyes forced shut. Then, the air was being pulled right out of her.

Her chest tightened with every draw the creature took, her body growing weaker. How strange that this was the closest to actual sleep she'd felt in so long. Just as she had accepted her fate, something distracted the shadow. It floated away, and the pressure on her chest lifted. She knew she was no longer immobile, but exhaustion and hopelessness weighed her down. Everything was just dark, depressing, useless. A feather-light touch brushed from her cheek to above her eyebrows. A faint breeze ruffled her hair. Something wet fell onto her cheek. From behind her heavy lids, she saw the faintest glimmer of golden particles floating above her. The pressure and hopelessness immediately melted away. Her breathing steadied.

It wasn't until she'd felt the kiss on her cheek that she could finally open her eyes.

"Dez."

She forced herself upright, seeing she was still alone, nobody else in sight. She could have sworn it was him. He was supposed to have been there by now. Pain throbbed behind her eyes as she stood. Dez wouldn't have abandoned her. The creature must have done something.

Feeling unsteady, she started walking to the castle. She needed to get to the book. If anything had happened, Dez would have written to her. Something felt more off than usual as she passed through the throne room. Everything was still there, unchanged, but duller somehow, as if a film had settled over the world.

Strange.

She shook off the feeling and continued to her room. She'd wanted to run right over to the book, but simply walking to the castle had been exhausting.

She flopped onto her bed, grateful for the royal comfort it held. She reached for the book and flipped past the pages of *Pride and Prejudice* Dez had sent a few days prior. It was definitely her favorite by far. Lizzie was captivating, and her love-hate dynamic with Mr. Darcy was delightful.

Aurora sighed, hoping her own Mr. Darcy was alright. Her breath hitched when she saw fresh ink on the next page.

Aurora? Christ's sake, please be okay.

She loaded her quill far too quickly, smudging her reply.

Dez, I'm here. I'm alright. Shaken.

The response came faster than ever.

Oh god, you're there. That thing came back.

Yes...

I tried to get to you, I tried so hard, I swear I did.

I know you did.

She hadn't seen him, but somehow, she knew he had been there.

I was stuck. I was in this room with a door and a window. I saw it attacking you, but was locked out.

Oh Dez.

And then somehow it got in. It came after me.

That's where it had gone.

I got out, but Aurora, I was so worried.

How'd you get out?

Kyra pulled the kill switch.

Kyra?

Who?

Oh, Christ's blood.

***

2026, The Museum of Historical Mysteries

"You didn't tell her about me???"

Dez cringed as Kyra snapped at him.

"You said you wanted to stay out of it!"

Kyra crossed her arms. "Initially, yes. But I figured the first thing you'd do after learning about the fairy shit was tattle to her!"

More words appeared on the monitor.

Dez? What's going on?

Dez gave Kyra a confused look. She groaned. "Okay, well, she knew me, but she knew nothing about the curse. And I'd like to keep it that way."

"Why?

"True Love has to be genuine, you dummy. Now, answer her."

Dez nervously exhaled and typed. "Sorry," he muttered, "I feel like I'm being ambushed."

"You kind of are. Tough titties. I need to make sure nothing else happens."

She stood with her hands on her hips, foot tapping, mirroring the night she had first caught him. She could understand why he hadn't told Aurora about her, to an extent. And she *had* said she would stay out of their connections.

But come on, Dez. All mighty magical being. Right here.

His reply appeared on the monitor.

Okay, so, you remember The Good Fairy from before you fell asleep? She's...here. She goes by Kyra now. She's head of your research team and has been trying to wake you too.

A pause.

That's a lot to process.

I know. I didn't want something else for you to worry about. And granted, I did only recently learn Kyra was a fairy. THE fairy, apparently. She's been pretending to be human this whole time.

Another pause.

Fascinating.

Kyra frowned. "She's mad."

No, she's not," Dez reassured her. "She's just taking it all in."

Aurora's reply appeared. *I guess if she hadn't figured out a way to connect with me before, that really does make you special.*

And Kyra melted again.

Dez was turning pink. She squeezed his shoulder.

"I'll leave you to talk to your lady, don't worry."

CHAPTER 42

2026, The Lab

"Everything alright?" Lila asked as Kyra returned to the lab. "You were in there way longer than usual."

"Equipment malfunction," Kyra lied. "We fixed it, but it set us back quite a bit. Dez is finishing up in the exhibit so I could come back here to go through my books. We're both staying late."

"Seeing that you haven't done that since Dez started, I'll allow it." Lila was gathering her things to head home. Surely it hadn't been that long? Kyra looked at the clock.

Yikes.

"Oh, by the way," Lila tossed some papers on Kyra's desk. "I think Voltav was somewhere on the coast of France. I'm not certain, but it seems the most probable."

"Hm," Kyra nodded. "d'Ambray, I guess that makes sense."

She really should have known exactly where the hidden kingdom was, but with the ever-shifting earth, she'd lost track of its location. At least there was still enough magic lingering that, if Aurora happened to be French, it would've implanted an understanding of English straight into her brain.

Lila shrugged. "I honestly swore it would be in Scotland, but what do I know?" She waved and headed out towards the exit.

"Lila?" Kyra called out. Lila faced her. "Thanks. Seriously."

Lila smirked and gave a quick salute. "All in a day's work."

Kyra waited until she was sure Lila was gone before frantically opening her desk drawers.

"It had better still be here and not at home," she grumbled. She pulled out various books; Greek Myths, Norse History, one of Galileo's old journals he'd left her…

"Aha!" She held the Mythical Creatures book up in triumph.

"Aha what?" Dez asked as he shuffled into the lab.

"Hopefully, this will tell us what our attacker is." She set the book on her desk. "Is Aurora okay?"

He shrugged. "She promised she'd be fine, said she'd rest in the dungeon if she had to."

"I don't like that."

"You think I do? I'd be there with her, but I can't risk trying to lucid dream again. That thing might be waiting for her."

"Or you," Kyra added. She blew a thick layer of dust from the book cover. "Which is why we need to do some research. Pull up a chair."

Dez dragged a folding chair over and sat next to her. "Is that from *the* Galileo?"

"Sure is."

"Do I want to know why you have it?"

She handed him the journal. "Read the inside of the front cover."

Dez opened it, his jaw dropping as he read.

Philippa,

Thee give my wholehearted thanks for thy dedication to our research. Thee am hopeful these words and notations will be helpful with thy future studies. Remain bright, remain strong, and continue learning.

"Philippa? Research?"

"Don't act so shocked," Kyra drawled, "It was a popular name in the fifteenth century. I wanted to learn from the best. He took me on as a pupil."

Dez shook his head. "Kyra, once Aurora's awake, you're gonna have to write a book."

Kyra laughed. "We can talk about that later. Now, mythical creatures."

Dez frowned. "I'm assuming you're gonna tell me all that nonsense is real, too?"

She sighed. "Some are, not all. Like manticores? Imaginary."

Dez whistled through his teeth. "That's a relief. Pictures of those things give me the heebie jeebies."

"Well, that's more because medieval painters seemingly couldn't draw animals." She shuddered at the thought of some of the cat drawings that came out of the Renaissance.

Dez peered over her shoulder. "What about griffins?"

"Very real, unfortunately extinct." She continued to flip through the pages. "People went after their feathers too much."

"That's sad."

"It is. My next goal is to clone one like Dolly the Sheep."

"Um."

She held up a finger. "*Later.* We have much more pressing matters at hand."

"Wait, I gotta know. Bigfoot?"

Kyra chuckled. "Amazingly, even my kind don't know. Stealthy, that one." She read through some descriptions. "You said it sucked the breath out of you?"

Dez nodded. "And I couldn't move. Aurora said the same."

"And you felt drained…?"

"Physically and emotionally," he groaned.

"So it was stealing your energy." It sounded vampire-like, just different…

Then it hit her.

"Oh dear lord, it can't be." She quickly flipped back a few pages before finding the right one. Her frown deepened.
"Crap."

Dez looked over her shoulder again. "What the hell is a boo hag?"

Kyra slumped back in her chair. "You know how people talk about sleep paralysis demons?"

"Yeah, I guess so?"

"Don't think too hard. Yes, most of them are purely neurological, but sometimes," she glared at the diagram, "sometimes it's a boo hag."

She handed Dez the book so he could read for himself. Not much scared Kyra, but boo hags gave her the creeps. The skinless creatures could reach their victims through the smallest crack, including keyholes. They'd sit on their victim's chest all night, stealing their energy through their breaths. And they called it "riding," which made the whole thing even creepier.

Dez looked up from the book. "I mean, it definitely sounds like this, but it didn't look like this."
Kyra scratched her head. The shadow figure Dez had described differed greatly from the bright red boo hag with throbbing blue veins.

"All I can think is that it's a dream version of one. Or maybe some of Carabosse's essence was left behind? So it's a ghost version? I don't know, but that would explain why the sun doesn't affect it."

Boo hags couldn't survive out in the sun. Their victims who resisted would meet a horrible fate—their skin stolen, used as a disguise during the day. If the boo hag didn't reach their skin in time after their night escapades, they would perish as soon as dawn hit.

Dez nodded slowly. "Okay. Boo hag."
He shut the book. "So… how do we get rid of it?"
Kyra scowled. "I have no clue."

CHAPTER 43

April, 2026, Wellington Bits, Lizzie's
Life Lessons by Elizabeth Hildegrant

Have I been quiet enough to be uncanceled yet?

For real though-do you know how hurtful it is to be bombarded with hate every single day. You're all acting like children; bullying a young woman in a male-dominated field. A woman who did nothing wrong.

I speak my mind? I'm annoying.

I ask questions? I'm a nag.

I was wrongfully removed from a public place? My perpetrators get applauded for it!

What's a girl gotta do to win anyway, huh?

Well, the joke's on you, you fools. Because whether you love me or hate me, I still get paid. Every comment, every angry share, every irresistible click on the *Wellington Bits*—it all keeps stuffing my pockets.

So go ahead. Keep running your mouths. I'll be laughing all the way to the bank.

#LizzieThePickMe

@user885: Wow, ur actually trying to flip that hashtag in your favor? Being a pick me has never and will never be a good thing.

@TrashTanya: She's dumb, but she's not wrong. We're literally feeding her engagement.

@DramaHawk: And yet, here we are. Talking about her. Again.

@BTL: #BoycottTheLizard

CHAPTER 44

2026, The Museum of Historical Mysteries

"Greg, was that you?"

"Was what me? I don't know nothing about nothing."

Dez chuckled. He had a pretty awesome best friend.

"I will say," Greg continued, "if I were to come up with a hashtag designed to destroy someone's career, I'd make sure it used a nickname close enough to their real name so they'd lose all traction."

"Well, whoever did just that is a genius. *Wellington Bits* activity is down by 40%."

"Huzzah!" Greg fistbumped Dez. "Why didn't I go into marketing?"

Dez smirked. "Because for whatever reason, you wanted to share the joy of education with children."

"Don't remind me," Greg groaned. "Speaking of which, I've got another tour. I'll see you later."

Ever since Greg called Lizzie out, he'd been the most requested tour guide at the museum. Dez hadn't even realized that could be a thing, but apparently, Greg and the museum as a whole were thriving. It meant he, unfortunately, wasn't around for research sessions as much, but there hadn't been much progress, anyway. Dez and Aurora had only communicated through text, both wary of encountering the boo hag again. Kyra theorized that if it was a dream boo hag, it could only enter through the connection formed during their face-to-face meetings. Unfortunately, she appeared to have been correct. Since Dez stopped seeing Aurora, the creature hadn't returned.

Dez missed her smile. Her laugh. Her eyes.

He'd almost asked if he could lie next to her in her bed, just to be closer to her. But he knew that'd definitely be going too far.

Meanwhile, Kyra had been obsessively researching the boo hag. The only way she could find to completely get rid of them, was to salt their skin to prevent them from getting back into it. This one wasn't skinless. Or maybe it was and they couldn't tell. Either way, they were stuck. There were odd ways to distract them; boo hags were obsessed with numbers and completion. Apparently, if one placed a broom beside their bed before sleeping, the boo hag would have to count every straw before attacking. If they lost count, they'd have to start over. Dez couldn't imagine *how* someone even discovered that.

There was also the fact that Kyra was certain the creature had been left behind by Carabosse in some way. She had mentioned that when she was killed, she dissolved into ash and black sludge. Was it possible that some remnants had crept into Aurora's dreams, lying dormant until they gathered enough energy to take on the form of a boo hag?

Dez wasn't concerned with the specifics—he just wanted to look into Aurora's eyes again.

"Hey Kyra, I had a thought," he said as he walked into the lab. "What if I took salt—"

He stopped mid sentence.

Kyra sat at her desk, head in her hands, shoulders trembling as she silently cried. Dez had never seen her like this.

"K-Kyra?" He slowly moved towards her. She lifted her head, face streaked with glittering tears. She sniffled. "Kyra, what happened?"

She sniffed again and pointed to her computer screen. There was an email pulled up. Dez leaned over to read, rubbing Kyra's back in the process.

Dr. Ellison,

I wish to offer my wholehearted congratulations on all your work on Exhibit Aurora. The progress over the past five months has been truly groundbreaking. Your determination, quest for knowledge, and passion

for this project have not gone unnoticed. My great-grandfather Otto would be proud to see where his museum stands today.

That is why it is with great sadness that The Museum of Historical Mysteries Board of Directors has made the tough decision to close Exhibit Aurora indefinitely.

Dez's eyes widened. "What? No! They can't do that!"
Kyra let out a choked sob. He continued reading.

This decision has nothing to do with your, or your team's, undeniable talent. It was based on discussions regarding whether what we are doing is morally and ethically right. As you know, the museum has faced these types of accusations for years now; unfortunately, in today's climate, it has become a much larger issue.

"I feel like maybe you should have been involved in this decision?" Dez muttered.
"I know…" Kyra sputtered, wiping her eyes. "I—"
Dez rubbed her back gently.

On May 1st, we will shut down Exhibit Aurora.
This will not affect your, or your team's, employment at the museum. We have arranged for Princess Aurora d'Ambray to be transported to a state-of-the-art hospice facility in Stockholm, Sweden.
We would like to extend an offer to the entire Exhibit Aurora team: any and all team members may relocate to Sweden with the princess and stay on as her caretakers. The museum will cover all travel and moving costs, and you will maintain your current salary.

For those who choose not to relocate, we will place them in other positions within the museum. However, we cannot guarantee an identical salary.
For those who wish to resign entirely, we understand. We will assist in finding new employment as best we can.

Dr. Ellison, your work has been remarkable. Thank you for being part of The Museum of Historical Mysteries.

Warm Regards,

Geraldine Pach

Dez's blood boiled. "Are they seriously expecting you to break this news to the entire team?"

Kyra nodded. This couldn't be happening. May 1st was next week. They only had a week to either stop this or fix it.

He couldn't lose Aurora. And he definitely wasn't about to uproot his life, move to Sweden, and watch her lie in a hospital bed until the end of his days. There was no way they'd allow him to bring all the dreaming equipment with him.

"We'll…we'll figure it out."

"Dez!" Kyra sobbed. "No we won't! I'm failing her again!"

Suddenly, Kyra's phone rang. She ignored it, burying her face in her hands once more.

It rang again.

"Could that be important?" Dez asked. It was strange having their roles reversed-Kyra was usually the composed one.

"If you think it's so important, you can answer it," she muttered.

Dez hesitated before picking up the phone. He unlocked it and pressed it to his ear. "Hello?"

"Who is this?"

"Uh, this is Desmond Buckley. Dr. Ellison is…indisposed at the moment. May I ask who's calling?"

"Pleasure to meet you over the phone, Dez," the voice replied. "This is Maura Arkin, I'm Kyra's therapist."

CHAPTER 45

2026, Dez's Car

"This is NOT FAIR!"

"Kyra, quiet."

"I WILL NOT BE QUIET!"

She couldn't remember the last time she'd been so upset. No. She did. Twice before. And they'd both been for similar reasons. The first was when Carabosse cast her initial curse. The second was when Phillip's kiss had failed to wake Aurora.

Now, she had well and truly failed. Whether the board had decided to close the exhibit because they simply gave up, or didn't want to fund it anymore, it didn't matter. The result was the same. The idea of Aurora wasting away in a glorified hospital was horrifying.

And now Dez had somehow wrestled her into his car and was driving her to her therapist's office.

"Dez, you said yourself that we'd figure something out. We can't figure something out if we're not in the museum!"

Dez had remained frustratingly calm. Normally, Kyra would have been impressed. But this was not a normal situation.

"Yeah, well, Maura was pretty insistent."

"So you're gonna listen to some shrink instead of the brilliant Dr. Ellison? I see how it is."

Dez shook his head as he exited the freeway. "You're being silly."

"Silly?!"

"Best word I could come up with." She crossed her arms and huffed. "Kyra, it's for your own good. Maura said you haven't had an appointment in two months. You said yourself you don't understand mental health. You're better at your job when you're in the right headspace. We'll get there. You'll have your appointment with Maura, and then we can go back to work."

"Or," she glared at him, "you can turn this car around right now so we can wake Aurora up sooner!"

"Again, you're being silly. Should I put some music on? Mozart's supposed to calm you."

"Mozart calms babies. And he was a dick."

She went back to pouting as Dez chuckled. "Of course you knew Mozart."

Dez pulled up to Maura's office—a cozy little cottage with ivy climbing the walls.

"Let's get this over with." He got out, walked around, and opened Kyra's door for her. "M'lady."

"Nope."

"Kyra, come on."

"Nope."

"Okay, you forced me to do this."

Before she could react, he unbuckled her seatbelt and hoisted her over his shoulder like a sack of potatoes. She shrieked. "What the hell?! When did you hulk up?!"

He shut the car door and started up the cobblestone path. "Aurora suggested I take up hammer throw. Greg knows a guy."

"Lovely. Wonderful. Now you have brains *and* brawn."

"I won't deny Aurora seems to have a thing for strong shoulders."

"Gross."

Dez reached out his free hand and rang the cottage doorbell. Maura opened it almost instantly, took one look at the scene in front of her, and burst into laughter. "I'm assuming she didn't want to come?"

"Not one bit," Dez grunted. "Now, may we come in? I'm stronger than I used to be, but this is not comfortable."

"I'll show you uncomfortable!" Kyra huffed.

Dez plopped her down as soon as they crossed the threshold. He turned to Maura, offering his hand.

"Dez. Maura Arkin, I presume?"

Maura shook his hand before pulling him into a hug. "That's me. I've heard wonderful things about you."

"Aw, Kyra, you say nice things about me?"

Kyra frowned. "I did."

Dez rolled his eyes and turned back to Maura. "I apologize for her behavior. She's had a rough morning."

"It's okay," Maura said. "We'll get her all sorted out."

***

"Ms. Arkin, aren't I not supposed to be in here?"

He and Kyra sat on a green corduroy sofa while Maura brewed some tea.

"Oh no, trust me, you're fine." Maura called.

"Hey! Shouldn't that be my decision?" Kyra retorted.

Maura strolled in with two steaming mugs. "This isn't a normal session, Kyra. Now here, drink this."

Kyra wanted to keep being petulant, but the tea smelled delightful. She calmed instantly after her first sip. "What's in this?" she muttered.

"Not a normal session?" Dez asked.

Maura settled into an oversized armchair across from them. "Not in the slightest. I hear you're dealing with a boo hag."

Kyra nearly dropped her mug. Dez blinked. "Uh… Kyra hasn't seen you in two months. How'd you know about the boo hag?"

Kyra smacked him.

"What?! She obviously knows already! And she somehow knows what a boo hag is!"

Kyra sighed. He had a point. "Sorry."

"It's okay. You're going through it," Dez said. He turned back to Maura. "Okay, boo hag."

Maura gave a knowing smile. "Watch out fuh da boo hag, my pickney. If it ride ya, you done fo'."

Kyra's jaw dropped. "Maura…?"

"Like all de women in my fam'ly dat come befo' me, I gots de power of witchcraft."

Kyra set her mug down before she dropped it. "You're a witch???"

"Witch???" Dez echoed.

Maura just laughed. "Yes, Kyra, I'm a witch. Witch of the Gullah people, if we're being specific."

Things were adding up. No wonder Maura had been so nonchalant when Kyra had first told her she was a fairy. Kyra stood and paced. "We are so talking about this later. But yes, like Dez said, boo hag. Do you have any clue how to get rid of one?"

Maura crossed her legs. "I'm going to assume this isn't a normal boo hag?"

Kyra and Dez shook their heads.

Maura sighed. "Well, that's unfortunate. Just need a bit of salt for the usual ones. No matter." She reached over to a small bookshelf next to her. "My great-great-great-grandmother was well known for helping people get rid of boo hags. I have her journals right here." She pulled a small, cloth-bound book out and opened it.

"Why therapy?" Kyra asked.

Maura kept scanning the pages. "I come from a long line of healers. Like the rest of my family, I wanted to help people. But I don't have the patience, or frankly, the stomach for traditional medicine." She stopped on a page and smiled. "I can help people with what's in their head, though." She tapped her temple with a finger. "Mus tek cyear a de root fa heal de tree." She handed Kyra the journal. "I think this is exactly what you're looking for."

Kyra skimmed the beautiful handwriting. Dez peered over her shoulder.

"This... this is not gonna be fun."

CHAPTER 46

Aurora's Dreams

Aurora glanced around at the dark, cold stone walls. It wasn't completely terrible.

She had told Dez she wouldn't come down here unless it was completely necessary. And it was.

Aurora didn't want to admit it to Dez, but it felt like her dream world was crumbling. The dull feeling in the throne room had spread throughout the castle, leaving her with the sensation of walking through a hazy smog. Her room, once a huge source of comfort, felt stale and unwelcome. Cloudy weather had become more frequent, making her reluctant to go outside.

That eerie feeling never left her, though she hadn't seen the boo hag since it hurt Dez. Yes, she had been attacked, but he had actually been injured. Still, she couldn't shake the feeling that the shadowy creature was lingering just beyond her dreams, waiting for the perfect moment to strike.

That was why she had come down to the dungeon. Well, what she had imagined the dungeon had been like. Her father had hated it and used it as little as possible, preferring rehabilitation over imprisonment for petty criminals. He had kept Aurora far away from the gloomy cells.

The dream version of the dungeon was a rough generalization. Aurora had built up the usual gray stone, iron bars, and chilly ambiance. But she had made it somewhat bearable. A bed almost as comfy as her own, a miniature candelabra, and a yellow tapestry to brighten up the space.
It wasn't ideal, but at least it was a change of scenery.

She had grown completely isolated again, and she hated it. The loneliness this time was so much worse. After being spoiled by Dez's affections, the solitude was unbearable. She felt like a prisoner in her own mind.

The only thing keeping her going was the magical book filled with Dez's words and the stories he still wrote out to her. She'd already read *Pride and Prejudice* multiple times and never tired of Jane Austen's words. One passage in particular always called to her—the moment Lizzie realized Darcy was her perfect match.

"She began now to comprehend that he was exactly the man who, in disposition and talents, would most suit her. His understanding and temper, though unlike her own, would have answered all her wishes. It was a union that must have been to the advantage of both: by her ease and liveliness, his mind might have been softened, his manners improved; and from his judgment, information, and knowledge of the world, she must have received benefit of greater importance."

Dez was her Mr. Darcy. There was no question about it. As far as she knew, they'd known each other for nearly seven months. It felt like seven years—no, seventy. Dez made her happy. He let her keep her independence while still making her feel safe needing someone. He gave her a reason to keep living.

She flopped back onto her makeshift bed, staring at the stone ceiling. So this was what love felt like…. Before, she'd never imagined wanting to share any portion of her life with anyone. Now she wanted to take Dez on adventures for the rest of their lives.

She had been wrong. It was fourteenth century men who weren't worth her time.

Dez was worth all the time she could spare.

Aurora pulled her book close, gently opening it to their first conversation.

You're certainly a peculiar one, Dez.

Peculiar good, or peculiar bad?

Most definitely peculiar good.

She smiled when new text appeared on the pages.

Aurora?

I'm here.

Are you alright?

As alright as I can be.

I miss you.

I miss you so much.

Tears pricked the corners of her eyes.

I have good news and bad news.

Bad news first.

Bad news…Kyra and I have to go away for a few days.

How long is a few?

Maximum, three.

She sneered. That was too long.

What's the good news?

We're going to find a root that should help us stop the boo hag. A witch helped us out.

First, I learn your superior is The Good Fairy, now a witch is helping you. This is insane.

I know. And we would just have the root delivered, but it won't get here until next week.

That's not too long.

It'll be too late by then.

Too late for what?

There was a very long pause. Aurora frowned. He wasn't telling her something.

Dez, you know you can tell me anything.

Still nothing. Then finally—

The museum is closing your exhibit next week. Your body's being transported to a new country.

It hit her square in the chest.

She would lose him. She couldn't lose him. She just couldn't.

Dez…

We'll figure this out. That's why I have to go. We'll be getting right down to the wire, but we need to do this.

Wire? Now wasn't the time for that. She knew this was important, but she couldn't stand the thought of losing contact for three whole days.

This is going to sound selfish, but please don't go.

Aurora...

Please.

Aurora, it's so important. I can't send Kyra on her own. It's just not safe.

Dez. Please. I'm... so lonely. I feel sad all the time. I don't care about anything except you.

Another pause. Now was the time. She needed to tell him how she truly felt. Right as she was going to write those three little words, his response appeared.

I'll figure it out.

CHAPTER 47

2026, Somewhere in Mexico

Kyra had wanted Dez to be the one to travel to Veracruz with her, but he had suddenly become insistent that he needed to stay behind. She was wary of traveling alone and hadn't been thrilled when he told her he couldn't go. He had been excited about the prospect of an adventure at first, so she was confused when he changed his mind.

But when she understood it was because of Aurora, she asked no more questions. The poor girl seemed to be going through a depressive state, only amplified by the possibility of another boo hag attack. Maura had already offered to give sessions to Aurora and Dez once all this was over. For now, he had to stay behind and keep her as calm as he could.

He loved her.

Kyra knew he loved her. It wasn't just in how he talked about her, how his entire demeanor changed when he wrote to her, or how his first instinct was to protect her. It was in the way he had become completely intertwined with Aurora's existence, the way he let her consume his thoughts, the way he refused to put anything else before her.

She had been watching it unfold for months now, and despite her usual tendency to tease Dez about his feelings, she hadn't been able to make a joke about it lately. It was too real. She had expected Dez to get attached to Aurora, but not like this. Not to where she could see the ache in his eyes when he had to be apart from her. And Aurora, the fiercely independent princess who had spent centuries with no human connection, had finally found something she wanted to hold on to.

Kyra sighed, gripping the controls of the plane a little tighter. Maybe, just maybe, this wasn't going to end in tragedy. Their best option was to keep the two's connection as strong as they could, even if currently it was only through text.

Which was why Greg was now clinging on for dear life in the passenger seat of the Pach family single-engine plane.

"I'm gonna puke."

"Please don't."

He leaned over and put his head between his legs. "Dr. Ellison, when did you get your pilot's license?"

"I didn't."

He lifted his head slightly. "Pardon?"

"I said I didn't."

He flopped his head back down. "You know, I don't care right now. I'm just gonna focus on not spewing my guts everywhere."

Kyra smirked. "Good man."

Otto had technically told Ashley that she was welcome to use the plane whenever she wanted, but wasn't around anymore to see who had actually been upkeeping the thing. He had taken a liking to Kyra's bright eyed TV reporter persona, encouraging her every step of the way. She'd even babysat Geri when she was little. Otto helped her scout museum exhibit locations for news stories—giving the museum traction and helping Ashley's career flourish.

Kyra hadn't been to Mexico in years and wished this trip was for something more vacation related. Instead, she was going to have to land a plane outside a tropical forest and go foraging for ipomoea purga. It just had to be the one plant Maura didn't have on hand, and they couldn't risk waiting on it being delivered.

Once they found the plant—and they *would* find it—they'd take the root, bless it, and turn it into an amulet. More specifically, a John the Conqueror root amulet, which yes, was quite the mouthful. Supposedly, it would help the wearer overcome obstacles, be lucky in love and amplify any other spellwork. Kyra was hopeful they'd be able to collect more than one; one for Dez's protection, one for Aurora's luck, and one for her own magic to be strengthened.

"Dr. Ellison?" Greg was desperately trying to hold it together.
"Yes?"

"Why couldn't you just teleport to Mexico?"

"Theoretically, I could have, but I haven't used magic over that much distance in a long time. I couldn't risk the exhaustion." She peered out the window as the lush, palm-lined landscape came into view. "Besides, this view is unbeatable. You should really take a look."

"I'm good." He gave a weak thumbs-up.

She shrugged. "Suit yourself."

"Wait—why not just poof the roots to you?"

"I can't summon something I have no prior knowledge of. Unfortunately, I'm unfamiliar with this plant."

"Fairies have too many rules."

Kyra looked out at the gorgeous expanse of green. Was this all finally leading up to the moment that Aurora would wake? Kyra had finally embraced true patience, allowing Dez and Aurora's relationship to grow naturally. She's enjoyed seeing them go from the stages of young love, to "dating," and now, to a deep connection. She only wished she'd encouraged Dez to just kiss the girl.

No. She couldn't think of the what ifs anymore. She had to focus on the now. And now she was going to save Aurora.

Kyra jerked the plane into a sharp, daring nosedive. Greg was immediately upright. "Dr. Ellison?!"

She focused on the landing area.

"Ohhh shit." Greg was gripping on his seat so hard his knuckles had gone white. "Not that I don't doubt your expertise, but GOD DAMN don't crash this plane!"

"Oh, shut up. I just have to make sure the military isn't aware of us. The Pach family will kill me if their plane gets shot down."

Greg sank down into his seat, clasping his hands together. "Queen Mab, if you're seriously real, please protect me and this crazy ass fairy flying the plane."

"Of course she's real, shut up. We're fine."

Kyra continued the nosedive before pulling up at the last second, leveling out smoothly and landing in a clearing. She slowed to a stop, then looked at Greg, who had amazingly kept himself from vomiting.

"I am deeply regretting agreeing to this."

Well," she said, unbuckling her seatbelt, "I'm glad you came. Come on, we've got a plant to find."

CHAPTER 48

2026, The Museum of Historical Mysteries

Any progress?

Unfortunately, no.

Dez tinkered away with the miniature MRI he had convinced his dad to let him borrow. He'd failed to come up with a decent enough excuse and had ended up just telling the truth; the girl he had wanted to ask out had actually been a museum exhibit, and Dez could enter her dreams. Dr. Buckley had been deeply confused, but his wife made him hand over the machine when she found out it had to do with Aurora.

"It's a girl, Cormac!" she'd exclaimed.

Dez rolled his eyes. A sleeping girl. Hopefully, a soon to be awake girl.

I'm pleased I've received the approval of your mother.

You've had it for years now. Pretty sure she's already planned our wedding.

Oh?

It's a joke.

Oh.

Shit, he messed up again.

Being married to you isn't a joke. The fact my mom is so eager for me to find a wife is.

You'd want to marry me?

Dez felt the familiar heat creeping up the back of his neck.

Is now the best time to talk about this?

I suppose not. We haven't even kissed yet.

Yeah. That. Dez had been kicking himself over it. He'd gotten ballsy when he kissed the top of her head, hoping the next time would be the real thing. Then the damn boo hag had to go and ruin things.

I'm sorry I keep interrupting things. I just miss you.

I know, I miss you too.

Kyra and Greg had barely been gone an hour when Dez got antsy. He started researching if anyone had successfully recorded videos of dreams. The closest thing he found was a study that matched brain activity to AI-generated images of what people might dream about. But that wasn't a live feed, so it wasn't what he needed.

Please don't be disappointed if you aren't able to make it work.

I won't be. Just figured I might as well experiment to pass the time. And when I still have you.

Dez...

Sorry, I know I said I wouldn't mention that.

He didn't want to think about being apart for the rest of their lives, either. That was another reason he was working—he needed a distraction. He was trying to combine the MRI and a variation of the EEG text speak, basically making it video chatting instead of texting. He had faith. After all, he'd been able to transport his dream self into Aurora's dreams. Surely that was more difficult than this, right?

That's what he had thought.

The real problem was the fact that Aurora didn't have an object to route the video call to. They'd gotten lucky with the book—smart phones weren't a thing in the medieval times, and rarely appeared in dreams at all. Something to do with subconscious perceiving them as a threat or something...he couldn't focus on that now.

If you figure this out, how do you think it would work?

I'm... honestly not sure.

Did I tell you I thought a miniature version of you was going to appear in my book when you first came here?

Dez had to laugh. The thought of being a tiny, pop-up version of himself…

Wait.

Aurora, you're a genius.

I know this.

He laughed again. God, he adored her blunt sass.

You just gave me an idea. I have to grab something, I'll be right back.

I'll be waiting.

***

Aurora's Dreams

Aurora rested her chin on her fist as she waited. She wondered what Dez had figured out this time. She gazed around at what had become her home over the past few weeks. She had expanded beyond her cell, creating different rooms out of the empty spaces. There was a kitchen, a drawing room, and even a very miniature ballroom.

Dez had told her she was most definitely suffering from depression. In the modern world, professionals apparently treated mental states medically. Healers—therapists, he called them—spent years studying the mind and the causes of emotional distress. There were ways of making one feel better through speaking with the therapists and taking specialized medicine. Aurora still didn't fully understand it, but she knew it was a good thing.

She recalled a duchess from a neighboring kingdom who had suffered similarly. The woman rarely made public appearances, sitting silent and withdrawn when forced to attend events. Then, one morning, she had thrown herself from a cliff, leaving five children behind. The youngest had only just begun to walk.

Aurora wondered if the children would have still had their mother if this form of healing had existed when she was awake. Dez had insisted the practice wasn't perfect, but things were better than they used to be.

She couldn't think about depression right now. Stretching her legs out, she slid off her bed and walked to the ballroom. It was small, but still lovely. She'd polished the stone floors, lined the walls with candlesticks, and placed a self-playing mandolin in the corner. She would twirl around the small area from time to time, imagining Dez was dancing with her. His tentative hands clutching her waist, fingers brushing her lower back.

She missed him so much.

"Hello?"

She froze. She could have sworn she'd just heard his voice.

"Aurora?"

She wasn't imagining it. That was his voice. Following the sound, she wound up back in her bedroom. Their book was open on her bed. And standing among the pages was a tiny Dez. Transparent and glowing pink, but it was definitely Dez. Aurora sat next to the book, just staring.

"Well."

Dez grinned up at her. "You look just as pretty as always."

She smiled back. "Thank you. Now, how are you managing this?"

"It's a little confusing," he scratched his head. "Do you remember how I tried explaining video chatting to you?"

She nodded. It was a modern way for people to see each other while communicating, even if they were far apart. "I thought that was what you originally tried to do before you figured out the lucid dreaming process?"

"It was." his brows furrowed. "This is crazy, but I'm mixing science and magic to do this."

Aurora's jaw dropped. "Sir Desmond Cathal Buckley, son of Dr. Cormac Cian Buckley, is using magic?!"

"How the hell did you remember my dad's middle name?"

She smirked. "One should know as much as they can about their in-laws, shouldn't they?"

The tiny figure was already pink, but Aurora swore he blushed magenta.

"I wanted to wait until we could speak in person, but…are we a thing?"

She grinned so hard that her cheeks hurt. "Are you referring to courting?"

"Oh, you learned that term," He looked at his feet, "from *Pride and Prejudice*, I assume?"

She nodded. This was ridiculous. They were dealing with her being asleep, speaking through dreams, The Good Fairy apparently being Dez's superior, and a boo hag. They hadn't even truly met in the physical world yet. But even with all that, she'd somehow fell for Dez. And he'd fallen for her as well. Hard.

"So," she prompted, "*are* we courting?"

Dez laughed nervously. "We usually call it dating now, but I'm sure you're enamored with the term. So, yes, I think we're courting."

Dez was hers. She was Dez's. Life was truly difficult and chaotic. But at least they still had each other.

CHAPTER 49

2026, The Museum of Historical
Mysteries

If you had told Dez that he would ask a literal princess to be his girlfriend
through a crystal ball seven months ago, he would have laughed. Yet, here he
was.

The museum had run a limited exhibit on mysticism the previous year
and had thankfully kept all the material in storage. The biggest hit from the
otherwise underwhelming exhibit had been a giant crystal ball, discovered in
the cellar of a Victorian house. Proudly displayed in the grand lobby, it had
distracted most patrons from the hired "clairvoyant", whom Kyra had
confirmed was a total fraud. Dez had always assumed the constant pink fog
swirling inside was some sort of asbestos trapped behind the glass. But after
accepting the existence of magic, he'd gone digging.

Kyra had also confirmed that the crystal ball was completely
legitimate. There were a select few practitioners of mysticism who could
actually do what they claimed, and apparently, the original owner of the
glowing sphere had been one of them. Kyra had somehow convinced the
museum to hold on to it for future decor use. When Dez asked why she had
just let it sit there, she'd simply said it was "pretty to look at."

As Dez had wheeled it out, the ball seemed determined to prove its
authenticity. Its pink glow flickered like a heartbeat and the fog danced
within its sparkling sphere. He wasn't positive about what he was going to
do with the thing, but figured it was worth trying to harness what little magic
he had access to at that point.

He'd connected both the EEG and the MRI to the crystal ball (which apparently had Wi-Fi, he didn't have time to question that), placed the small bore around his head like a crown, and powered everything on. Somehow, his brainwaves were being transported into the crystal ball, converting into a visual image. Aurora's book acted as her version of the setup, casting her image within the pink smoke.

He was going to take copious notes later on. For now, he was just glad to see Aurora's smiling face again.

"You're brilliant, Dez." Aurora said, beaming.

"Nah," he muttered. "I know nothing about magic, so this was just pure luck."

"Luck or not, you're still brilliant." She adjusted in her bed. "Can you imagine what you'll be able to do if you can mix science and magic like this?"

The idea had crossed his mind.

"Aurora, how much do you know about magic?"

"A little bit. If you weren't gifted, you learned more about magical history. I obviously wasn't."

He hummed. "You're gifted with everything else."

She smirked. Dez continued on.

"Seeing that I've got a fairy and a witch in my corner now, I'm thinking we'll be able to learn more."

"This is wild, Dez."

"I know."

He put his hands on his hips and stared up at his princess's dream image. Yes. His princess. He wanted to reach out, stroke those golden locks, intertwine his fingers with hers, shower her with kisses…

"Dez?"

He blinked. She giggled.

"You did that thing where you get lost in admiration again."

"I did not." He faked a pout, which quickly turned into a smirk. He couldn't deny it.

"What time is it there now? Shouldn't you be at home?"

"Trying to get rid of me already?"

She rolled her eyes. "You know I'm not. I just worry about you getting in trouble."

"I don't give two shits about that at this point." She laughed again. "I know you don't want to hear about this, but if this whole root thing doesn't work, I want to spend as much time as possible with you."

She frowned. "It will work, though."

He nodded. "I know. We have to stay positive."

She sighed. "I know you have to consider all outcomes. I don't expect you to follow my physical form to another country, especially if you can't bring all your equipment."

"I will follow you to the ends of the earth."

Aurora's eyes widened. Yup, he just said that.

"Dez, you know I always thought you were caring, but you're being… dare I say, romantic."

He was blushing furiously now. He didn't care. Was now the time?

"Aurora, I—"

"What the hell?!"

That voice. That shrill, screeching, horrible voice.

Aurora's jaw dropped. "Dez, who is that?"

Lizzie stomped over and reached out for the bore around his head. Dez dodged the attempt and held out a long arm.

"Lizzie, you had better move back right this moment."

She put her hands on her hips. "And who's gonna stop me?"

Dez could feel the familiar anger boiling up inside him. The museum should have been closed at this point. How had she gotten in? And why was she there?

"Well, I was going to try to get another interview with you, but it looks like I stumbled upon something juicy." She smirked. "I'm sure your parents are just gonna love this."

"Dez?"

Aurora's voice calmed him a bit.

"I'll handle this, don't worry," he said, keeping his gaze locked on Lizzie to prevent any sudden moves.

"Lizzie, as official staff of The Museum of Historical Mysteries and a member of the Exhibit Aurora team, I need to ask you to leave right now."

"Ohhh, don't pull that official mumbo jumbo on me. Is that the crystal ball from the mystic exhibit? And is that…" She stared up at Aurora's image. "Oh my god, that's Aurora!"

Aurora's eyes narrowed. "Dez, is this Lizzie?"

He nodded, hoping she could still see his form.

"Are you Elizabeth Hildegrant?" Aurora asked, her voice taking on a regal edge.

Lizzie just stared, mouth agape.

"Answer my question."

"Y-yes," Lizzie sputtered.

"Yes, what?"

"Yes, Your Highness."

Dez would have killed for a camera right now. He wondered if he could save crystal ball footage to a hard drive…

"Mademoiselle Hildegrant, may I ask why you think it is acceptable for you to parade around a location you are not allowed to access?"

Lizzie bit her lip. "Um…"

"How dare you? How dare you invade this space, and how dare you intrude on a private conversation? Have you no decorum?"

"Well, I—"

"There's absolutely no excuse. You'd be in the stocks by now if you were one of my subjects. You deserve to be made a mockery of, considering how much you revel in others' embarrassment."

"Your Highness, please, if you'd just let me explain—"

"Why should I?"

God, she would have made an amazing queen.

Lizzie starting rambling, and Dez noticed Aurora's eyes shift slightly to the side. She was looking at something. Could she see into the exhibit? He followed her gaze. He saw the glass dome bed, the machines, the crystal ball…ah. Was that it?

"Elizabeth, I do not for a moment believe that you have an ounce of humility within your body. You should be ashamed of yourself."

"Okay, what the hell is happening?! I cannot be getting yelled at by a princess in a bubble!"

Dez lunged, wrapping Lizzie in one of the exhibit's heavy tapestries.

"It's a crystal ball, you idiot."

Somehow, he wrapped her within the thick fabric like a burrito, sitting on top to keep her still. Her muffled shrieks barely registered as he gazed up at Aurora, who was grinning devilishly.

“We make a great team,” she beamed.

“Oh yes, we do, my sweet princess.”

“That is disgusting, and I should place you in the stocks instead.”

CHAPTER 50

2026, Veracruz, Mexico

Kyra was not a happy camper.

Yes, she and Greg had found the root—multiple roots, to be exact. And thankfully, it hadn't taken too long.

What had taken up a majority of their time was Kyra tripping over a tree branch and sliding down into a ravine. Wanting to conserve her magical energy for emergencies, Greg had been the one to drag her out, complaining the entire time.

"All I'm saying is you've been relying on your magic a heck of a lot more lately. Surely you're used to the drain by now?"

She was currently riding piggyback, forcing him to hold both of their backpacks on his front like twin babies.

"You greatly underestimate my abilities," Kyra replied. "Unless it's my tears, it takes a lot for a fairy to heal themselves."

Greg groaned. "It's a twisted ankle. It can't be that bad."

"Oh, and as if I weigh that much."

"I'm not saying that. It's just a little bit more difficult when I'm lugging a fairy and two backpacks full of equipment through a muggy forest in the middle of Veracruz."

"See, this is why I've spent more time with computers instead of people."

Greg rolled his eyes. "You and Dez both. You two need to get laid."

"I won't disagree with that."

"Hey, I can set you up with someone when we get back. If we get back."

She sighed. "We're almost to the plane, then we're home free."

"You said we were almost there an hour ago. I swear, Dr. Ellison, if you got us lost...."

He continued to lumber on as Kyra sniffed. They weren't lost. They weren't.

"Whoa, what's that?" Greg stopped in his tracks and pointed to the ground. Kyra peered down and gulped. White footprints were scattered on the forest floor.

"Shit. Greg, move faster."

"Wha—"

"Move."

Miraculously, Greg managed a slow jog, Kyra bouncing on his back like a newborn.

"Dr. Ellison, do I even want to ask?"

"Nope."

"So it's bad."

"Ye—" she got cut off as Greg screeched to a halt. In front of them stood a short, tanned-skinned man, completely naked. He crossed his arms.

"*Uan kanke timoiljuia tias?*"

Greg tensed. "Dr. Ellison?" Kyra narrowed her eyes. Her Nahuatl wasn't great. "*Um... amo tijnekij timitschiuilisej tlen amo kuali.*"

"*Pero tijneki tikijtos tlen amo kuali ipan tepetl!*" he spat back.

Greg glanced quickly between her and the stout creature in front of him. "Should I be worried?"

Kyra shook her head. "Not yet."

"Yet?!"

The creature uncrossed its arms, becoming less threatening. "Is English better for you?"

Kyra sighed in relief. "Yes, thank you."

"Don't assume I'm going to just let you go."

Greg frowned. "Let us go? I'm pretty sure I could drop kick you to the stratosphere."

"Threatening isn't the best idea, Greg," Kyra muttered. "That thing will steal your soul in a flash."

Greg swallowed. "I feel like being aware of magic makes everything harder."

"Welcome to my life."

"Excuse me?" the creature interrupted. "I'd suggest you return those roots to me."

Damn it.

"Sir, we need them."

He shook his head. "You have disrespected the forest and the earth by taking what does not belong to you."

"There's plenty of them!" Greg protested.

The creature attempted to lock eyes with Greg, and Kyra clasped her hands over his face. He tried to shake her off. "Dr. Ellison? What gives?!"

"Greg, shut up. I told you, it'll steal your soul. Then we're really screwed."

Greg groaned. "Hey, dude, I'm sorry. Please don't take my soul."

"Return the roots and I won't."

Kyra looked at the creature. "Look, I can assure you there are plenty of the plant to go around. I even pollinated the flowers so they could grow more."

"And why should I believe you?"

Queen Mab, she really had tried to conserve her energy. But she supposed this was an emergency. Squeezing her eyes shut, she focused on the space between her shoulder blades, calling on what had been deeply buried for centuries. She gripped Greg harder and moaned—this hurt. This hurt badly. Kyra suppressed a scream as wispy, lilac, glowing wings sprouted from her upper back. She lightly fluttered them, letting them breathe.

"Uh, Dr. Ellison, I don't know what you just did, but you're gripping my face."

She was still covering Greg's eyes. She quickly dropped her hands. "I'm so sorry."

Greg turned his head to look at her, jaw dropping. "Whoa." The sun reflected off her wings, casting a purple shimmer over Greg's cheeks.

"I know we're in a serious situation, but that is really cool."

She grinned, then faced the creature again. He stared with wide eyes.

"I do apologize, Ms. Fairy, but I still need something to make up for taking the root."

Kyra scowled. "Greg, give him your granola bar."

Greg was flabbergasted. "What?"

"Just do it."

Greg dug through his backpack on his front, searching furiously for the snacks he'd packed. "I think I ate them all…oh! Here, will this work?" He pulled out a blueberry pie protein shake. Kyra had to laugh.

"Sir, I believe this offering will be more than enough."

Greg tentatively handed the shake to the creature, who snatched it away, sniffing at the plastic packaging. "Unscrew the top. It's one of the best flavors, I promise."

He opened the shake, took a swig, and licked his lips. Then he began to chug.

"Geez, okay."

"Greg, I repeat, shut up."

He finished the shake, wiped his mouth, and loudly belched. Looking up at Kyra and Greg, he gave a nod of approval. "Carry on. Your plane is about a half of a mile east." He gave a small bow before running back into the brush, leaving more white footprints behind. Greg stood there for a moment, dumbfounded.

"Dr. Ellison, what the hell was that?"

Kyra sighed. "A Chaneque. They're Mexican cryptids that protect nature. If I had known there were any around here, I would have had us wear our clothing inside out."

"I'm just more confused, so we can worry about all that later." He adjusted her on his back. "Hey, since those are out now, can you fly?"

Kyra grinned. "I certainly can. In fact–" She flapped her wings, lifting both her and Greg from the ground.

Greg couldn't help but laugh. "Fairy perks rock!"

CHAPTER 51

Aurora's Dreams

Aurora wished she could somehow mute Lizzie. She'd been wrapped up in the tapestry for what had to be two hours now, yet was still screeching like a banshee. How this woman shared a name with one of the best fictional characters was beyond her.

"Dez, I assure you, a couple of right hooks should knock her unconscious."

Dez rolled his eyes. "Aurora, you're hysterical, but I'd rather not add assault to what I'm sure is already a long rap sheet."

She smirked. Lizzie was just as terrible as Dez had described—shrill, uncontrollable, a complete brat. But Aurora had to appreciate her gumption; the girl simply refused to give up. And she *had* shown Dez that he didn't need to wear the bore like a halo, given Aurora had seen and heard her clearly. Too clearly. He'd been able to place the bore next to the crystal ball.

"Turn her to face me."

Dez arched an eyebrow, but did as she said. She could see two beady eyes and pig-like nose peering out from the small opening of the tapestry wrap.

"I would appreciate if you could be quiet."

Lizzie spat. She actually spat. Aurora's blood boiled.

"How. Dare. You?!"

Lizzie's eyes widened. Florestan would have been so proud of his daughter—she'd maintained an imposing presence, even through a pink fog.

"This will all be a lot easier if you keep that giant mouth of yours shut."

Lizzie didn't reply. She just lay there in the tapestry, her mouth set in a tight line.

"Thank you."

Dez grinned at Aurora. "You're incredible."

She couldn't help but smile back. "Thank you."

Another tiny figure joined her book. It was a shorter, older woman with gorgeous, braided hair. Dez jumped. "Sorry Maura, I didn't expect to see you here. And how did *you* get in?"

She brushed some dust off of her shirt. "Don't worry about that. But you won't have to deal with this one," she pointed at Lizzie, "trying to sneak in again."

Dez scratched his head, then his eyes widened with realization. "Did… did she come in through the air duct?"

Maura shook her head. "Of course not. She hid in the mummy's sarcophagus when it got delivered earlier. Apparently stayed put until the museum closed."

Dez just stared in disbelief. "You can't be serious."

Maura shrugged. "Just don't move anything that looks like an indigo talisman if you see it."

"Indigo talis—you know what," Dez held up a hand, "I'm not even gonna ask." He gestured to Aurora. "Maura, this is Princess Aurora d'Ambray. Aurora, this is Kyra's therapist, Maura Arkin. The witch."

Aurora hummed. "Pleased to make your acquaintance, Maura."

"The pleasure is mine," she replied, giving a small curtsy. "Dez, how are you doing this?"

"Long story short, a mix of magic and science."

"Magic?!" Lizzie shrieked.

Maura frowned at the tapestry. Aurora saw her pull something out of her bag, lean down in front of the opening with her hand outstretched, and blow. There was a snorting sound, then silence again. Maura stood and looked up at Aurora.

"That should shut her up for a while. I unfortunately can't mind wipe, so we'll have to wait for Kyra to get back for that. Speaking of which," she pulled a little rectangle out from her pocket. The front glowed as she pressed on it as if it had buttons.

"Dez, is that a phone?" she asked.

Dez nodded. "Yes."

"Fascinating."

Aurora stretched her legs out. She'd been sitting for far too long, but she desperately didn't want to leave the tiny Dez out of her sight. They were not only making up for lost time, but were possibly spending their last moments together. She stood up from the bed and looked at her surroundings. While she'd been able to make the dungeon more homey looking, there was no denying what it truly was; a prison.

She'd been attempting to distract herself, but the lingering possibility that none of this would work and she'd remain asleep for the rest of her days was always there. She'd be alone again. Alone, bored and in constant fear of being attacked by a boo hag. That couldn't happen. It wouldn't happen.

"Aurora, dear?" She gazed back down at the book. The tiny Maura was waving at her.

"Yes?"

"Good news! Greg and Kyra located some roots. They're on their way back right now."

Aurora frowned. That meant six more hours of waiting, give or take.

"Don't worry, Kyra's apparently sped up the plane's engine, so they're moving quickly."

"How quickly?"

"Quickly enough that I could hear Greg dry heaving over the phone," Dez added.

Aurora sat back on her bed. This was it. This had to be it. She would wake. She'd be with Dez. She'd be in the real world. Before she knew it, tears trickled down her cheeks. By God's bones, she hated crying. People had seen it as a sign of weakness when she was awake, especially for a woman. She had held her emotions in for far too long, trying to prove that she was just as strong as her father.

She clenched her fists in her lap. If this failed, what would be left? Centuries had already slipped through her fingers. She couldn't bear another era of waiting for something, anything, to happen.

"Hey."

She looked back to the book to see her miniature Dez looking at her.
"I know."

She released a loud sob as more tears fell. She let them. She had waited long enough.

CHAPTER 52

2026, The Museum of Historical Mysteries

Kyra limped down the museum hall, leaning up against Greg. He wasn't faring much better and looked like he would pass out any second. It had taken an immense amount of energy and magic, but Kyra had gotten them back within two hours. She knew they had to get back before the museum opened to the public to avoid being caught. It was 4 A.M. and the eerie nighttime silence still lingered. Poor Greg hadn't even been able to vomit since they had been flying so fast.

"Dr. Ellison?" he asked, weakly.

"Yes?"

"You owe me an actual vacation when all this is over."

She had to laugh. "What, hiking, foraging and Chaneque not your jam?"

"Not at all, oof—" He stumbled slightly, gripping his stomach.

"Please don't throw up now. We don't have Dez mopping the floors anymore."

The duo stumbled into Exhibit Aurora, basically falling into Dez's and Maura's arms. Kyra looked up at the giant pink crystal ball. Well, that hadn't been there before. What also hadn't been there before was the image of Aurora among the pink fog, staring in horror at her and Greg's state.

"Dez?"

Oh my god, her voice. She could hear her voice.

"Dez… is that The Good Fairy?"

Dez smiled and gripped Kyra's arm. He helped her to her feet and gently led her closer to the crystal ball. She gazed up at those familiar twinkling eyes for the first time in centuries.

"Hello, Your Highness."

Aurora scoffed. "Please, call me Aurora. It… it *is* you."

"You can call me Kyra now." She managed a smile.

Dez grinned. "I thought you changed your image?"

Kyra slowly nodded. "I did, but I'm guessing I finally ended up going with a persona that looks similar enough to my original form." There were only so many faces one could come up with.

"Highness, you look well."

"Please, *Aurora*. And I'm alright. I'm hopeful this all works."

"Oh, yes," Kyra said, digging the roots out of her backpack and handing them to Maura.

"Perfect. Just give me one moment." Maura retreated into a corner, holding the roots close to her. Kyra looked back at Aurora.

"It'll work."

***

The moment Maura had taken ended up being close to an hour. While they were all on edge, Kyra was grateful for the time to speak with Aurora.

"This is all my fault. I'm so sorry."

Aurora tilted her head. "Pardon?"

Kyra took a deep breath. It was now or never.

"Aurora… when you were a baby, your parents invited all fairy kind to your christening to offer blessings. I was there. Right when I was about to give my gift, Carabosse appeared."

Aurora scowled. "The Wicked Fairy?"

Kyra nodded. "Yes. Your parents hadn't invited her because…well… for obvious reasons. She was so furious, she put a curse on you."

Aurora's face fell. "Curse?"

"She proclaimed that on your twenty-first birthday, you would prick your finger on the spindle of a spinning wheel and die."

Aurora blinked. "But Dez said I'm definitely not dead."

Kyra shook her head. "You're not. I counteracted the curse so that you would just fall asleep… only to be woken by True Love's Kiss."

Aurora sat back and furrowed her brow. "So that's what that sharp thing was… wait! That's a memory! I remember that!"

Dez moved closer. "What happened?"

She squeezed her eyes shut. "It…I needed to get away from my party. I heard a voice. I was in a room with some object with a spinning wheel." Her eyes popped open. "There was a cloaked figure. It had to of been Carabosse. I knew I shouldn't be in there, but she coerced me into touching the spindle."

Kyra knew it. Aurora was far too smart to enter random rooms and touch things. Carabosse had manipulated her right into her clutches.

"So that's where the kissing lore came from?"

Kyra nodded.

"And that's why I'm not awake."

She nodded again.

"Kyra… what became of my family?"

Her heart sank. She should have known that the question was coming.

"Aurora…" she was cut off by Maura, finally dangling three amulets in front of her face.

"Sorry that took so long. I've never had to do three at once before."

"It's alright." Kyra took the amulets in her hand. "So, the proper people just need to wear them?"

Maura nodded. "I can't help you after that. This is obviously a unique situation."

Kyra took a deep breath and looked at Dez. He managed a small smile and nodded.

"Let's find ourselves a boo hag."

"Do you think we can maintain this connection, too?" They looked up at Aurora's concerned face.

"I don't know if right now is the best time to be experimenting," Dez answered in a sad tone.

Aurora grimaced. "Dez."

"Aurora."

They both were silent, just staring at each other. Kyra's heartstrings were being pulled at. She gently touched Dez's back.

"It'll work."

He glanced at her, managed a smile, then looked at Aurora again. "It'll work."

CHAPTER 53

2026, The Museum of Historical Mysteries

Dez laid back on the bench, cap on, amulet resting against his chest. They still hadn't given him something comfier, but hopefully, he soon wouldn't need anything else.

Kyra, also wearing an amulet, was typing away at the on the EEG keyboard. Greg was opening up the dome on Aurora's bed to place the third and final amulet underneath her pillow. Maura had been assigned Lizzie duty, ready to knock her right back out if she woke up.

"That woman really is a leech," Kyra quipped.

"More like a roach," Greg replied. "We can't get rid of her. She actually hid right up against a dead person just to get in. Who does that?"

"An insane person, that's who. I should put the thought in her head to check herself into a mental hospital."

"Hey Kyra," Maura chimed in, "you're The Good Fairy, emphasis on good."

Kyra rolled her eyes. "It'd be for the greater good."

Maura chuckled. "That well may be, but psychiatrists don't like being terrorized either."

Greg unlocked the last padlock on Aurora's bed. The hiss of the dome opening sent shivers down Dez's spine. He watched as Greg carefully slid the amulet under Aurora's pillow. This was it.

Dez was about to be thrown back into the worst nightmare he'd ever had. He swallowed hard, remembering the suffocating darkness, the blaring red lights, and the agonizing pain that had left his head throbbing. The boo hag's attack hadn't just hurt—it had emotionally drained him, leaving him feeling despair deeper and darker than anything he'd ever known.

Kyra gently placed her hand on his chest. "Let's go over the plan one more time."

Dez gnawed at his lip and nodded.

"Your amulet should strengthen you within the dream world. Just in case, I'll be continuously casting a protection spell on you. Hopefully, my amulet will transfer the magic into the dream. If the boo hag appears, Aurora's amulet should shield her."

It was a lot of "shoulds" and "hopefullys," but it was the best they had.

"Greg?"

Greg looked at Dez quizzically.

"If anything goes wrong, save Aurora first."

Greg's face hardened. "Dez, no offense, but you've been my best friend for fifteen years. She's your girlfriend who I've barely spoken to."

Dez exhaled sharply. "But you know I love her, right?"

The words slipped out easily.

Kyra squealed.

Dez smirked. "Your good fairy's showing again."

She was literally glowing. "I don't give a shit, I love love!"

Greg rolled his eyes at Kyra's enthusiasm, then looked back at Dez. "Dez, I think I knew you were head over heels before you did."

"Then you'll do this for me."

"Dez—"

"Greg, promise me."

Greg grimaced, but held his hands up in surrender. "Okay, fine. I promise."

Dez nodded, took one more deep breath, and closed his eyes. Kyra powered on the machine and entered the code.

Program activated.

***

?

Dez woke to complete darkness. He blinked rapidly, trying to get his eyes to adjust, and pushed himself to his feet. This time felt different. No headache. No relentless beeping making his heart race. But also, no red light or brainwaves dancing across the walls. Meaning he couldn't see a damn thing.

He reached his arms out in front of him, hoping to find a wall to move across. From there, he'd hopefully find the door. His arms met only empty air. This wasn't right.

He wondered if the amulet was doing too good of a job protecting him. Was it shielding him from everything?

Just as dizziness began settling in from the endless black void, the metal door and circular window materialized right in front of him. He grinned. "Didn't like me doubting you, amulet?"

Pressing his hands against the door's cool surface, he peered inside. The fog swirling behind the glass shifted, revealing the dungeon Aurora had transformed into her safe haven.

A sudden scream cut through the silence—a battle cry, not one from fear. He turned toward the sound just as Aurora and the boo hag came into view. She wielded a massive, flaming sword, swinging it with fierce precision. The creature twisted and dodged each strike, but fire reflected in Aurora's eyes, making them sharper, wilder, completely determined.

He slammed his fists against the door. This time, the metal actually dented. A good sign. He stepped back, scanning for the crack he'd made in the glass during his last nightmare. Light glinted off of Aurora's sword-there, the crack was there. Dez gritted his teeth and started punching. The crack splintered further, but the glass refused to fully break. His knuckles throbbed, the skin threatening to split open. He stopped his assault on the window. The last thing he needed was blood loss.

Another yell echoed from inside. Dez looked just in time to see Aurora back the shadow figure against the wall. The flames danced along the blade as she lifted her sword high above her head.

His heart swelled with pride. She was going to destroy it. That was *his* incredible princess. Then, at the last second, the boo hag dissolved into smoke. Aurora's sword slashed through the air, missing completely. The creature re-materialized behind her and grabbed her hair. She yelped, this time in pain.

That did it.

Blood loss be damned.

With a battle cry of his own, Dez sprinted towards the door and slammed into it. The metal tore free from its hinges, glass shattering in an explosion of shards. And then he was inside.

CHAPTER 54

Aurora's Dreams

The loud crashing sound echoed through the dungeon, momentarily distracting the boo hag. It released Aurora's hair and stalked towards the intrusion. Relief flooded through her when she saw Dez sprawled on the cold stone floor. A tiny shard of broken glass had embedded itself just below his eye, far too close for comfort. She couldn't imagine never seeing the spark in his green eyes again. The shadow figure approached Dez, but he was too dazed to notice.

"Get away from him!" she shouted.

The boo hag turned back toward her, tilting its head unnervingly. Aurora clenched her fists, rage flaring throughout her body.

"Come and get me!" She spun and sprinted down the corridor. The flickering candlelight, caused by moving air, indicating it was following her. She didn't exactly have a plan, but she knew she had to keep it away from Dez.

A cold feeling washed over her. A clammy hand clamped around her forearm, numbing her fingers instantly. Her flaming sword slipped from her grasp, clattering against the stone. She turned just in time to see the boo hag's other hand shoot forward, gripping her face. She could feel the amulet's power pushing back against the force, but the protection felt thin, like a thread fraying under too much strain. The boo hag leaned in right against her face.

"Stop resisting. Your energy's mine."

That voice. It was the same voice that had entranced her so long ago, drawing her into the abandoned room in the castle, forcing her to prick her finger. It *was* Carabosse. Aurora's blood ran cold. The pressure was crushing. Maybe this was it. Maybe this time, she wouldn't win.

No.

With every ounce of strength she had left, she kicked her leg up, catching the creature square in the jaw. It shrieked, loosening its grip just enough for her to dart away. She stumbled back, her heart hammering in her chest. Her sword, where was her sword?

"AURORA!"

She whipped around just as Dez tackled the creature to the ground, hitting the stone with a loud thud. The boo hag thrashed about, trying to force him off, but he had wrapped his arms around its throat. Blood trickled from his cheek like a crimson tear, but he either didn't notice or didn't care. Aurora's breath hitched. He was fighting for her. This man, who always claimed he wasn't athletic, was wrestling a demon creature to protect her.

He met her gaze and gritted his teeth. "Aurora! Salt! Think of salt!"

What on earth?

"Salt?!"

"JUST DO IT!"

The boo hag backed up and slammed him against the iron bars of a cell. The force of the impact made him grunt as he released his grip and slid to the floor. It turned on Aurora again, moving too fast for her to react. In an instant, it pressed its palm against her chest. The heavy feeling threatened to knock her over, but she could fight it off this time.

"Just give in," it whispered, its breath hot and suffocating. "It's so much easier."

No.

Aurora squeezed her eyes shut and forced herself to picture salt. Tons of salt. Mountains of salt.

The boo hag recoiled, the weight vanishing from her chest immediately. The ceiling above them had cracked. A glimmering cascade of salt poured down like a waterfall, coating the floor in a thick, glistening layer. The boo hag screeched, writhing as the salt clung to it like a living thing, creeping up its body. Its form blackened and burned, holes eating through its shadowy flesh. A foul stench filled the air. Across the hall, Dez stared in wide-eyed shock, frozen.

The boo hag let out one last, guttural wail before collapsing in on itself, its body dissolving into a tar like sludge. The remnants oozed into the salt, sizzling into nothingness.

It was gone. It was actually gone. They sat there for a moment, the only sounds being their jagged breathing. Finally, they locked eyes.

Dez grinned.

"Hello."

A breathless laugh escaped her. "Hello."

Before either of them could think, they closed the distance between them in a desperate embrace. Dez's fingers ran through her hair, holding her close.

"I missed you," he murmured.

She clung to him, burying her face against his neck. "I missed you too."

For a long moment, they stayed like that, neither wanting to pull apart. Then, slowly, Dez moved away enough to meet her eyes.

"I love you."

Aurora froze.

"Wha...what?"

Dez cupped her face in his hands. "Aurora, I love you. I don't care how it happened, or how strange this is, or that we've only ever met in your dreams. I love you, I love you, I love you—"

She cut him off by pressing her mouth to his.

It wasn't her first kiss, but it felt like the first time she had ever truly kissed someone. Dez's lips were soft and warm, molding perfectly against hers. He pulled her even closer somehow, as if he was afraid she'd disappear. Aurora couldn't help but smile against his mouth.

As they finally parted, she gazed into his beautiful green eyes.

And then... darkness.

CHAPTER 55

2026, The Museum of Historical Mysteries

Dez opened his eyes to find Kyra, Greg, and Maura standing above him, concern etched on their faces.

"Well?" Kyra muttered.

He rubbed his eyes, flinching as he felt the cut on his cheek. "Well, what?"

"Did you… I don't know, defeat the boo hag?" Greg asked.

Dez shot up. Yes, the boo hag was gone. He'd told Aurora he loved her. They'd kissed. But didn't that mean—

"Aurora?" Dez pushed through the group and ran over to the bed. She still lay there, apparently sound asleep. He slumped. Shouldn't that have worked?

A soft moan escaped from the princess's lips. His eyes widened, and he leaned over her. Aurora's arms stretched above her head as she yawned, then slowly opened her eyes.

"Queen Mab," Kyra murmured.

Aurora shielded her eyes from the museum light. "That's awfully harsh, isn't it?"

It was still her voice. Raspy, dry, but unmistakably hers. Dez inched closer, finally looking into her eyes in the real world for the first time. She peered up at him, then burst into a grin.

"Am I awake?"

Dez released the breath he'd been holding. He scooped her into his arms, holding her close. "Yes. Yes, you're awake."

"Oh HELL YES!" Greg cheered from the corner.

***

After mind wiping Lizzie yet again, implanting a false memory of her never leaving her house, and having Greg dump her in her yard, the group reunited at the exhibit. None of them really knew what to do next.

Kyra had thoroughly exhausted herself by showing her wings again, speeding the plane's engine, casting a protection charm, and performing countless other fairy duties. Now she lay sprawled in Aurora's exhibit bed, snoring lightly.

Maura had headed home, hoping to catch a few hours of sleep before her first morning client. Before leaving, she slipped Dez her business card. "When you're ready," she whispered.

Greg, unable to sit still, had packed up all the equipment (crystal ball included), and now paced around the museum aimlessly. Before heading off, he'd scooped Aurora up in a giant bear hug. "I know we've not really met, but you make Dez the happiest he's ever been. So, you're automatically one of my favorite people."

Now, Dez and Aurora sat together on his bench. He had a hysterical, dinosaur Band-Aid on his face, covering the only remaining damage left by the boo hag. He hadn't been able to stop touching Aurora, needing the reassurance that she was truly, physically there. Their fingers were intertwined, her head resting on his shoulder.

"Well, Sir Desmond, what do we do now?"

He smiled, weakly. "Would you be disappointed if I said I had no clue, Your Majesty?"

She turned her head, kissing his cheek. "You could never disappointment me."

He gave her a quick peck. "Even if I hadn't woken you up?"

Her eyes twinkled. "No, because I know you would have found a way."

She snuggled into his shoulder again, and he wrapped his arm around her waist.

He'd done it. And she'd known he'd be able to do it.

Dez looked up at the clock and chuckled. "It's May 1st." It had technically been since midnight, but who cared?

"Right on time," she quipped.

There was so much they needed to figure out, but Dez was perfectly content to just sit there with his princess in his arms. Nothing could ruin this moment.

"Uh, guys?" Greg's voice echoed from the hall, tinged with concern.

Dez and Aurora turned to see Geri Pach entering the exhibit, Greg sulking behind her. Geri's gaze swept around the room before landing on Aurora. Her mouth fell open.

"I…. what…. how?!"

Kyra stirred, rubbing her eyes. "Hm, what?"

"Dr. Ellison, I believe you have some explaining to do."

Kyra lifted her head, scoffed at Geri, then rolled over. "Geri, I apologize, but I had a very long night. I need to catch up on my sleep."

"Kyra!"

"Talk to Dez."

Geri turned on her heel and marched up to Dez and Aurora, arms crossed. "Well?"

Dez was surprised at how little he cared. He had Aurora. That's all that mattered.

"Hello, Ms. Pach."

"Don't 'hello Ms. Pach' me! What on earth is going on? How are you," she gestured wildly at Aurora, "awake?!"

"I kissed her," Dez answered nonchalantly.

Geri gaped at him, at a loss for words.

"I mean, if you want to get technical about it, I combined the EEG and lucid dreaming equipment so I could communicate with Aurora. We fell in love. I kissed her. *Tada*." Aurora couldn't help but giggle. He stroked her arm gently.

"Oh, also, I graduate next week. I think I need you to sign some forms, Ms. Pach."

Geri rubbed the back of her neck. "I…good lord." She leaned against one of the exhibit pillars. "Not that I'm not thrilled—trust me, I am—I just…"

She exhaled slowly. "I honestly don't know what to do now."

"Let me go home?" Aurora offered.

Geri blinked. "Your Highness, this has been the only home you've known for years."

Aurora shook her head. "My home's with Dez."

Geri ran her hands through her once perfectly styled hair. "That's very sweet. I just need to figure out the ethics of all this. Just…don't move."

Aurora shrugged.

Geri quickly left the exhibit, already digging her phone out of her purse and dialing frantically. Greg dashed over to Dez and Aurora.

"Well. This is a clusterfuck."

Dez just grinned. "Hey, I got the girl."

Aurora lightly slapped his shoulder. "Princess."

Dez laughed and kissed the top of her head. "My princess."

Greg rolled his eyes. "Is this what I get to deal with now? Jesus."

CHAPTER 56

*May 2026. Wellington Bits, Lizzie's
Life Lessons by Elizabeth Hildegrant*

I TOLD YOU ALL. I said something was fishy about Exhibit Aurora, and somebody needed to get to the bottom of it.

I had the courage to investigate because I knew it was my duty as a journalist. I told you Desmond Buckley wasn't just randomly hired; he got onto that team for a reason. I was harassed for doing my job, but I never stopped speaking the truth.

But did anyone listen to me? Nooo.

In case you've been living under a rock—or in a deep sleep yourself— you've probably heard the news: Princess Aurora d'Ambray, the mysteriously sleeping, never aging woman, has woken up.

Let's review the facts:

- Her birth records date all the way back to the 14th century.
- It is believed that she lived in the lost kingdom of Voltav.
- As far as we know, she is the sole surviving member of the d'Ambray family.
- She lay in a state of suspended sleep for over fifty years inside The Museum of Historical Mysteries.

And yet, despite this groundbreaking discovery, the public has been told almost nothing! The museum released one measly announcement, and then, radio silence.

What are they hiding?
Dr. Ellison? Desmond Buckley? Geraldine Pach?
I'm looking at you.

@User02: Okay, I know we've been standing firm with the whole #BoycottTheLizard thing, but I gotta say something. Lady? What the heck? You're bordering on stalking at this point. Take a chill pill and maybe find something actually worthwhile to obsess over. The girl's been asleep for lord knows how long, maybe let her breathe?

CHAPTER 57

2026, The Museum of Historical Mysteries

"Dez, if you were to ask me, I don't believe anyone here has a clue what they're doing."

Dez sighed. He, unfortunately, had to agree with Aurora. "This *is* getting pretty ridiculous."

Geri and the rest of the board had adamantly refused to allow Aurora to leave the building. It had now been three days since she woke up, and aside from a quick physical examination by a member of the medical staff, they'd heard nothing. Since they wouldn't let her leave, Dez had refused to as well. There had been no pushback, so he and Aurora had spent the past seventy-two hours together. If it weren't because she was essentially being held hostage, it might have felt like they were playing house. Aurora had fallen asleep right before coffee became a staple in Europe. Dez had taken it upon himself to play barista, letting her test various brews. Her current favorite was a vanilla latte.

Greg was still stuck giving tours (to much less enthusiastic kids as of late), but had gone grocery shopping for them the night after Aurora woke. Dez claimed the use of the giant kitchen in the museum basement to cook their meals. It was only used for catered events, anyway. Aurora had been delighted to find that the dishes she'd had in her dreams tasted even better in real life.

He'd slowly been introducing her to technology. While he'd explained some of it to her in her dreams, having the physical devices in front of her was a completely different experience. Unsurprisingly, she was obsessed with the tablet Dez had gotten her. She said it felt like their communication book in her dreams, but better. He had finally taken advantage of his library card, giving her access to nearly any book she could think of. *Pride and Prejudice* remained her favorite, and she was thrilled when Dez introduced her to not one, but two screen adaptations.

"It's like a play, but not religious! And I can watch it over and over again!"

Apparently, most plays in medieval times were church related.

The two of them were currently walking hand in hand through the aquatic exhibit. One good thing about being trapped in a museum was… well, being trapped in a museum. Especially considering how bookish they both were. Dez was obviously familiar with every exhibit, but he was enjoying playing tour guide for Aurora.

"You're telling me this creature doesn't have a brain? How is that possible?"

She was watching the hologram recreation of a group of Moon Jellies.

Dez nodded. "Not my best subject, but I think they just have a set of nerves? It's apparently enough for them to get around. They don't live that long, anyway."

"Well, there *is* the immortal jellyfish."

Dez and Aurora turned to find Greg standing there, a gaggle of fourth graders trailing behind him. A younger group than usual, but more grades had been requesting tours.

"Sorry," Dez apologized. "We'll get out of your way."

"Wait, immortal jellyfish?" Aurora asked.

A short girl pushed her way to the front of the group, eyes locked on Aurora.

"Are you The Sleeping Beauty?" she asked in a small voice.

Oh boy, Dez should probably get her out of here. Before he could reach for her hand, Aurora knelt down at the girl's height. "Do I appear to be sleeping?"

The girl shook her head.

Aurora smiled warmly. "I am Princess Aurora d'Ambray. What's your name?"

A hint of a smile crossed the girl's lips. "Stella."

"Stella, that is a beautiful name."

"Thank you, Your Majesty."

"You can call me Aurora."

The other kids gathered closer, murmuring questions and compliments.

"Do you like being awake?"

"Your hair's pretty."

"Isn't that Mr. Dez?"

Dozens of children's eyes shifted to Dez. Greg smirked. "Yes, that's Mr. Dez Buckley."

Stella lightly tapped Aurora on the shoulder. "Is he your boyfriend?"

And just like that, Dez turned pink. Aurora giggled. "He's my beloved, yes."

"Beloved?"

"It means we love each other very much."

A chorus of "awwws" erupted from the group. Dez shot Greg a pleading look. Taking pity on him, Greg snapped his fingers. "Hey kids, we gotta get back to the tour."

"Can Aurora and Dez come with us?"

"Uh…" Greg looked up at the couple.

Eh, why not?

"We're game, if you're okay with it," Dez offered. "I was just showing Aurora around, but I'm sure she'd get a better experience from a professional."

Greg smirked. "I *am* the most requested tour guide at the museum, after all. Alright, join the group."

Dez took Aurora's hand, and they fell in line with the kids.

"BIGFOOT EXHIBIT!" Greg announced.

Dez rolled his eyes so hard he was amazed they didn't fall out of his head.

About two hours later, Dez, Aurora, and Greg stood by the main entrance, watching the students board their buses. It had been the most entertaining afternoon since Aurora woke up. She truly was royalty. She had been so genuine and kind, even when faced with silly questions like "Did you have to brush your teeth for a whole hour after waking up?" Her warmth was infectious, putting even the once crabby looking teacher in a wonderful mood.

Greg clapped her on the shoulder. "You're coming for my job."

She laughed. "I have no interest in your job. You're still the one who answered all their museum related questions." She took Dez's hand again. "I'd very much like to make some mac and cheese and watch a movie."

Greg groaned. "And she's an introvert. Dez, she really is your perfect match."

Dez gave her a quick kiss. "I think so."

Greg blew a raspberry.

"You're just jealous."

CHAPTER 58

2026, The Board Room

"Geri, you're being completely unreasonable."

Kyra stared down the table filled with board members. Lila sighed for what felt like the three hundredth time that day.

"Actually, you're *all* being completely unreasonable."

She had only argued with the museum's board of directors since they had granted her the short nap.

"Dr. Ellison," Ryan Woodmier, the vice-president, interjected, "we're simply attempting to make sense of a day we never thought would come to be."

"It's been FOUR DAYS, Ryan!"

"Dr. Ellison—"

"No! I've done nothing but speak in circles with you all this whole time! My team has documented everything for the past three years, and the teams before us did the same. This should be a straightforward sign off." She crossed her arms. "It seems you all have concentrated solely on the financial side, ignoring Aurora's well-being."

"Hey now!" William Fowly, the treasurer, called out. "Do you know how much we've invested into this exhibit throughout the years?"

"Oh sure, Bill, and how many times have you personally visited the exhibit in the past decade?"

"Dr. Ellison, don't push it—"

"Don't you dare threaten me," Kyra growled.

Lila finally took that moment to speak up. "You do all realize that we have nothing to lose, right?"

All attention shot to her.

"Dr. Killenger," Geri hissed, "what do you mean?"

Lila leaned back in her chair, very apparently not giving a shit. "Aurora's awake. Her entire team, in essence, is due to be unemployed."

"Okay, that's not true," Geri tried to interject.

Lila held up her hand. "But isn't it? Sure, you'll probably try to offer us other positions within the museum, but every single member of the team has better prospects elsewhere. Think about it," she actually put her feet up on the conference table, "the entire Exhibit Aurora team has worked harder than anyone else in the museum. We achieved our goal. We're successful. Any top tier company will not only hire any of us in a second, they'll pay us at least 30% more just to lure us away. What's stopping us from speaking out about the museum board's blatant lack of care for a beloved historical figure?"

Silence.

Kyra had to hold back her giggles. Lila was an absolute bad ass.

Ryan finally sighed. "I suppose Dr. Killenger has a point."

Lila arched an eyebrow. "So, what are you going to do about it?"

He took a seat and stared at Geri, who looked about ready to melt into the ground.

"Seeing that we can't seem to reach an understanding—"

"More like you *refuse* to, but carry on," Kyra snapped.

Geri scowled. "I feel that our best option is to bring in a group of non-biased individuals to mediate."

Kyra groaned. "Whyyy?"

She sounded like a four-year-old, but truly didn't care. Lila touched her shoulder. "Kyra, it's not ideal, but it's better than dealing with these chicken heads."

"Dr. Killenger, that is uncalled for."

"Mr. Fowly, how about I go give Lizzie Hildebrant that juicy info she's been after? I can picture it now, 'Museum Board Doesn't Care About a Beloved Princess.'"

Bill turned green. Lila and Kyra shared a nod of agreement before Kyra addressed Geri.

"We accept."

***

Kyra's House

"Why aren't there more women on the board?"

Lila was enjoying a glass of wine on Kyra's couch. Kyra had resorted to shoving her face in Sigmund's belly to calm down. The familiar was purring ferociously and bathing her hair.

"Because," Kyra mumbled into white fluff, "the patriarchy is still a thing."

"It's bullshit, is what it is."

Kyra flopped on the couch next to Lila. "I agree. Although, Geri has done a mostly good job so far. I truly think they didn't believe Aurora would wake up, so they don't know what to do."

"They didn't have to keep us there for four days, though."

Sigmund chirped.

"See, your cat agrees."

Kyra smirked. "He just agrees because Greg didn't give him enough of his favorite treats when mommy was gone."

Sigmund hopped off Kyra's chest and went on a yowling rampage down the hall. Apparently, Greg really hadn't fed him enough.

"So, who do you think these 'unbiased individuals' will be?" Lila asked.

Kyra shrugged. "It'll probably be just one. And I'm guessing a magistrate or something from a state over."

Another yowl sounded from Kyra's office, followed by what sounded like a thundering herd running back down the hall. Sigmund hopped onto Lila's legs, dropped something in her lap, and then was gone again.

"Oh, he went hunting for you."

Lila laughed and held the object up. "Hey, isn't this that famous reporter?"

Kyra gulped. Sigmund had retrieved one of her old persona photos. "Um."

Lila stared at her quizzically. Kyra let out a heavy sigh. Now was as good a time as ever.

"No, that's me."

Lila snickered. "You have her eyes, but that's about it."

"Lila," Kyra reached out and touched her arm, "that's me."

Lila just stared, completely baffled. Kyra stood from the couch and stretched her fingers.

"Promise me you won't freak out."

Lila nodded. Kyra took a deep breath, summoned her magic, and felt the buzzing in her fingertips. This time would hopefully be easier, seeing that she hadn't done anything fairy related in four days. Sparks ignited under her fingernails. A steady stream of blue fog poured from her hands. Kyra collected it into a cloud and blew.

A clear image of Ashley appeared among the smoke. She was standing in a room, looking at a photo album, a green salamander perched on her shoulder. Ashley smiled as she passed her fingers over the photographs. She reached up and petted the salamander's head.

This was a pretty good life, Sigmund.

What was clearly Kyra's voice came out of Ashley's mouth.

Ashley closed the album, sighed happily, and shut her eyes. Identical sparks formed at her fingers. Fog seeped from her fingertips and climbed up her body, completely engulfing her. As it dissipated, a new woman came into view.

Kyra.

The cloud evaporated, and Kyra looked back to Lila. She was clutching her wine glass, eyes wide.

Before she could stop herself, Kyra let her wings appear. The pain was thankfully gone. Their lilac glow cast flickers of light throughout the room. Lila continued to stare.

Kyra bit her lip. "Well?"

Lila gently set her wine glass down and placed her hands in her lap. She furrowed her brow in thought before meeting Kyra's gaze.

"I feel like I should be surprised, but I'm honestly not."

CHAPTER 59

2026, The Museum of Historical Mysteries

"Are you sure you'll be okay?"

Aurora nodded, eyes twinkling. "Dez, it's only for a few hours. I'll be fine. This is important."

It was Dez's graduation day, and Aurora still could not leave the museum. Dez had offered to skip the ceremony, but she'd insisted he go.

Well, and so had his parents. Speaking of which, Dr. and Mrs. Buckley entered the now closed off exhibit to pick up their son. This was their first time seeing Aurora awake.

"Hey Dez," Dr. Buckley greeted.

His mother wasted no time sweeping Aurora into a tight embrace. Aurora could hardly breathe under the intensity of the hug. "Oh, Aurora, dearie! You're even prettier when you're awake!" She pulled back just enough to cup Aurora's face. "Goodness… it's remarkable."

"Sloane, give the girl some room." Dez's father gently pried his wife away before extending his hand. "Dr. Cormac Buckley, it's a pleasure to finally meet you." Aurora gracefully took his outstretched hand and curtsied. Dez grimaced.

"Aurora, I said you didn't have to do that."

"I know," she said, rising, "but it's going to take a while to break something that was instilled in me for twenty-one years."

Dr. Buckley reached out and lightly lifted her chin, studying her. His eyes were just like his son's: green and twinkling with a constant state of curiosity. He grinned.

"Absolutely fascinating." He turned to Dez. "You did good, son."

Aurora smiled. "He knows he's fortunate."

His parents laughed as Dez blushed.

"Glad to see you three get along so well," Dez said, checking the time. "But we need to get to campus or you'll be late."

His mother sighed. "You're sure we can't sneak her out?"

Dez shook his head. "Unfortunately, no. We already broke enough rules waking her up…"

"I heard nothing," Dr. Buckley interrupted. "Let's hit the road. Aurora," he took her hand again, "we'll visit with you more later, I promise."

"Oh yes," his wife agreed, "We need to know everything about you."

Aurora smiled. It wasn't her parents, but they felt like family already.

Dez leaned over and kissed her cheek. "Last chance, I won't go."

She huffed. "You're going. It's important."

He kissed her again. "Okay."

***

"Your Highness?"

Aurora lifted her head, barely able to make out Maura's form through her tears. Once Dez and his parents had left, she'd begun to cry. And cry. And cry. She didn't know how long she'd been crying, but it felt like a long time.

"Why… are… you here?" she managed to gasp out.

Maura sat beside her and wrapped an arm around her shoulders. "I was double checking on some security updates I made. Now, what's wrong?"

Aurora just shook her head, voice choking with sobs. "I… I don't know."

Maura rubbed her arm. "What happened before these tears started?"

"It's Dez's graduation. His parents came to collect him and go to the event. They're so lovely and were so nice to me…." More tears spilled down her cheeks.

Maura pulled her close. "It made you think about your parents."

Aurora nodded.

"Aurora," Maura turned to better look at her. "It is perfectly normal for you to feel this way. You were your parents' only child, correct?"

"Yes."

"From what Kyra has said, they weren't only incredible rulers, they were incredible parents. They loved you very much, and you loved them back. After everything, they're gone and you feel a bit guilty?"

"Yes...."

Maura held out a handkerchief, which Aurora graciously accepted.

"It's called survivor's guilt," Maura explained gently. "You came out of a traumatic event when others didn't. That kind of loss leaves scars."

Aurora sniffled.

"I'm sure they raised you to keep your emotions hidden as a royal," Maura continued, "but you don't have to do that anymore. You'll do better if you allow yourself to truly feel those feelings."

"How do I do that?"

"You can talk to me, to Dez, to Kyra. She's probably the only one who can truly understand what you're going through."

Aurora frowned. "How?"

"Do you know why she stuck around this whole time?"

Aurora had barely seen Kyra since she woke up. "No..."

Maura gave a small smile. "She blamed herself for everything. She thought she didn't do enough to save you from the initial curse. Didn't do enough to save your parents, or the rest of the kingdom."

"She tried?" Aurora asked.

Maura nodded. "The best she could do was put your parents and the rest of the entire kingdom into a hundred years' sleep. She figured that'd be more than enough time to find someone to wake you. And then...it just didn't happen. Despite her doing everything in her power."

Aurora squinted. "She couldn't have possibly expected to find my True Love that way."

"Of course not. But she felt responsible and was willing to do anything to fix things."

"It was out of her control."

"She knows that now. Well, somewhat." Maura sighed. "She's really like your fairy godmother. She's been here for you this whole time. What you need to understand is, Kyra cares for you deeply, and she's dealing with similar trauma. It might help you both to spend time together.

Aurora nodded slowly. "I understand." She looked into Maura's kind eyes. "Is this mind healing?"

Maura laughed. "We call it therapy, but yes. Do you think continuing on will help you?"

Aurora couldn't help but hugging the woman. "I do, thank you."

"It's best not to keep everything inside, especially when it's trauma like this."

Aurora wiped her eyes. "I'll try."

"That's all you can do."

CHAPTER 60

2026, The Museum of Historical Mysteries

"Aurora?"

Dez peered into the reptile exhibit, but she wasn't there either. He'd returned from the graduation ceremony alone—his dad had faked a headache to escape the swarm of graduates pushing their resumes at him—only to find Aurora missing from her exhibit. He'd searched everywhere he thought she might be, as well as places she might not be. But the princess had disappeared.

"I just got you back, where'd you go now?"

He chewed at his lip. Kyra would kill him if Aurora had run off. Had he done something wrong? They'd only been together a week and a half. Surely he hadn't messed up already.

Dez wandered out to the lobby, his footsteps echoing across the marble floor. He'd checked the lab, the archives, the damn Sasquatch exhibit....

Oh. There was one place he hadn't checked, mostly because he usually forgot it existed.

As he approached the planetarium, he saw light flashing under the theatre door. Hopefully that meant Aurora was in there and not some art thief.

He breathed a sigh of relief when he saw her familiar golden locks in a middle row. The presentation on Greek Mythology and their corresponding constellations was playing. Stars danced across the ceiling, narrated by a calm British voice. Lights reflected in Aurora's eyes, making them look like stars themselves.

The show was nearly over, so Dez quietly slid into the seat beside her. She gave him a quick smile before gazing back up at the Milky Way swirling overhead. He had to admit, the astronomers and media designers had done a bang-up job with the visuals. The stars above all merged at the center of the ceiling, forming a red supernova. The fiery mass burst into brilliant, shimmering sparks that cascaded down the walls before fading into darkness. A moment later, the theatre's houselights came up slowly. Aurora closed her eyes and smiled.

"People nowadays are able to create such beautiful things."

Dez reached for her hand, and she gratefully accepted it.

"How did you figure out how to start the show?"

She gave him a sly grin. "I picked the lock to the control room and found the user manual."

Dez raised an eyebrow. The security system to the booth was just the same as the labs; swipe card, fingerprint scan, and a door code. Aurora's smile turned smug. "Did you know the library has books on hacking?"

He let out a hearty laugh. "You've been part of the modern world for ten days and you're already an expert hacker."

"Did you expect any different?"

"Of course not." He kissed her forehead. "You're brilliant. Is this how you spent your time when I was gone?"

"No, I cried first," she said, completely nonchalantly.

Dez blinked. "Why?"

She shrugged. "Your parents were so kind. When they left and took you with them, I felt abandoned. So, I cried."

"Oh, Aurora…" He pulled her closer.

"It's alright. Well, somewhat. Maura paid a visit, and we did that mind healing you told me about. She said I had survivor's guilt and the best thing I can do is talk about it. So, here I am, confessing to you I cried a lot because I miss my parents and don't understand why I'm the only one left—" she took a shuddering breath. Dez squeezed her hand gently. He knew that feeling all too well. Being logical never really helped when one experienced emotional distress.

"You know you can talk to me about anything, right?"

She nodded. "I know. Just… be patient with me?"

He smiled. "I waited for you for quite a while. Patience isn't a problem."

She chuckled and leaned her head back against the seat.

"So, after your therapy session, did you just do this for the rest of the night?" Dez gestured to the planetarium.

Aurora closed her eyes. "No, I did some studying and work. This was my reward."

"Work?" Dez asked.

She smirked. "Seeing that my kingdom is no longer around, I figured I should seek employment."

"I'll take care of you."

She opened her eyes and gazed at him. "I don't doubt that, but you know me. I need to keep my mind busy."

"So, what have you been up to, Your Majesty?"

A light smack.

"Ow."

"That did not hurt," she quipped. "I took the General Educational Development test."

"What?!"

"I passed."

"WHAT?!"

Dez just stared at her, mouth agape. She laughed. "I don't just read and watch movies all day. You're not the only one who does research. Making my way around a computer is still difficult, but Greg helped me get to the proper website." She yawned. "I passed all the practice tests, which allowed me to take the real thing. I passed, easily."

He planted a stream of kisses on her cheek, making her giggle. "I'm so proud of you. Wait... how did you pay for all that?"

"Dr. Killenger gave me some random numbers. Said something about the museum's credit card? I didn't know what it was, but it worked."

Killenger, that devil.

"So what's next? College?"

She yawned again. "I haven't decided yet. I'm just glad to know I do have that option."

Dez stood and took her hand. "Let's get you to bed. You've had a busy day."

She nodded. "Congratulations, by the way. Is your title 'master' now or something?"

Dez gulped. "Uh, no. And never call me that ever again."

CHAPTER 61

2026, The Museum of Historical Mysteries

Aurora smiled as Dez's chest rose and fell slowly underneath her head.

She hadn't told him, but sleeping had been a struggle since waking from the curse. It surprised her, seeing she had never slept in her dream world. She'd assumed all she'd be able to do now, was sleep. But it turned out to be completely the opposite.

It probably had to do with the guilt Maura mentioned. She hoped if she continued on with the mind healing (she knew it was therapy, but mind healing sounded more interesting), the ability to sleep would eventually come easier.

For now, she used the extra hours to her advantage. Studying for the GED had been a good distraction. It was amusing how little education had changed; most of it was just new information and she'd caught on quickly with the help of others. Now that she'd passed the test, she'd probably look into psychology. Maura was great, but if she could understand more about the mind, maybe she could heal faster.

When she wasn't studying, she explored the vast quantity of library books on the tablet. *Pride and Prejudice* remained her favorite, but *The Pillars of the Earth* was an easy second. She'd already finished the first two books and was close to finishing the third. Apparently, there was a video game adaptation, but she hadn't quite figured that kind of technology out yet.

Then there were the peaceful moments when she just watched Dez sleep. She knew that might seem ominous, but considering thousands of people had watched her sleep for over fifty years, she gave herself some grace. She'd never slept next to someone before now, but it felt completely natural, just like everything else had with their relationship.

As peaceful and adorable as Dez looked, Aurora needed to get out of bed. No point in attempting sleep when her body was clearly awake. Carefully, she slipped out from under the blankets, found the slippers Greg had gifted her, and crept away from the exhibit.

The hallway to the main lobby had become all too familiar to her. The area reminded her the most of the Voltav castle's ballroom, so she often found herself drawn to it.

Aurora stared out one of the large windows, pressing her palm lightly against the glass. She longed to see the world past the museum shrubbery. In all honesty, she could escape if she wanted to. The only reason she was still there was to protect Dez; if she ran, he'd most likely be the one blamed. So, for now, she stayed.

She sank into one of the bright red couches and let her thoughts wander. While she missed her parents and her old life dearly, she was trying to stay optimistic. She'd spent some time reading about the politics and current events. While nowhere near perfect, she had real opportunities now with education and employment. She didn't know if she would apply for university anytime soon, but knowing she could made her feel better.

The sharp sound of heels clicking against the floor brought her back to reality. Who on earth was there at this hour? She turned to find Dr. Ellison and Dr. Killenger walking toward her, both looking concerned.

"Highness—" Kyra started.

"Kyra, please, call me Aurora."

Kyra smiled. "Aurora, why are you up so late?"

"More like early," Lila muttered, checking her watch. "It's 3 A.M."

"I could ask you two the same," Aurora countered.

"I've been going through all my lives with Lila for the past few days," Kyra explained. "We didn't really know where else to go, so figured we'd come in early."

Lila grinned. "I know about the whole fairy thing now."

Aurora blinked. "Sorry, I keep forgetting fairies aren't common knowledge in this time."

Kyra sat beside her. "Well, the plan is to make them common knowledge again."

Lila sat on her other side. "Seeing that Dez was so successful utilizing both science and magic, we have a good feeling about Kyra going public."

Aurora nodded. These were all good things.

"Not to undermine this, because I think it's wonderful," she said, squeezing Kyra's forearm, "but do you have any idea when they will actually let me leave?"

Lila and Kyra exchanged a look.

"We finally have an update on that," Lila said.

"The board is basically holding court," Kyra added. "They're bringing in an outside source to deliberate."

Aurora frowned. "I don't understand why I can't just leave. I've been stuck here for so long, I just want to start a new life."

"With Dez?" Lila teased.

"Of course with Dez," Aurora smirked. "So, after this court session, we can go?"

Kyra sighed. "If they rule in your favor, yes."

Aurora crossed her arms. "Kyra, this doesn't seem fair."

"I don't disagree with you," Kyra admitted. "But unfortunately, it's the only option we have."

Aurora groaned. "Fine then. When will this happen?"

"We just found out. Two days from now," Lila replied.

Kyra rested a hand on Aurora's knee. "I know it's short notice, but—"

"It's not."

Kyra and Lila just stared at her.

Aurora shrugged. "Father used to have to hold court at a moment's notice. I sat in on enough sessions to understand how it works."

"Aurora," Kyra sighed, "this isn't the same as royal court."

"That's where you're wrong." Aurora straightened. "Two parties have a disagreement. We have evidence to present our case. And our argument should be enough to put the magistrate on our side."

Kyra smiled. "Your confidence has always been admirable."

"That, and I'm more intelligent than the typical princess."

Lila laughed. "You were right, Kyra. She's definitely special."

"If you trust us," Kyra said, "that's what matters."

Aurora arched an eyebrow. "You're acting like I'm not going to represent myself."

Kyra and Lila exchanged another look.

"We weren't planning on it, no," Lila finally admitted.

"Oh no," Aurora stood, "that simply won't do."

"Aurora—"

She held up a hand. "No, Kyra. Listen to me. My father put so much time and energy into my education and training. He prepared me for something exactly like this." She lifted her chin. "I'm Princess Aurora d'Ambray, and I will successfully advocate for my release from The Museum of Historical Mysteries to be with Desmond Buckley." She looked between them, unwavering. "Am I understood?"

The women just blinked for a moment. Then Kyra gave a small, amused nod.

"Absolutely, Your Majesty."

Aurora rolled her eyes. "I do suppose I earned that title this time."

CHAPTER 62

2026, The Board Room

"All rise, for the Honorable Judge Mitre."

The room stood as the judge entered, making his way to the head of the long conference table. Dez had half expected the board to drag them to a full-fledged courtroom, but wasn't surprised they'd opted for the museum's meeting room instead. They likely assumed that keeping things on their home turf would give them the upper hand.

If they thought they could control the situation, they were sorely mistaken.

Dez stole a glance at Aurora. Even in modern day clothing, she radiated regal poise. She'd donned a sleeveless navy dress with gold detailing, paired with matching stilettos. When he'd voiced concern over the height of her heels, she had only laughed.

"Dez, you should have seen some of the footwear nobility attempted to get away with. These are nothing."

She wore her blonde hair slicked back in a low ponytail, better showcasing her striking features. She'd somehow perfected a makeup look on her own.

"I watched a YouTube tutorial," she'd announced proudly. "It's amazing what you can learn on that site."

Her eyelashes looked even longer with the mascara she'd applied, and Dez just wanted to kiss her mauve tinted lips…

Nope.

Focus, Dez.

"You may be seated," Judge Mitre instructed as he settled into his chair.

Dez took stock of the room. The entire board sat on one side of the table, apparently attempting to look intimidating. On the other side sat Aurora, Dez, Kyra, Lila, and Greg. Dez wasn't entirely sure how they'd got Greg there, but he was grateful for the extra support.

Aurora used the moment of silence to make eye contact with every member of the board. Each one, including Geri, looked away once her piercing blue eyes met theirs.

How Dez had earned her love, he'd never understand.

Judge Mitre lifted a thick binder. "I've thoroughly reviewed the case file, and I must say, it is quite remarkable."

Aurora's case was so well known, they'd had to appoint a judge who had the least exposure to it. Judge Mitre was from across the country and typically focused more on small claims cases.

"It is my understanding," the judge continued, "that this hearing revolves around unique ethical and legal concerns."

Bill sighed audibly.

"Do you have something to add, Mr. Fowly?"

"No, your honor."

"Then I suggest you refrain from unnecessary commentary."

Dez and Greg locked eyes, both suppressing giggles.

Judge Mitre pressed on. "The Museum of Historical Mysteries' Board of Directors has expressed concerns regarding Princess Aurora d'Ambray's release from their care. Given that she fell into an enchanted sleep in the 14th century and remained unchanged for centuries after that, the board asserts that ongoing supervision is necessary for her reintegration into modern society."

A few members nodded in agreement.

"Conversely, Dr. Kyra Ellison, head of the Exhibit Aurora research team, maintains that Princess Aurora is fully capable of independent living. If released, she will reside with a designated team member, Mr. Desmond Buckley, and comply with any reasonable reintegration protocols set forth by the court."

Dez tensed at the implication that the board would still have any say in Aurora's future.

"The floor is now open for arguments," Judge Mitre said. "Ms. Pach, will you be speaking on behalf of the board?"

Geri stood. "Yes, your honor."

"You may proceed."

Geri clasped her hands in front of her. "For over fifty years, the Museum of Historical Mysteries has had custody of Exhibit Aurora. As with all our exhibits, we maintain legal ownership regardless of whether they change, close, or remain on display. While Aurora is undeniably a unique case, our primary concern is ensuring she has the best possible quality of life. We firmly believe that should be under our supervision."

With that, she took her seat. That was it? Dez almost scoffed. They were really banking on the judge simply agreeing with them?

Judge Mitre turned his attention across the table. "Dr. Ellison, I assume you will be speaking for your team?"

Kyra stood. "No, Your Honor." Then she immediately sat back down.

A flicker of confusion crossed the judge's face. Dez's fingers brushed against Aurora's leg as she rose to her feet.

"Your honor, I will be representing myself."

Judge Mitre nodded. "Unconventional, but permitted. Proceed, Your Highness."

Aurora offered him a polite smile before clasping her hands behind her back.

"First and foremost, Your Honor, I'd like to thank you for your time today. I have chosen to speak on my own behalf because, as Ms. Pach indicated, I am a living, breathing person. While I acknowledge that the museum has, in effect, had ownership over me, I am now awake. I am fully capable of making my own decisions regarding my life and, as such, am entitled to autonomy and privacy."

She stepped away from the table, once again locking eyes with each board member. "I recognize that my circumstances are highly unusual. However, the choices that were made concerning my body and my future were made without my consent. That alone should render any prior agreements between myself and the museum invalid."

Dez fought back a grin. *That's my girl.*

"I am more than competent, Your Honor. In the twelve days since I awoke, I have immersed myself in learning about the modern world. I have already obtained my GED, developed a strong understanding of current technology, and begun the legal process to obtain a birth certificate and social security number."

She pulled a neatly stacked set of papers from her file and held them up. "All documentation is available for review."

Judge Mitre gestured for the paperwork, which Greg quickly delivered. Aurora continued as the judge examined the documents. "I won't deny that Desmond Buckley and I have developed a romantic relationship. He has offered me a safe and stable home, where I can continue my adjustment. If necessary, I am willing to seek employment to demonstrate financial independence. Additionally, I have the unwavering support of Dr. Kyra Ellison, Dr. Lila Killenger, and Mr. Gregory Taft."

Each of them nodded in agreement.

"I have also enlisted the assistance of Ms. Maura Arkin, a licensed therapist I have been in contact with, to help me navigate this transition. I understand that I am experiencing symptoms of survivor's guilt and post-traumatic stress disorder. The very fact that I recognize the importance of prioritizing my mental health should be further evidence of my ability to function independently."

"That may be," Ryan interjected, "but she has been asleep for centuries. She has been under the Pach family's and museum's care since the moment she was discovered, and we maintain that ongoing supervision—"

"Oh," Aurora interrupted smoothly. "Regarding that. Your Honor, may I call a witness?"

Judge Mitre arched a brow. "This is not a trial, but I see no reason to object. Proceed."

Aurora walked toward the meeting room's entrance and cracked open the door. "They'll hear what you have to say." Dez's breath caught as Dr. Henry Pach stepped inside.

CHAPTER 63

2026, The Museum of Historical Mysteries

At precisely 2 A.M. the morning of the court session, an elderly man slowly wandered into the museum lobby. He walked with a pronounced hunch, relying heavily on a jade colored cane. Aurora half expected a frantic nurse to come rushing in to retrieve him, assuming he had strolled out from a retirement home. But instead, the man made his way directly in front of her, extending his hand. Aurora tentatively took it, suppressing a gasp as he bowed and pressed a reverent kiss to her fingers.

"What a gentleman," she remarked.

The man's eyes twinkled. "You are a princess, after all."

He was clearly of sound mind.

"I apologize. Have we met?"

"May I sit?" he asked, and Aurora patted the seat beside her. He lowered himself onto it. "In a manner of speaking, yes, we've met."

Aurora arched a brow. "I assume you mean while I was asleep?"

The man chuckled. "I discovered you, my dear."

Aurora's eyes widened. "Dr. Pach?"

The man nodded. "Dr. Henry Pach, to be exact. My father was Dr. Otto Pach."

Aurora's lips curled into a smile. "Thank you for bringing me here. Without you, I would likely still be alone in that castle."

He rested his chin on his cane. "My father was adamant about it. I had my reservations at first, but I felt it was my duty to attempt to solve your mystery.”

“I’m glad you did. I might not be awake right now if you hadn’t. I certainly wouldn’t have Dez…” Her gaze drifted to her lap.

Henry smiled knowingly. “How is Mr. Buckley?”

Aurora’s face brightened. "He’s wonderful. Intelligent, dedicated, passionate, handsome—" She cut herself off, blushing.

Henry chuckled again. “I had a good feeling about that one. He treats you well?”

Aurora nodded enthusiastically. “I truly believe he’d worship the ground I walked on if I allowed him.”

Henry’s chuckle turned into a hearty laugh. “You are royalty, after all.”

“He still holds me accountable, though. We’re equals where it matters, and complete opposites where we need to be.” Aurora’s smile broadened. Her love for Dez continued to amaze her.

“Sounds like quite the perfect relationship.”

“It is. Which is why I need to get us out of here.”

“Ah,” Henry sighed, “about that….”

***

The Board Room

“Grandpa?!”

Geri leaped to her feet, rushing to Henry’s side.

“None of that, Geri,” he chided, waving his cane. “I’m perfectly capable of walking to a chair.”

“But —”

“Sit, Geraldine.”

Geri immediately sank back into her seat. Henry approached the table and took a seat beside Judge Mitre.

“I apologize, Your Honor, I would stand, but…” He waved his cane again.

“Perfectly acceptable,” the judge said. “May I ask you to identify yourself for the records?”

“Dr. Henry Pach.”

"Thank you, Dr. Pach. And what is your involvement in this matter?"

"My father and I were the ones who initially discovered Princess

Aurora d'Ambray in Voltav Castle. We established Exhibit Aurora and served as co-leads on her research team until my father's passing in 1997."

Judge Mitre nodded. "And will you be providing a witness statement regarding this case?"

"Yes, Your Honor."

"You may proceed."

Henry took a steadying breath. "My father, Dr. Otto Pach, founder of The Museum of Historical Mysteries, had only one wish: to see the princess awake. He dedicated his life to making that happen. Unfortunately, he passed before witnessing this miracle." He gestured toward Aurora with his cane, smiling. "When he died, I made it my life's mission to continue his work. When it became clear that I would not be the one to succeed, I ensured a team was in place that shared the same goal. The research teams before Dr. Ellison laid a strong foundation, and thanks to her and Desmond Buckley, we have achieved what was once thought impossible." He turned to Dez. "Mr. Buckley, my father would be incredibly proud of you. You have my deepest gratitude."

Dez nodded his head in appreciation.

Henry faced the judge again. "While I am 'technically' retired, even my granddaughter has always emphasized that Exhibit Aurora is a Pach family endeavor. The princess is awake, her case has been thoroughly documented, and she has demonstrated her ability to live independently. Not only is it my personal wish, but I firmly believe my father would have wanted this as well —to see her fully released from the museum's jurisdiction."

Henry leaned back in his chair, hands clasped over his cane. Judge Mitre reviewed the documents once more before speaking. "I will be candid; I had already reached a decision prior to Dr. Pach's statement, but it has only reinforced my ruling." He set the files down and folded his hands before him. "In my professional judgment, I find that Princess Aurora d'Ambray should be fully released from The Museum of Historical Mysteries' supervision to reintegrate into society."

Bill moved to object, but Judge Mitre swiftly cut him off. "My ruling is final." He turned his gaze to Dez.

"Mr. Buckley, are you prepared to provide a safe and stable home for Princess Aurora?"

Dez stood. "Absolutely, Your Honor."

"Very well." The judge placed his hands in his lap. "This matter is hereby concluded."

A moment of silence.

Aurora finally spoke up. "So… I'm free to go home?"

Judge Mitre offered a small smile. "Yes, Your Highness. I wish you all the best. This hearing is adjourned."

Chaos erupted on the Exhibit Aurora side of the room. Greg swept Lila off her feet, twirling her around in celebration. Kyra approached Henry, thanking him profusely. Dez swore he saw the old man slip something into her pocket, but Aurora quickly distracted him by wrapping her arms around his neck.

He gazed at her. She was his greatest achievement, his greatest love. And now, she was fully and completely his.

Aurora's blue eyes twinkled.

"We did it."

He finally kissed her in front of everyone. He didn't care.

"We did it."

CHAPTER 64

May 2026, Wellington Bits, An Announcement from Paul

To our readers,

My name is Paul Shimmer, and I am the majority owner of *Wellington Bits*. I do not regret to inform you that Elizabeth Hildegrant, my former business partner, is no longer affiliated with this publication.

When *Wellington Bits* was founded, our goal was simple: to deliver important, factual news to the people of this city as quickly and accurately as possible. Unfortunately, over the past year, Ms. Hildegrant has deviated from that mission. While I have always valued journalistic integrity and encouraged her to maintain ethical reporting standards, I have become increasingly concerned with the shift in tone and direction of her work. *Wellington Bits* is a professional news outlet, not a gossip blog.

As the majority owner, I have made the decision that I believe will restore the credibility and quality of our reporting. Until I find a new partner —someone who shares my dedication to Wellington and its people—I will feature guest writers to bring fresh, responsible journalism to our readers.

To those who have remained loyal to *Wellington Bits*, I sincerely appreciate your continued support. And to those who have distanced themselves from us because of recent editorial choices, I ask that you give us another chance. We are committed to rebuilding your trust.

Thank you,
Paul Shimmer

@User219: Paul, thank you for listening to both the readers and your gut. Let's get back to actual journalism.

@YakityYak: What's the real story here? Did she leave willingly, or was she forced out?

@TruvalT44: Will there be any statement from Lizzie? I'd like to hear her side of things.

@User00001: Y'all, Lizzie was trash. We don't need to hear from her, I think it's pretty obvious what happened.

@9sixty: Looking forward to the guest writers. Willing to give you guys another shot.

CHAPTER 65

2026, Somewhere in Ibiza

Lizzie stood by the car, watching Monty stagger out of the seedy club. He was barely holding it together, grinning like an idiot. She could already feel the fury building inside her. Monty heaved, seemingly forced the vomit back down, and then continued stumbling toward the passenger side.

"Oh hell no," Lizzie snapped, immediately pressing the lock button on her key fob. Monty uselessly pulled on the handle, too drunk to realize it was locked.

"What the hell?" he hiccupped.

Lizzie crossed her arms. "Either you puke on the sidewalk right now, or we wait for you to sober up. You are not getting any of your barf in my car."

Monty swayed. "Come on, Lizzie, lighten up."

"There's nothing to lighten up about!"

She stomped her foot, and instantly, the heel of her shoe snapped. Monty giggled.

"Oh, you've got to be kidding me…"

When her article views began dwindling and Paul basically broke up with her, Lizzie's finances took a serious hit. She'd been wandering a local park in Wellington, wallowing in self-pity, when an SUV pulled up beside her. It felt just like something out of a movie. An action movie. Someone had quickly yanked her inside before the car sped off.

Once inside, she found herself face-to-face with Millie and Franklin Monjurse. They explained they were looking for someone to basically babysit their son, willing to pay top dollar to keep him out of trouble. When Lizzie asked why she would even consider such an offer, they threatened legal action for the multiple defamatory articles she'd written about their family.

She had written nothing untrue, but the Monjurses had more money and time than she had, and they could easily drag her through endless court battles until she was bankrupt.

Looking at her depleted bank account, she knew she couldn't afford a fight like that.

And so, she had found herself in Ibiza with the Mongoose.

"Lizzie Lizzie bo bizzie, banana fana fo fizzie," Monty sang as he tried to once again open the car door.

"I can't believe I'm doing this crap," Lizzie muttered under her breath.

"Oh, come on, Fizzie...bo bizze… just have some fun. What else are you going to do?" He swayed dangerously and Lizzie reached out to steady him, but it was too late. Monty collapsed into a heap in the grass. She planted her hands on her hips and glared down at him.

"You are exactly why I can't have fun! The only reason I'm here is to keep your parents from having to deal with another museum ban or paparazzi feature. I can't exactly have fun while I'm busy babysitting your ass!"

"You're pretty when you're mad. You ever thought of being a dominatrix?"

Lizzie gritted her teeth. "Absolutely not." Although, a whip was mighty tempting at that moment.

"Whoaaa, the ceiling's spinning," Monty slurred.

"We're outside, you dimwit," Lizzie hissed.

Monty responded by rolling over and puking. Lizzie wrinkled her nose, disgusted. "Well, at least I can take you back to the rental now."

"Nooo, let's find another party," Monty whined.

"You're lucky your parents are rich," Lizzie muttered, though she knew that wasn't the only reason she was stuck with him. She looped her arms under his armpits, dragging him to the car, narrowly avoiding the vomit puddle. Once she got him into the backseat, she saw she'd ripped her skirt in the process.

"Aw Lizzie, don't be sad…."

Lizzie clicked her seatbelt and started the car.

"If this is the rest of my life, I'm going to be sad. Now shut up."

"You really know how to kill the vibe, you know?"

"Yeah, well," Lizzie said, smirking, "It's my job now. If you throw up in my car, you're paying to have it cleaned."

And with that, they drove into the night.

CHAPTER 66

2026, Dez and Aurora's Apartment

"Ding dong, the witch is dead," Greg sang to Sigmund, who chirped back.

Lila raised her wine glass like a toast. "You think Paul actually came to his senses, or Lizzie quit sleeping with him?"

"Who cares?" Greg danced around with Sigmund more. "She's gone where the goblins go."

"Your singing's offending him," Kyra deadpanned.

Greg mocked offense. "How dare you! He thinks my singing's brilliant. Don't you, Sig?"

Sigmund yowled and clawed at Greg, who had no choice but to let him go.

Kyra laughed. "Even you can piss him off, of all people."

"Can I get a Band-Aid?" Greg mumbled.

Sigmund wandered to the couch and jumped on Aurora's lap. She scratched under his chin. "Hard to believe you were that milk snake at one point," she cooed. "Dez, we should get a snake!"

Dez shuddered. "I love you, but no. I'll gladly take a fat, clingy cat over a snake."

Sigmund flicked his tail in Dez's face, apparently offended by the fat comment.

"What? You are fat," Kyra agreed.

"It's because you insist on giving him so many treats," Lila groaned.

Dez glanced around the room. He truly loved this little family they had created. Three weeks had passed since Aurora's release from The Museum of Historical Mysteries. They were in Dez and Aurora's new apartment, finally celebrating their housewarming. Sigmund had somehow shrank himself down and crept into Kyra's bag, so he was happily crashing the party. He'd gone right back to his fluffy huge self as soon as he popped out of the bag.

"I still think you could have just stayed in your place." Greg quipped.

Aurora rolled her eyes. "Trust me, I said the same thing. But *someone* insisted that I deserved better for my first home in the modern world."

Dez wrapped an arm around her. "You do."

"Aw." She gave him a quick kiss.

"Again, ew. You two are sick," Greg muttered.

Kyra clapped her hands like a little kid. "Sickly sweet!"

Lila joined in the eye rolling. "You're such a fairy."

Greg sat on Dez's opposite side. "You gonna be able to afford this long term? It's awesome, but I'm sure the rent's not cheap."

Dez grimaced. "I should be. I've got another job offer this morning. Aurora and I need to talk about which contract makes the most sense and which position would be best for overall happiness."

After details of Dez's communication methods with Aurora leaked, multiple companies contacted him. He had a sneaking suspicion that Henry had something to do with it before he passed.

The man had died only two days after the court case, further proving he had been waiting for Aurora to wake up before he let go. His funeral had been surprisingly joyful, filled with people who spoke about how he had helped them in some way.

Greg clapped Dez on the shoulder. "Not gonna lie, I'm proud of you for finally letting your parents help you out."

Dez squirmed. For the first time in his life, he accepted an offer from Dr. and Mrs. Buckley. The couple graciously covered the first three months' rent on the apartment. Dez had every intention of paying them back at some point, but knew they wouldn't hear of it.

"Think of it as a graduation present, bud," his dad had insisted.

"And your fiancée deserves the best," his mom had grinned.

No, he and Aurora were not engaged.

"You aren't going to accept Geri's generous offer?" Kyra said sarcastically.

Dez laughed. "I thought you two made up?"

Kyra rolled her eyes. "We did. But I'll never forgive her for making us go through the whole rigmarole to get to this point."

Dez nodded. "No, I turned her down."

Geri had offered him a prestigious position overseeing multiple research teams at the museum. While the job would have given him everything he could have asked for, he knew his time there was done. He and Aurora would gladly still be patrons, but thirteen years of basically working there had been enough. He needed to explore what else was on the horizon.

"Kyra," Lila said, "if money is an issue, I think now is the time to tell them what you've been up to." Kyra grinned slyly. She retrieved a file folder from her kitchen island and presented it to Aurora.

"Highness, this is yours."

Aurora groaned. "Kyra—"

"Just look at it."

Dez peered over her shoulder as she opened the file. The first document was a brand new birth certificate.

Aurora d'Aumbray, dimanche 26 septembre 2004.

"I obviously couldn't put 1420, so I had to make it accurate to your current age," Kyra explained.

Dez squinted. "Uh, Kyra, why's it in French?"

Kyra smirked. "Because Aurora *is* French."

Dez, Aurora, and Greg just blinked. Lila swirled her glass. "Henry gave Kyra the exact location he and Otto found you. Kyra went there after his funeral. The castle's still there."

Dez was still stunned. He knew he'd seen the old man slip Kyra something.

"So…" Aurora said, "where exactly in France?"

"Le Lavandou," Lila answered. "Right on the coast, tons of dolphins."

Aurora gazed at the document. "And the castle's still there?"

Kyra grinned more. "Take a look at the next document."

Dez leaned in as Aurora flipped to the next page. It had been laminated, thankfully, because otherwise, it might have crumbled apart. Though yellowed with age, the beautiful manuscript remained legible. A wax crest of a diamond intertwined with a briar was pressed into the corner. Aurora ran her fingertips over it.

"That's…that's my family crest."

"What is it?" Greg asked, gently.

Dez studied the page. "It appears to be the deed for Voltav Castle. It states that ownership transfers to the current living member of the d'Ambray family."

Greg's jaw dropped. "Yo, Aurora's got real estate!"

Aurora just stared at the deed. "Kyra… the castle's still there?"

Kyra walked to her side and gently touched her shoulder. "Yes."

"Intact?"

"For the most part. It certainly needs a little TLC, but the foundation is strong."

Aurora looked to Dez. "Didn't that science museum that offered you a job have an architectural preservation program?"

Dez squeezed her arm. "That it does."

Kyra smirked. "Well, it sounds like karma is on our side. Look at the final document."

Aurora shuffled to the last few pages.

Dez, Greg, and Lila all peered and gasped.

"Oh, I didn't know about this part," Lila murmured.

Aurora's eyes widened. "Is… is this true?"

Kyra smiled warmly. "Yes. I presented your family's vault records to the French government and provided proof that you are alive and well. The vault, the land, the castle, and a trust that was somehow still maintained; it's all legally yours."

Aurora launched herself at Kyra, wrapping her in a tight hug. "Kyra, thank you."

Kyra smiled. "It was the least I could do."

Greg now swept Dez off his feet. "You're rich! Well, your girlfriend's rich! Time to propose, dude!"   Aurora punched his shoulder.

"OW!"

Dez laughed. "Shut up, Thor."

"No, OUCH, that legitimately HURT. Your girl's got an arm."

Dez grinned before lifting Aurora into a spin. "That she does."

She gazed at him, her blue eyes full of love and mischief. "Do you not want to marry me?"

Dez smirked before kissing her. "We'll get there, I promise."
"I know."

CHAPTER 67

June 2026, Exhibit Aurora, Final Update, by Dr. Kyra Ellison

When Aurora d'Ambray was first placed in The Museum of Historical Mysteries, the world believed she was nothing more than an artifact. Experts treated her like an enigma to be studied, explained, and categorized. But thankfully, individuals came along who knew better. She was never just a relic of the past; she was a living, breathing person with a story far greater than any exhibit could contain. Now, as she steps away from the museum, it's time we acknowledge something that many have long ignored: Magic is real. It always has been. And I, for one, am done pretending otherwise.

People treated science and magic as opposing forces for too long, but Aurora's journey proves they never were. Her existence challenged logical understanding, yet it was science, heightened with magic, that helped her find her place in this new time. It's time we stopped looking at magic as something imaginary and started recognizing it as a fundamental part of our world.

I have spent many lives hiding. I've seen humans lose faith in magic, something that was once universally accepted and respected. The rest of my kind have retreated to our home world, their trust in humans completely gone. Because of this, the idea of magic and magical beings has turned into nothing more than children's stories.

But now, more than ever, the truth needs to be told.

I, Dr. Kyra Ellison, am a fairy.

I have not only been here for Aurora for the past three years; I was there when she was born, when a curse was put on her, when the rest of her kingdom aged and passed away as she continued to sleep…I've been here for it all.

While I'm sure most may know me as a biomedical engineer, I was also a TV reporter named Ashley, a lawyer named Betty, a government clerk named Denise, and the list goes on and on. (You can find a link to a website at the end of this article with plenty of proof.)

I dedicated my life to helping Aurora wake, as I felt responsible for her slumber in the first place. Through tireless investigation, we uncovered the true origins of her kingdom, the fate of those lost to time, and most recently, the existence of her family's castle, which still stands. That discovery was not just a historical breakthrough; it was a moment of reclamation, returning centuries' worth of history to Aurora.

Much of this progress would not have been possible without my mentee, Desmond Buckley, whose work led us to multiple breakthroughs once thought impossible. His research and communication methods proved it doesn't have to be either science or magic. Instead, when combined, they allow us to explore the world with a deeper, more complete understanding. His contributions have laid the groundwork for future interdisciplinary research, and I have no doubt his work will continue to inspire those willing to look beyond the boundaries of traditional study.

Aurora's departure is not the end of her story; it is just the beginning. She embarks on new and exciting adventures with Mr. Buckley at her side. Hers is a story of hope, something more of us should continue to believe in.

And as for me? I'm sure many of you assume I'm now unemployed. That is far from the case. I will be traveling the world, assisting the brightest minds in incorporating magic into their practices. Who knows what we can accomplish now?

To our loyal patrons who have followed Aurora's journey, thank you.

To those who doubted her tale, I truly hope you're okay with being proven wrong.

And to Dez and Aurora, I wish you both well. Your relationship was built on history. Now, it's time for you to write your own story.

EPILOGUE

September 2026, Le Lavandou, France

"Mademoiselle d'Ambray?"

Aurora looked up from the blueprints she'd been studying.

"Yes, Amédée?

"They've nearly restored the ballroom floor; would you like to take a look?"

She rolled up the blueprint. "Of course."

The ballroom had been the biggest undertaking, so she and Dez decided to tackle it first. Amédée walked ahead, a spring in his step. The Frenchman was actually an elf who'd recently gone public thanks to Kyra's article. It made sense that he'd gone into the architectural field, given elves' pension for craftsmanship. Amazingly, most of the general population had been incredibly accepting of magical beings walking among them. Magic made life easier. Who didn't want that?

She walked along the overgrown but familiar path to the castle. The gardens would be beautiful once they'd been brought back to life. And the horses! She couldn't wait for the stables to be fully functional again.

Her mouth fell open as she entered the ballroom. Workers were placing the last of the refurbished floor tiles. Kyra had been right—the foundation was still strong. They had simply removed each section of flooring, cleaned them, patched any problem areas, and placed them right back where they belonged.

More light than necessary poured in through the smashed windows. The reflection on the now pristine floor was absolutely blinding.

"Uh, Amédée?"

"Oui?"

She shielded her eyes. "Could we make the windows the next priority?"

Amédée squinted as well. "Oui Mademoiselle, that would be wise. The original glass is unsalvageable, so we will need to replace it entirely."

She nodded. "That's fine. It's not like I have any emotional attachment to the originals." The only window that truly mattered to her—the stained glass one in her room—had remained untouched. In fact, Kyra's enchantment had held up so well that her entire room looked brand new.

"Christ's fingernails!"

Aurora turned to find Dez stepping into the room, instantly blinded by the floor. He was furiously digging through the pouch strapped to his waist.

"Here," he said, shoving a pair of dark-lensed glasses with an elastic strap into her hands. She slipped them on without hesitation. Much better. She glanced at Dez, who had donned an identical pair, and burst out laughing.

"What?" he asked.

"You look like a bug."

"You're wearing the same pair! So you look like a bug too, then."

She smirked. "Lovebugs."

Greg had made a comment on how their "honeymoon phase" would eventually fade. So far, that wasn't the case. Dez took her hand as they walked toward the grand staircase. The team had made incredible progress, and they'd be able to start work on the second floor soon.

"We picked the right job for you," Aurora mused.

Dez laughed. "You're just saying that because I technically work for you now."

The Bloomsburg Science and History Museum couldn't offer Aurora a position, as she still only had her GED. But eager to acquire the Voltav Castle, they named Aurora the official client for the restoration project. She owned the castle, after all.

Dez was juggling his role as the project's lead researcher with his work developing lucid dream communication technology. It turned out that his machine could be used on coma patients, yielding results similar to

Aurora's. One woman, who had been unresponsive for nearly two years, had finally woken up to the joy of her family.

Kyra had already reminded Dez to thank her in his Nobel Prize acceptance speech.

"You know," Dez mused, "I find it funny that we rented our first apartment, and they immediately shipped us off to France three weeks later."

"You bought it," Aurora corrected.

"My parents did. I'm paying them back."

"You are not. Sloane will never agree to that."

"The fact you're on a first name basis with my mother is alarming."

She threw her head back in laughter. "It's a good thing."

Dez smiled. "I know."

Aurora's phone buzzed in her pocket, making her jump. She still hadn't gotten used to that. She pulled it out and squinted. "I can't see anything with the light and these ridiculous glasses."

"They're protective gear," Dez corrected.

"Regardless of what they are, I can't read my email. Let's head back to the hut."

The "hut" was actually a cottage the museum had provided for them when they were in France. It was just a short walk from the castle, and Aurora was already considering purchasing it.

"Amédée?" Dez called out.

The head restorer walked over. "Oui Monsieur Buckley?"

"If it's alright, Ms. d'Ambray and I will be taking the rest of the day off. Did you need anything else?"

Aurora blinked. A day off? They hadn't talked about that. Amédée gave a knowing smile. "We've got it covered from here. Enjoy your afternoon."

Aurora barely held back a squeal as she stepped into the cottage. Sparkling streamers hung from the ceiling, balloons covered the floor, and a large cake sat on the dining room table between two bouquets of roses. Dez wrapped his arms around her waist from behind.

"Happy twenty-second birthday, my dear princess."

Aurora leaned her head back against his chest.

"You've outdone yourself, Sir Desmond."

He tickled her, and she swatted his hand. "Come on, let's have some cake."

Her mouth watered as Dez slicked into the strawberry shortcake. She'd developed a sweet tooth for modern desserts, but this one smelled particularly delicious. He handed her a plate with a generous slice.

"Wait," she said, suddenly remembering, "what did that email say?" She pulled her phone out again, scanning the screen. Her eyes widened, and she grinned.

"I got into school."

Dez nearly knocked over a bouquet in his rush to her side. "You did? I'm so proud of you!" He peppered kisses over the top of her head.

After showcasing her skills in court, Aurora had decided that law was the right path for her. Unsurprisingly, multiple schools had offered her full-ride scholarships for her bachelor's degree. In the end, she applied only to the University of Hawaii, home to the William S. Richardson School of Law, where she hoped to enroll after earning her philosophy degree. The school's part-time programs would allow her to pursue her studies while continuing to travel.

Aurora had also come to realize she wasn't exactly a "people person." The idea of being crammed into a classroom with unfamiliar students held little appeal. Luckily, she and Dez shared that sentiment. They were both happy to thrive in their respective fields, as long as they could end their days with mac and cheese and a movie.

Dez kissed her again. "I have one more present for you."

He disappeared into their bedroom, practically bouncing with excitement.

"Dez," she called after him, "you do too much."

"Not enough!" he shot back.

A moment later, he returned, carrying a large picture frame. Carefully, he set it on the floor.

"I didn't wrap it because it's fragile, so close your eyes."

Aurora smirked and obeyed. She heard him shift the frame around. A pause. Then, softly, he said, "Okay, look."

She opened her eyes. Before her was a beautifully restored portrait of King Florestan and Queen Matilda, framed in gold, the d'Ambray family crest embossed in the corner.

"I hope you like it," Dez murmured. "The archaeologists found it two days ago, and Amédée helped me restore it."

Aurora blinked, tears welling in her eyes. Dez leaned the portrait against the table, then stepped to her side, touching her hand gently.

"Is it too much?"

She shook her head. "No. It's perfect." She smiled through her tears and cupped his face. "They would have adored you."

Dez smiled back. For a moment, they stood silently, observing what had been lost. Thanks to Maura, Aurora had learned to accept the past—not with grief, but with gratitude. She had been lucky to know the love of two parents for twenty-one years. Now, it was her turn to honor them by living her best life.

"Dez?" she whispered. "What if I had never woken up?"

He smiled. "I would've just kept on dreaming with you."

She pressed her forehead to his. "You are far too sentimental."

Dez grinned. "And you love it."

She wiped away a few lingering tears. "I can't help it."

He gave her a quick peck. "Well, birthday girl, how do you want to spend the evening?"

She hummed. "What's the most ridiculous movie you can think of?"

He pursed his lips. "I don't know, *Dodgeball?*"

"Perfect. I think we should end the day with something comedic."

He smirked. "Comedic is one way of describing that film…"

"Could we just make frozen pizza?"

Dez raised an eyebrow. "Pizza? In France? Shouldn't we make, I don't know, ratatouille or something?"

She stood and extended her hand. "Overrated. And it takes too long to make."

Chuckling, he took her hand. "Fair enough. It's your special day. You get whatever you want." Hand in hand, they headed toward the living room, leaving the portrait in a place of honor, where it belonged.

ABOUT THE AUTHOR

Kylie Casino

Kylie Casino is a dance educator, choreographer, and emerging novelist whose work explores the intersection of movement, memory, and storytelling. Her original stage productions often draw on folklore and mythology, blending classical forms with contemporary expression. Exhibit Aurora is her debut novel, inspired by a lifelong fascination with reimagining fairy tales through a speculative lens. When she's not writing or choreographing, Kylie can usually be found reading or daydreaming new stories on long walks through downtown Columbus, Georgia, where she lives with her husband, stepdaughter, two dogs, and eleven cats.

www.ingramcontent.com/pod-product-compliance
Lightning Source LLC
Chambersburg PA
CBHW060302310726
48976CB00007B/2179